WITHDRAWN

Praise for *The Maze of Cadiz*

'*The Maze of Cadiz* is a splendid debut mystery . . . Monroe provides terrific and convincing historical atmosphere; I am delighted that she is writing more Peter Cotton novels' *The Times*

'Aly Monroe has created an impressive novel with an extraordinary, dream-like atmosphere . . . The next can't come too soon' *Financial Times*

'Aly Monroe is a newcomer to crime writing, whose accomplished debut, *The Maze of Cadiz*, is set in 1944 . . . Monroe's portrait of Cadiz in the aftermath of the civil war is atmospheric, and in a surprising twist the mild-mannered Cotton turns out to be as devious as his adversaries' *Sunday Times*

'Cotton's investigating is clever and fascinating' *Guardian*

'Addictive' *Sunday Telegraph*

'[Monroe's] writing is skilful and evocative . . . *The Maze of Cadiz* is a stylish and impressive debut' *The Economist*

'I have been quite captivated . . . The book had me totally convinced that Ms Monroe knows her Spain and, more to the point, knows the Spain of 1944 . . . wonderfully atmospheric, very well-written' *Shots*

Washington Shadow

Also by Aly Monroe

The Maze of Cadiz

Aly Monroe

Washington Shadow

JOHN MURRAY

First published in Great Britain in 2009 by John Murray (Publishers)
An Hachette UK company

1

© Aly Monroe 2009

A CIP catalogue record for this title is available from the British Library

Hardback ISBN 978-1-84854-034-7
Trade paperback ISBN 978-1-84854-035-4

Typeset in Monotype Sabon by Servis Filmsetting Ltd, Stockport, Cheshire

Printed and bound by Clays Ltd, St Ives plc

John Murray policy is to use papers that are natural, renewable and recyclable
products and made from wood grown in sustainable forests. The logging and
manufacturing processes are expected to conform to the environmental regulations
of the country of origin.

John Murray (Publishers)
338 Euston Road
London NW1 3BH

www.johnmurray.co.uk

To Iain
born 18 March 2009

I

ON SUNDAY, 26 August 1945 Peter Cotton flew from Hamburg in Germany to London in a DC-3 with four nurses, a lieutenant on compassionate leave, a number of bags of post and a regimental mascot – a well-behaved goat called Ajax – and his handler. In his battle jacket pocket, Cotton had orders to present himself at the temporary office of the Economic Warfare Unit the next day.

On Monday, Cotton found the office three floors up in a narrow building behind the Oriental Club in Hanover Square. For a moment he thought they were still moving in, but then saw that two girls in uniform were emptying shelves and packing boxes with files.

'We're being entirely wrapped up,' said D, 'and archived. Moira?'

Cotton had never seen his boss in anything but a naval commodore's uniform. Now he was dressed in an elderly blue tweed suit, bagged at the knees, looking like a bad-tempered country solicitor.

One of the girls went to a desk, opened a drawer and took out an envelope.

'Read what's in that,' said D, 'and sign it.'

Cotton opened the envelope.

It contained a three-page joint statement from the heads of MI5 and MI6, drawing 'Urgent Attention' to the differences between WAR and PEACE.

It is not – and never will be – the policy of His Majesty's Government to instigate, carry out, be part of or otherwise sanction, permit or condone the taking of human life by any member of His Majesty's Intelligence Departments in time of peace.

Cotton paused.

'They're clearing out the farouche, the louche and the schoolboys,' said D.

Cotton looked at him. It was D who had originally picked him out, then overseen his training. D had always been extraordinarily focused and insistently to the point in wartime. Today, there was no sign of that. He looked drawn, as if his skin had fused to the bones behind his face.

Cotton read on. The second page was mostly one long, particularly opaque paragraph on the terms 'covert' and 'clandestine' as they were forthwith to be understood. The third page merely contained a reminder that the reader had already signed the Official Secrets Act.

Cotton looked up. 'About "covert" and . . .'

'What can and what cannot be attributed to His Majesty's Government,' said D.

'Quite which is which?' asked Cotton.

'I think "covert" means the government can deny any involvement. "Clandestine" means the government doesn't have to deny it.'

Cotton thought this was probably accurate but extremely cynical from someone about to give him his new orders.

'You do have to sign before I can proceed,' said D.

Cotton signed. D beckoned and they went through to his office. D shut the door. He frowned.

'Why on earth are you dressed as a major?' he asked.

'The military authorities decided that for personal security and ease of identification in Germany I should put on uniform.'

D shrugged and sat down. 'Well,' he said, 'now you're being sent to the States, to our Embassy in Washington.'

'When will I be leaving?'

'Just as soon as you can be got on a ship or a tin can that floats.' D checked himself. He sighed. 'Are you au fait? Mm? With events of the last month . . . and a day?'

Cotton nodded. 'I think so,' he said.

On 26 July the Labour Party had been declared winners of the British general election. To the surprise of many foreign observers and some British – 'including Lord Keynes' as D said – Winston Churchill had been replaced as Prime Minister by Clement Attlee. Cotton had voted Labour himself – and the election result had been no surprise to troops, who thought they had fought for some measure of justice and reward.

'Right enough,' said D. He started counting off on the fingers of his left hand. 'Hiroshima. Nagasaki. On August 15th the Japanese finally surrender. World War Two is entirely over.'

Cotton nodded. 'Yes.'

D leaned forward. 'Then two days later, on the 17th or hangover day' – more than a whole week before the Yanks even arrive in Tokyo – President Truman calls time on lend-lease.' He snapped his fingers. 'Gone! Not a cent more to keep his British allies afloat.' D almost smiled.

'Well, I'm not saying the British government is shell-shocked,' he went on, 'but . . . Let's say it's a little optimistic to call them merely rattled.' D cleared his throat and leaned back in his chair.

'Four days ago, at a crisis meeting held at Downing Street, our new government decided to send a mission to Washington under Lord Keynes. He's leaving today on a Canadian troopship. We're sending a begging bowl delegation. Huge bowl, rather small delegation. You're following on.'

D opened a drawer of his desk. 'Drink?'

It was eleven in the morning and Cotton could still taste the powdered egg he had been given for breakfast. 'No, thanks,' he said.

D poured whisky into two glasses and pushed one towards Cotton. He had a milk jug filled with water and poured some in until his glass was nearly full.

'Cheers,' he said and drank about a third of it.

Cotton nodded but did not drink.

D put down his glass and sat back. He looked up at the ceiling. 'In 1939,' he said, 'the American government sat down and made a shopping list of what they wanted from the war others were about to fight. On one side of paper. Clear?'

'Yes.'

'Priority one? Naturally, the annihilation of Nazi Germany. Priority two? The defeat of Japan, of course.' D lowered his eyes and looked at Cotton. 'Any ideas on priority three?'

Cotton shook his head.

'The destruction of the British Empire,' said D.

Cotton nodded. 'I see,' he replied. 'What was priority four?'

D smiled. 'What I have been trying to get over to our side is that American policies have been entirely consistent with this list. I think they are still horrified by the one-sheet-of-paper business. They'd have preferred two bits of paper, one for enemies, one for allies, I suppose.

'As you know, lend-lease was designed to keep us fighting. But it was also arranged to make sure we were never an industrial power again. The Americans were "spending" us – mostly in their own interest – and now we are pretty much spent.'

D took another mouthful of his whisky and water.

'I sometimes think the Yanks are being awfully polite about it. If the British want to see 31.4 billion dollars as proof of disinterested friendship in the fight for civilization, well that's Britain's affair. Or if we see ourselves as a not quite equal but proud, loyal partner, in need of a loan to get us back on our feet, that's our mistake as well.'

D downed the rest of his whisky.

'The truth is however that a reverse colonization has taken place. Once we colonized the States; now they are making us a dependency.'

Cotton nodded. He had heard this take on things before, but never with quite such dispatch. D poured himself some more whisky and poured water on top of it. Cotton could not work out whether the stuff was exacerbating D's exasperation or soothing his contempt.

'Our politicians are in shock but unable to see, let alone accept, what has happened. That's partly because they have chosen to cower behind public reaction. They can't actually say "Well done, everyone, we've won – but now, sorry about this, chaps, we're utterly broke and have to start all over again exactly as if we had lost. Well, just like those people we've been fighting."' He groaned. 'I can see us rattling about in a hollow victory for generations.'

Behind Cotton in the office Moira's voice rose.

'Rosalind! Have you used *all* the string?'

D smiled and tapped himself on the chest. 'I don't really know how long I've got left here,' he said. 'If our masters borrow some American vigour I've got about two days. If they are being British about it, I could be hanging about here for weeks and weeks. Keep in touch till then.'

Cotton nodded. 'Very well.'

'In Washington you'll be under the wing of Geoffrey Ayrtoun. Know him?'

'No, I don't,' said Cotton.

'Yes, it's the kind of name that begs a sir in front of it.' D pulled himself up, shook his head. 'Late thirties perhaps. Very effective, I understand. Was in Propaganda and Misinformation. Advertising before that. Sausages and soap powder. You will take your orders from him.'

Cotton nodded.

'You don't know Washington DC?'

'No.'

'It's a provincial town that doubles as a national capital. I can't really think of an equivalent. It's false, like Berlin or Madrid or Leningrad, in the sense that somebody plonked it down somewhere with a rotten climate. A Frenchman's Cartesian plan was kicked off but then the proportions aren't quite right, the domes aren't part of a circle, the columns look more like cake decoration than genuine supports . . . it's like an essay with too many not quite accurate quotes at the beginning. So it is top heavy and then has notes and straggle and later considerations that have nothing to do with the plan.'

D looked up. 'Mind you, it is a boom town. The population has doubled with the war. And the place is crawling with foreigners trying to worm their way into America's favour and join in making the new world.'

6

'What about the British Embassy?' asked Cotton.

'Ah,' said D. He gave himself a moment. 'The Ambassador is Lord Halifax, an aristocrat who has never let his idleness and love of hunting cloud his right to high office. People forget he was Foreign Secretary at Munich and the alternative to Churchill in 1940. He never did quite manage to appease Hitler, not after mistaking him for a footman at their first meeting, but I dare say he'll be able to tone down Lord Keynes' more intemperate outbursts.'

Almost despite himself, Cotton was impressed. It was one of the briskest hatchet jobs he'd heard.

'The rest of the Embassy crew is made up of mealy-mouthed diplomats, family dead wood, communist toadies, ferocious snobs – those last two sometimes the same – and of course I mustn't forget the pillow-diddlers.'

Cotton had never heard the expression 'pillow-diddler'.

'No?' said D. He shrugged. 'A cocksman for information and influence.'

'How does that work exactly?'

'Well, it is true that sperm serves as invisible ink – though the sheet is usually of paper or, at most, a nice silk scarf. Every man is his own pen, as they used to say. In DC, stuffed with bored wives and daughters no longer able to partake of foreign travel, our pillow-diddlers saw themselves as part of the Allied war effort. They diddled for Victory. One attaché diddled Clare Booth Luce whose husband runs *Time* magazine. I think the logic was that a little bit of sheet shrieking would turn the American readers of *Time* pro-British.'

D barely bothered to shake his head. 'By the way, they're keeping you in uniform,' he said.

'Really? Why?'

7

'The policy is to "show them our medals" apparently,' said D.

Cotton frowned in disbelief. 'But why would we do that?'

'Mm. It's quite one of the stupidest things I've ever heard. Can you imagine why the Americans should consider their medals as having less value than ours? But that's the reaction. We are going to impress them into understanding our contribution. And Keynes has decided to be optimistic. Apparently pessimism is something you give in to. Optimism is useful hope.'

'So what will my role be?' asked Cotton.

'You'll be an academic sort of soldier, a brave economist. And you've got a promotion. You'll be a half-colonel.'

'Are you serious about this?'

'Yes! You're part of the policy, part of the medal rattling. And don't forget the economist part. You get to be a shaman before a charlatan.'

'You're putting me off?'

'Absolutely not! You don't have much of a choice anyway. Let's say the situation is "awfully fluid".' D imitated someone who spoke in a holy drawl. 'Ayrtoun will give you the specifics of what they want from you when you get there. But in general terms we are trying not to disappear in the Coronation of the US as winners of the world war. We've had some trouble over the atom bomb, you know, even though some of our scientists worked on it. Like lend-lease, formal co-operation has now ended. They just forgot to send some of the papers on. Nothing too mean in that, just forgetful, because the Americans like to believe they are awfully practical.'

D looked at him. 'I'm drinking too much,' he said. 'Look, on a personal level you'll get out of Britain for a while. We're utterly whacked and fingering our morals while wondering how much power we've lost. You may get some time to think about your future, and DC won't look too bad when you're job hunting. With luck you could be demobbed early next year. Or . . . you can see what you are capable of.'

'Why have I been chosen?' asked Cotton.

'I really wouldn't want to depress you,' said D but then decided to do so. 'You got three ticks. One was for Madrid and your work on the Nazi–Argentinian connection. They liked your paper on that.'

Cotton dipped his head.

'That was one tick. And in Germany you wrote another paper on the effects on the British Army of ending European lend-lease. I take it you said "not good"?'

'Yes, I did.'

'Two ticks. And then, I suggested you. Third tick. I said you are quiet, cautious, reasonably resourceful and you are, as much as economists ever are, capable of a larger view. In the Embassy, people will ask you lots of questions about how it is all going with Keynes and company.'

'They're not going to know?'

'My dear chap, its *sauve qui peut* and pass the parcel out there. If you don't know, you can't be responsible. And that's our side. Oh, by the way,' he added. 'You'll be travelling with another man.' He looked down at a paper on his desk. 'Yes, chap called Tibbets.'

Later Cotton made his way to Waterloo. Nothing much had changed in London since he had last been there in June. The standing buildings were still black with soot, the bomb damage and rubble looked very much as it had done. The only difference Cotton saw was in Waterloo Station, where some German prisoners of war had been put to clearing away the sandbags and were making brisk, quite cheerful progress. Some of them were scrubbing the red brick.

Cotton took a train to Dorking and a cab to his father's house in Peaslake.

He found him outside by the apple store priming a smoke gun. Since the death of his wife in 1938, James Cotton would begin conversations as if they had been going on for some time or as if his son had just been round the corner fetching something.

'I was a bit of a worshipful husband, you see.' He looked up. 'What do you think you'll be?'

Cotton smiled. 'That would depend on who I marry, don't you think? I'm being sent to Washington DC.'

'Yes,' said his father. 'You're quite right. I do think I was lucky. How long will you be gone?'

'Not sure. But at least a couple of months?'

'So you might see Joanie.'

'No might — I will.'

'I'd better get writing then. You can take some letters for the grandchildren.' He paused. 'I always thought Halliday was an extraordinary name for a child. Foster is a bit better. Your mother used to laugh a little at Stephen Foster songs, but rather liked them, I think . . . and Emily is quite perfect, of course.'

'I've brought you some bacon and I filched some sugar from the RAF.'

'Good. I've been getting the apple store ready, you know, and waging my own little war on wasps. They spoil the fruit, you see. I have no choice. I have to take it as a kind of robbery.' He looked up and smiled. 'It must be pretty exciting, eh? You are going to see your sister and the grand-children.'

Cotton put his arm on his father's shoulder. 'We'll get you to see them as soon as we can.'

His father beamed. 'Oh, Isla would have loved to have seen those children!'

Cotton sucked on his teeth. Though he had not been drinking, they felt as if he had. He turned away from the fusty, cider smell of the apple store.

2

COTTON HAD not seen his sister, who lived in New York, since 1936 – and he had an American brother-in-law, a niece and two nephews he had never met at all. He could not see, after docking in New York City on 11 September, with a train to catch to Washington DC, that he had enough time to visit them. He was intrigued, then, to watch Jeremy Tibbets dash off to Brooks Brothers to order a Botany 500 suit, some shirts and a quantity of 'proper socks'.

Tibbets wriggled down the gangplank past the GIs. Cotton wondered what was on the paper he was waving, then heard his plummy tones:

'Coming through! Diplomatic business!'

They had crossed the Atlantic on an American troopship from Le Havre.

'American steel around you now, gentlemen,' the captain had said when they went on board. 'You're welcome but you will keep an eye on that headroom, won't you? Have a good trip.'

They had been given one-half of a four-berth cabin and Tibbets immediately claimed the lower bunk.

'I'm a restless sleeper,' he explained. 'I wouldn't want to disturb you from the upper berth.'

Tibbets was so slender, he looked taller than he was, with a long, smooth, young, rectangular face and lots of dark, floppy hair. He wore a hairnet when he went to sleep. Cotton was not aware his face had even twitched but Tibbets explained he had the advice from his father. 'It protects the follicles,' he said.

Tibbets also soon volunteered that his mother was from 'the wallpaper family'.

Wallpaper was not something Cotton knew about but the name Sanderson came to him.

'No, no, no,' said Tibbets forgivingly, 'not those,' but he did not give a name.

Tibbets described himself as being 'purely on the research side'. In such cramped quarters, however, it was not difficult to see that he spent a lot of time fiddling with numbers and Cyrillic characters in a kind of grid, and that he was finding his code book, F. Scott Fitzgerald's *The Great Gatsby*, rather strange.

Cotton went back to his own reading. Before he left, he had been given Henry James's *The Ambassadors* as his code book for communicating with D. It was a story of European freedom for some Americans, and different kinds of betrayal on both continents. James described his moral hero Strether as a 'fine central intellect' but what struck Cotton as he read in the thrum of the ship was the extraordinary sensitivity of so many characters to shades of meaning as they talked on and on.

Cotton had also been given quantities of figures on the British Colonies – demographics, GNPs, exports, main crops and production figures, all from before the war, with guesses since. This was to be his cover. He would say he was working on the economic implications the Anglo-American negotiations would have for the colonies and the sterling area.

In a third, much slimmer file was a job D had advised him to palm off on someone else. It was a civil servant's 'Consideration' in civil servant's language. It suggested that:

> given the schedule of work and social engagements, the likelihood of one or more of the British delegation providing what will be denominated a distraction (in other words, causing a scandal) approaches levels of some certainty.

The 'consideration' also mentioned that 'much of the US press is hostile towards us and not above underhand methods'.

The British were, however, well looked after on the crossing, given quantities of chicken, steak, mashed potato, spinach and corn – what Cotton knew as *maíz*, from his childhood in Mexico. Tibbets was particularly fond of tinned peaches and ice cream for dessert and would then smoke his cigarette of the day, a Lucky Strike.

'Fabulously comfortable,' he said. 'One could get used to this.' Tibbets liked to use 'one' from time to time.

Round them, the ship played music for the troops going home. Harry James, Perry Como, Les Brown and his Band of Renown, and a singer called Doris Day.

'*Gonna take a sentimental journey, Gonna set my heart at ease . . .*'

'The musical equivalent of saltpetre.' Tibbets sniffed.

At Charterhouse, Cotton had pretended to be more tone-deaf than he was – the school was proud of its choral tradition. It had been one of his cheerfully admitted failings. That did not stop him finding Perry Como's song 'Till the End of Time' a dirge every time it was played.

'Mozart's my thing,' said Tibbets, though Cotton had not asked. 'And Bach, of course.'

'*Never thought my heart could be so yearny . . .*' Cotton found it irritatingly catchy.

The GIs themselves sometimes preferred songs by Ethel Merman and Celeste Holm. 'Why is a Private called a Private?' and 'Three Day Pass'. They had adapted the words, as they had for the Gershwins' 'Let's Call the Whole Thing Off', and sang them with gusto :

'*You say teste and I say tasty . . .*'

This upset the chaplain but it struck Cotton as quite inventive. He found the troops better-humoured than the British, a bit noisier and not quite as stiffly disciplined.

New York City appeared first as a smudge on the horizon, then as a low, dark, convex button. There was a kind of visual fizz above the button and then, shrouded in a morning mist, possibly of its own making, New York sprouted a series of what looked like immensely tall, very slim pencils. On a calm sea and under a pale blue sky they watched the famous skyline take on detail.

'A mammon-made atoll,' said Tibbets. He said it with relish. 'These people have completely moved on from Vitruvian Man.'

Cotton laughed. Tibbets appeared to admire, envy and resent the Americans, but it did not stop him being pompous or patronizing. For most of the GIs, seeing New York from the new immigrants' point of view was a source of excitement and pride. Some of them were calling out the names of the tallest skyscrapers. 'Singer! Woolworth!'

'No! That's the Bank of Manhattan!'

Tibbets later had a story that he had heard one of the young soldiers identify the Statue of Liberty as 'the Liberty Belle'.

When they had docked, Cotton went to thank the ship's captain for both of them.

'You're welcome, Colonel,' said the captain. 'You're on the west side of Manhattan. That's the Hudson River. Glad to help out.'

Cotton organized their baggage and asked the cab driver to take him to Pennsylvania Station.

'Penn Station,' said the driver. 'Canadian?'

'British.'

The driver grunted. The sound was not one of approval. Cotton waited a little to see if there would be more than a grunt – but the driver said nothing.

Inside the cab Cotton was taken by how clammy the heat was. He could smell hot asphalt and warm rubber, a mix of acrid and sweet through the open windows. He tried to settle back to look out, but the ride was jerky, the driver dashing for the next traffic lights and pulling up sharply. Cotton didn't take this to be aimed at him. He could see this was how New York drivers drove. They stopped by a display of fruit and vegetables outside a shop, perhaps fifty feet long, strips of colour and piled, plump shapes, something he had not seen since Mexico and never in such quantity. He almost asked the driver what 'rationing' in the US meant.

After London at the end of the Second World War, New York looked to be not just on an utterly different scale but in a different world. This world was brisk, noisy, scrappy, confidently self-centred and too busy to clean up. It wasn't so much that the buildings towered far higher than any

16

tower in Britain, or that the automobiles were fat and had metal to spare. This was a place that had been to war but not *in* a war. There were uniforms about, of course, but the shops looked full of goods, people buying, the streets crowded. Most striking, after the drabness of Britain, were the flashes of bright colour. This mass of people was not huddled. They had never been bombed and couldn't even begin to imagine it. Things were good and they were pushing on with them. The British had won but had become huddled and reduced in the process.

But somehow it was Penn Station that impressed him most. An enormous structure on an enormous area, the main waiting room extended over seven acres, as big as a park, but based on the Roman baths of Caracalla. It was imperial in scale but not, somehow, in purpose. The architects had exchanged washing for travel. This was pre-First World War America, its references still to Europe, but its functions adapted. Since then, Cotton knew the USA had cut free of Europe as a standard, that the references were all beginning to go the other way, but it wasn't until Penn that Cotton quite understood, despite the films and the newsreels, that the American century had begun thirty to forty years before.

'Wonderful to get some style into life again!' said Tibbets when he arrived, looking very flushed. 'Marvellous shop! I got a pale yellow tie. In silk!'

There were other novelties. The cheerful Negro attendant, dressed in a striped shirt and what looked rather like a kepi hat, who saw them on to the train listened to them speaking.

'May I ask a question, sir?'

'Of course.'

'Have I the pleasure of attending British gentlemen?'

'Well, we're certainly British,' said Tibbets, 'but I'm not sure if that is such a good thing to be in the United States just now.'

'That would depend on who you are talking to, sir.'

'All right,' said Cotton. 'Who are we talking to now?'

The attendant smiled. 'You see, sir, you've just proved it. My nephew told me there was no racism in Britain. Not even the girls are racist. All he got was respect and gratitude. That's what I had heard. That's what I'm seeing.'

'I'm glad to hear it,' said Cotton. He put his hand in his pocket.

The man shook his head. 'No, no, sir. Some things are a pleasure.' He leaned a little closer. 'When my nephew got back he was put in a segregated train, had to watch German prisoners of war get a comfortable carriage.'

'I say,' said Tibbets.

'May I shake your hand, sir?'

'Of course. Peter Cotton.'

'Moses Campbell.'

They shook hands. The attendant showed emotion and pleasure. He separated both hands and feet, then brought everything together in a clap and a click. 'Yes, sir!'

'What on earth was that all about?' said Tibbets when Moses Campbell had gone.

'He didn't think we were racist in Britain.'

Tibbets frowned. He sat down and languidly crossed his legs. 'Oh, surely not,' he said. He sighed.

Tibbets behaved as if New York were an island in the USA and Washington another.

'I understand there is quite a lot of nothing in between.'

'How do you know that?'

18

'Isn't that what people say?' He shrugged. He smiled. 'Wonderful tie,' he said.

The journey to Washington DC took a little under four hours via Philadelphia and Baltimore. The train was higher-set than they were used to and decidedly wider. In Philadelphia there was a longish stop and there Cotton ate a club sandwich and drank a beer. For a couple of days, two of the delightful sounds of America were the noise of cold beer bottles being opened and the rattle of ice cubes. The club sandwich contained turkey and bacon and lettuce and came with mayonnaise. The beer was sweet. Tibbets ate a bagel with cream cheese, then tried a muffin. He found the first 'interesting', the second 'extremely good'. He then ate a roast beef sandwich and drank root beer.

'Have you noticed that the train has a slightly cleaner sound than ours?' said Tibbets when they were going through another Aberdeen, far from Cotton's mother's birthplace, this one before Baltimore. 'In the wheels I mean.'

From Union Station in Washington they took a cab to the Statler Hotel on 16th Street, two blocks north from the White House. The Statler was new — three separate, short, brick towers rising from a single high ground floor. It was factory-plain and functional on the outside but with quite grand interior décor: crystal chandeliers, a plethora of mahogany-clad columns, highly polished dados, pale leather-buttoned booths in a bar, deep red and green velvet coverings for other chairs and the atmosphere of a gentlemen's club on ladies' day.

'Like someone's idea of a neoclassical aquarium,' said Tibbets.

At the reception desk they were given notes instructing them to present themselves at a formal reception that evening at the British Embassy to mark the beginning of Keynes' negotiations. They agreed to meet in the lobby at six.

Cotton sent a telegram to his sister:

```
ARRIVED WASHINGTON DC STOP AT STATLER STOP
WILL ARRANGE VISIT AS SOON AS SCHEDULE KNOWN
STOP LOVE TO ALL PETER
```

He was pleased to get away from Tibbets for a while, and delighted to have a room to himself. The room, while not large and rather over-draped for his taste, was air-conditioned and had its own bathroom. He showered and then sat for half an hour wrapped in a towel sipping the cold water provided. Then he dressed for the reception. Even in air conditioning the formal clothes felt heavy.

Tibbets was already in the lobby when he went down. He beckoned Cotton and indicated that he look through an interior window. A hugely stout man dressed in a brown suit with a startlingly bright tie of red, gold and white, was cutting into a very rare plate-sized steak with two fried eggs on top. 'Look! That fat fellow there is eating at a sitting what looks like more than the British meat ration for a month.' Tibbets sounded as much thrilled as incredulous.

'Your transportation, gentlemen,' said a bellboy, 'is waiting.'

The British Embassy in Washington DC, 'all Wren and Williamsburg by Lutyens', in other words redbrick neo-Georgian with white stone detailing, sits in four acres below the Observatory summit on Massachusetts Avenue hill. Though not yet needed, candle lamps had been lit outside. A number of uniforms were handling arrivals, saluting as doors opened.

Cotton and Tibbets were checked against a list, then went into the reception hall.

Geoffrey Ayrtoun was waiting for them. Short, five foot six or seven, he looked as if he had been neat and athletic, but had now slackened a little. His wavy, thinning hair had been plastered down and, judging by his eyebrows and especially the red-blond fuzz on his freckled hands, much darkened by hair oil. His nose was long and had a pea-sized bump on the bridge. He had been waiting for them, head down, hands behind his back, but came to life when he saw them. His voice was clipped and his extraordinary laugh began with a rapid snorting from the nose and then a staccato bray from the throat, easily loud enough to attract attention.

'For someone in an organization with the motto "*Semper occultus*" – always hidden – that is quite a bark,' muttered Tibbets.

Ayrtoun was in evening dress. During the day they would find he always wore blue, double-breasted suits and a Wykehamist tie. He sat very upright when writing and often played with a tin of fifty Senior Service cigarettes as he spoke, rolling the thing, sometimes tossing it from hand to hand. Occasionally he would open it – 'as if he were wringing a chicken's neck,' said Tibbets – then sniff at the cigarettes. No more than ten times a working day, he would light one, sucking hard, then picking flecks of tobacco off his tongue, even when there were apparently none there.

He wore turned-back shirt cuffs – 'rather too much

showing,' said Tibbets – and gold, oval cufflinks with his initials engraved on them. But, given his colouring, the most unexpected thing about him was the colour of his eyes. They were extraordinarily dark, 'like hard treacle' complained Tibbets.

Ayrtoun welcomed them both, then turned to Cotton.

'Is the idea that we have been a bit unlucky? Mm? That if we had had a year to make use of lend-lease we'd have been able to convert back to peace in relative comfort? But as it is we're fucked? Have I got that right?'

'Something like that,' said Cotton.

Ayrtoun snorted and laughed. The sound was as startling as a flashbulb popping. 'Then why is Keynes sending mixed messages? He tells the Americans our food supplies aren't really so bad, then says we are about to go bankrupt. You can have ermine or you can have cap in hand. Ermine cap in hand is a little confusing.' He stared at them. 'The Embassy says he is absurdly optimistic. How much is he asking for?'

'Nine billion dollars,' said Cotton.

'And how much will he get, do you think?'

To Cotton's surprise, Tibbets answered, 'I'd imagine about six.'

Ayrtoun looked at Cotton.

'Not less than three and a half billion, probably no more than four and a half.'

Tibbets was indignant. 'What do you mean by that?'

'My father managed a bank.'

Ayrtoun grunted in amusement.

'What's that got to do with it?' said Tibbets.

Cotton dropped his voice. 'Banks prefer you to pay them back. Here the Americans have to lend money that at least looks as if it might be paid back, an amount they can sell to the public as being fair, but businesslike.'

'What? Are you suggesting they think we might welsh on it?'

Cotton nodded. 'We did after the First World War.'

'I say, did we?'

'Yes, we did,' said Cotton.

One of the fussy, bouffant-haired men in charge of receptions at the Embassy was called Drey, possibly Dré. Also known as the P & Q, as in Protocol and Queen.

'Chop, chop!' he called as he passed. 'Now move along! The high-ups will be along any second.'

Ayrtoun paid no attention whatsoever. Drey did a stagey kind of double take.

'I said chop, chop, chaps! Now, please.'

Ayrtoun glanced round, very briefly, but saw nothing interesting,

'Oh, dear boy, you'll have to do much better than that. I've moved junior royalty, you know.'

As he said this he raised his hands to clap. He did not manage it. In a ferociously quick but somehow almost discreet movement, Ayrtoun had Drey's wrist caught and down with enough force to make him tilt and wince. Ayrtoun did not let go. He leaned forward towards Drey's ear.

'Don't,' he whispered, 'make that mistake again. Clear?'

Drey was in pain but also indignant.

Ayrtoun sighed and applied more pressure. 'No, I'm not going to have your fingernails removed and made into a charming necklace but you might find your wrist movements severely limited.' He smiled and let go.

There was a sad moment before the P & Q retreated.

'I say!' said Tibbets again.

'You're going to tell me the war's over, are you?' Ayrtoun shook his head. He turned to Cotton.

'I understand you're still doing your national service.'

'Yes.'

'Any job offers?'

Cotton shook his head. 'A PhD or my father's old bank.'

'There's always this.'

'What is this exactly?' said Tibbets.

'Fascinating stuff!' said Ayrtoun. 'Shall we go in now? Mm? Have either of you managed to catch any theatre recently?'

Cotton remembered D had told him that Ayrtoun's nickname was Rikki-Tikki-Tavi.

'Like Kipling's mongoose?'

'Quite. Though the 'Tavi' is from Tavistock, the clinic.'

Cotton frowned. 'I thought that was a hospital for shell shock, battle fatigue, things like that.'

'Oh, they've moved on since the First War,' said D. 'Some of them are about to start a Tavistock Institute to allow them a little more . . . leeway in their examination and management of the human psyche.'

Cotton let Ayrtoun lead the way.

3

THERE WERE two levels of guest at the reception and, in consequence, two areas of the ballroom. The chief delegates of the US and British governments, their partners and guests near the windows – and a much larger one for everyone else.

Tibbets suggested this had been done 'quite subtly, really'.

Geoffrey Ayrtoun looked at him before he snorted. It was not a laugh. 'What would you call a large arrangement of flowers on a table set between the pilasters? A pretty barrier or a clear barrier?'

Cotton had never liked formal receptions and loathed formal evening wear, particularly the military kind, and now that he had been again 'reassumed' into the Army, he was particularly uncomfortable. The dress uniform itself felt very heavy and tight. It smelt of old wool and moth-balls in the very humid heat of Washington. The Embassy being British soil – a kind of over-warmed Wiltshire where the roses in the garden drooped and looked blowsy and smelt more of horse manure than roses – there was, of course, no air conditioning, and as the room filled up, the heat grew oppressive. Sweat started to trickle down Cotton's back. The portraits on the walls, by Hogarth and Gainsborough, made him wonder why the British insisted on evoking the time of the American Revolution – when something glimmered at him.

An elderly lady in a grey moiré gown dimpled and tripled her chins at him while fingering a necklace of blue stones. He wasn't sure what was on her head, something between a tiara and a fascinator. It took him a second to understand she was adding twinkle to her eyes. He smiled politely in welcome, as at a grandmother.

'Now where did you get those quite remarkable pants, young man?'

Evidently he had misjudged her. 'From the British Army, madam.'

'I bet they have their own name.'

'They're called trews. It's Scots for trousers.'

'Is that pattern plaid?'

'We say tartan, I think. Argyll and Sutherland Highlanders.'

'Well now,' she said, 'they're certainly bright.' She leaned back and considered him below the waist. 'And quite remarkably snug. What do you call the jacket?'

'A short jacket.'

'Really? I thought you called them bum freezers.'

'Not in this heat, I promise.'

She laughed. 'Oh thank God! You sound like fun. I had thought the Scots for trousers was breeks.'

'If trews are trousers, I suppose breeks might come from britches?'

The old lady smiled. 'Ah, the Scots "r". The English have problems with it.'

'In what way?'

'They sometimes miss it out. Don't mind me, I am just an old broad as we Americans say. What's your name?'

'Peter Cotton.'

'I'm Evelyn Duquesne. My late husband Gerald was in

wood pulp, for newspapers, you know, and now I am invited to receptions as part-payment for my political donations. And some shares in radio stations. What's this one for exactly?'

'Our respective governments are due to talk about money. I believe we are going to ask for some.'

She raised her chin. 'Well, how direct and unstuffy. I'll keep my eye on you, young man. But do remember, a sense of humour can be a disadvantage if you have political ambitions.'

'I have none whatsoever, I assure you,' said Cotton.

She looked mock-shocked. 'No, no, no! You can't say that. Not in Washington. Though you might like to tell Maynard to keep the humour to himself. But he is quite incorrigible, of course. I understand our journalists – on the whole quite a hardbitten crowd, you know – well, they do find his refinement a little long-winded and his jokes more than obscure.'

Cotton smiled. 'Mrs Duquesne, I had the privilege of hearing Lord Keynes speak when I was at university but the relationship has not progressed out of the lecture hall.'

She laughed. 'You really are refreshing. Not as much as air conditioning would be, but your honesty provides an atomizing tingle. Ah,' she said, 'now you must tell me what you think of this.'

Coming towards them were two men, one in evening wear, the other in a US Navy dress uniform. They were flanking a blonde girl in a dark red velvet gown. Cotton did not know who they were but Ayrtoun beamed.

The girl detached herself from the men and approached Cotton's companion.

'Mrs Duquesne, good evening.'

'Katherine, darling, lovely to see you. Miss Ward. This is Colonel Cotton. Don't you think his pants are just too much? Almost divine.'

Cotton inclined his head. 'Miss Ward.'

The girl smiled pleasantly. 'Colonel, I believe you are Trustee to the Colonies.'

Cotton had never heard this title. 'That sounds very grand.'

'I have to warn you, Katherine,' said Mrs Duquesne, 'that he talks himself down.'

'Are you the anti-Trustee?' said Cotton.

She shook her head and smiled. 'I'm with the State Department,' she said. 'We don't have colonies.'

Cotton grew aware of a kind of shifting around them from the men, what Spanish calls 'peacocking' and his mother had termed 'shuffling like overdressed cavemen'. Cotton learned that the navy captain was called Jim Lally, the other man Emilio, but didn't catch his surname – Col something, possibly Colati. He spoke first.

'What? The British are leaving their Empire?'

'I understand there is a possibility we don't believe in it any more,' said Ayrtoun.

'That's not our information.'

'I think it is because we can't afford it,' said Tibbets.

'But you are not leaving it to us,' said Captain Lally.

'You're saying you don't want us to have it but you don't want it?'

'That's about right,' said Katherine Ward. 'Self-determination, Colonel Cotton. It's an American enthusiasm.'

'And very admirable.'

'Oh darling, he means our Indians are not his Indians,'

28

said Mrs Duchesne. 'Nobody asked Sitting Bull what he felt about Holy Cows. Around 1908 I had a suitor with the first name Custer. Custer Dean. Oh, I was a looker then.'

Mrs Duquesne suddenly leaned over and put her face, all wrinkle and smile, beside Katherine Ward's, as for a photograph, or perhaps to demonstrate what happens to everyone eventually. There was a moment when Katherine Ward's green eyes struck him as very expressive but then he became aware of her promising cleavage.

At the entrance to the ballroom something stirred. The principal guests, the Ambassador Lord Halifax and Lord Keynes for the UK, and Will Clayton and Fred Vinson for the US, came in with their various partners. The crowd stepped back to allow them through and they proceeded down the ballroom towards the windows and the air.

Cotton had not seen John Maynard Keynes since university. He had become a very old man and had difficulty walking. Clayton at six foot six, his white hair centre-parted, looked to be attentively helping him along. Fred Vinson, walking in with Lady Keynes, was acknowledging people he knew. Lord Halifax had been born with an atrophied left arm and no left hand.

The Embassy First Secretary, a man called MacLean, accompanied them looking unsteady and flushed. He did not seem to know whether he was an actor in, or director of, the procession.

'I say, our side looks a bit battered,' said Tibbets. Cotton glanced at him, unsure whether or not Tibbets was aware he had spoken aloud. 'Keynes looks like some sort of marine mammal,' murmured Tibbets. 'What are those things in Florida? Manatees?'

The Keynes and Clayton procession passed and Mrs Duquesne waved as she followed them.

'They say,' she whispered as she left, 'that Lady Baba Metcalfe is too fatigued to attend.' Evidently this was good.

'Lady Who?' said Captain Lally.

'I have no idea,' said Cotton.

'Lady Baba is Viscount Curzon's third daughter,' Tibbets explained, but none of the Americans looked wiser.

'The Ambassador was rather upset to have his holidays interrupted for these negotiations,' said Ayrtoun. 'Lady Alexandra is a kind of compensatory old chum.'

'Did he have far to come?' asked Katherine Ward.

'Yorkshire in England. Shooting.'

'Lady Baba is often called Baba Blackshirt,' said Tibbets. 'Her husband is Fruity Metcalfe, equerry to the last King, now Duke of Windsor. Her brother-in-law was Oswald Mosley, the fascist. Also her lover. Her sister killed herself.'

'Well, isn't this all bluff and cosy,' said the navy captain.

Cotton had some sympathy. As well as the clothes, the other thing he disliked about formal receptions was the conversation. It was almost always excruciatingly dull or overly facetious, rarely useful, accurate or surprising. Katherine Ward surprised him.

'You're not quite British, are you?'

Cotton smiled. 'It can't be the uniform,' he said.

'I meant your accent.'

'Really? In what way?'

'No haw-haw,' said Captain Lally.

'That's true,' said Tibbets. 'I had rather taken you for an Indian.'

'What are you talking you about?'

'The Cotton family in India. Madras I think. Judges and so on.'

'Most people ask if I am related to Henry Cotton, the golfer. I'm not as far as I know.'

'I'm guessing you speak another language. And you've done that for a long time,' said Katherine Ward.

Cotton smiled. 'You really do your research.'

He was surprised she should look a little hurt.

'No,' she said, 'I was listening.'

'Then I'm sorry. You're correct.' He smiled again. 'What?'

'I am thinking what language. Say something with a lot of vowels.'

Cotton shrugged. 'Your motor cars are large and fast but not in Manhattan where the flow of traffic can get . . .'

'. . . jammed tight as a racoon's head in a licked out jar of peanut butter,' said Captain Lally.

'We say automobile,' she said. 'South American Spanish?'

'You have a good ear.'

'Where?'

'Mostly Mexico. Though I was in Spain not long ago.'

'Your colleagues say "cah",' said Jim Lally.

'They don't have the Scottish "r", according to Mrs Duquesne.'

She frowned. 'You're Scottish?'

'Not particularly,' said Cotton, 'not by accent anyway. I usually find I adapt till people understand me.'

'That has to be a deliberate policy,' said Emilio.

'Of course. At prep school, junior school, they called me "bananas".'

'Buhnaaahnas,' offered Tibbets.

'Because?'

'Oh, because I had a South American home address? At the next school they called me "Gringo".'

'That's us,' said Emilio.

'But my favourite was "Sorrow" – for "*Zorro*".'

She laughed – and moved on. 'Lovely to meet you all.'

Tibbets barely waited.

'I say,' he said, 'she liked you, all right.'

Cotton considered him. 'Do you have a sister?'

'Well I do! But not like that!'

'Neither's mine. But she did let me in on quite a lot of things that allow me to understand. Miss Ward was just doing her job. I think my sister said men tend to misjudge the quality of attention women lend them.'

Ayrtoun raised his eyes. 'Time to circulate, gentlemen. Get to know people. Introduce yourselves.'

Noise level rose, as alcohol worked and people competed to be heard over laughter and clinking. There was no air conditioning, but the British had given way on ice and Cotton got through the reception by raiding the ice bucket with a single whisky that someone later took for gin.

At the end of the reception, as Cotton was pretending to listen to an American marine drone on about the future of aircraft carriers, something caught his eye. Mrs Duquesne was beckoning. Cotton excused himself and went over.

'Colonel, dear, I'm having a little dinner at home on Thursday evening. Do come. You'll get the average age down and make it harder for the older men to drop off to sleep. They get competitive, you see, and they stir themselves when faced with youth.'

'You're very kind. I'd be delighted to come.'

'Where are you staying, darling?'

'The Statler.'

'Like Maynard?'

'In another part of the building.'

She laughed. 'Lovely. I'll have you . . . collected.'

Cotton inclined his head.

'We've built you up a little, old boy,' said Ayrtoun behind him, 'made you into a brain box with a future.'

Cotton said nothing.

'Mrs Duquesne was rather stoutly on the side of the Allies, you see, and quite figures herself as a modern version of one of those *grandes dames* of the French Enlightenment. You might want to cultivate her – as a soul mate, of course. Her contacts are legion, high up and they always pick up the telephone.'

Cotton still said nothing but turned round. Tibbets had appeared.

Ayrtoun frowned. 'Where are you two staying?' he said.

'At the Statler.'

'They'll move you out.'

'But we've only just arrived,' said Tibbets.

'The Americans haven't given us any money yet. Eight a.m. tomorrow, gentlemen. Sharp.'

They watched him walk away and then filtered out into the hall.

'What do you think of him?' said Tibbets.

'I was told he was very ambitious.'

'Really?' said Tibbets. He nodded. 'Do you know what you are here for?'

'Not yet.'

Tibbets sighed. 'I suppose we'll be down the car-pecking order,' he said.

In fact they were soon called. On their way back to the Statler, Tibbets changed the subject.

33

'Mm. Do you mind if I ask you a question?'

'Go ahead.'

'Are you good with women?' he asked.

'Haven't we had this conversation?'

'Well, I was really asking for a bit of advice, you see.' Tibbets sounded put-out.

'All right.'

'Are you sure?'

'Yes. Of course I am,' said Cotton.

'Well, you see, I am rather keen on this girl. Joyce. She's very, well . . .' Tibbets made fumbling, roundish gestures in front of his chest '. . . she's dashed attractive.'

'Yes.'

'And very bright, of course. That's not common, you know. She was at Lady Margaret Hall.'

Cotton nodded. 'So what's the problem?'

'She's lively and gay and all that but . . . she just doesn't seem very interested. I don't know if that's a general thing or just me.'

'How specific has your interest been?'

'Oh, God, not very. Not at all.'

'Do you have her address? '

'Oh absolutely. She's almost a neighbour. I've known her for a long time. And all her family. She read biology and we have a shared interest in music. She's a flautist and I play the viola.'

'Right,' said Cotton. 'Why don't you try a letter then? Keep the first one general and chatty, talk about music, that kind of thing.'

'You think so?'

'It's a suggestion only. Say something here made you think of her and see what she replies.'

34

'Can I think about it?'

'Well, of course. And you certainly don't have to take my advice.'

Tibbets grunted. It was an odd, hopeless sound, as if he had no choice.

Cotton thought Tibbets had to be a wonderful mathematician.

Back at the hotel reception there was a telegram for Cotton.

WELCOME STOP LOOK OUT FOR OCTOBER 12 AND
WEEKEND STOP CHILDREN VERY EXCITED LOVE JOAN

'Not bad news, I hope,' said Tibbets.

'What? No. The reverse.' Cotton smiled. 'I'll say good-night then.'

'Really?' said Tibbets. 'Well, all right then.'

Cotton walked to the main door and stepped outside.

'Cab, sir?' the doorman enquired.

'No, thank you,' said Cotton. 'I was only thinking of stretching my legs.'

'The doorman shook his head. 'I wouldn't advise that, sir.'

Cotton raised his eyebrows. 'What?'

'We try to help, sir. It's night and you're in the South, and I've only got you in view a short way.'

Cotton blinked. 'All right,' he said.

In his uniform the heat was almost tropically humid but, after a day of ship, cabs, train and Embassy, he wanted at least to be outside.

He strolled across the sidewalk or pavement and looked right, then left along 16th Street. Cotton breathed in and shut his eyes. He had an impression he was getting rid of aches, smoke, the smell of pink gin and perfume, when the hairs on his hands stiffened. Very close by, a motor gunned up. Cotton jerked backwards but remembered to keep his head up, like some inept matador avoiding a wing mirror rather than a horn. A fraction later his fly buttons shuddered, a wisp of tartan wool away from the swerving car. The car swept on and he heard, but had to wait to make out the words – 'When I sees a turkey I just aims for it, man' – followed by high-pitched laughter. He saw a black face grinning back at him and felt the tingle where his middle finger had flicked against the window.

He felt shock creeping over his scalp, swore, but then, a pleasant surprise, he began to laugh. He turned and walked back into the hotel past the impassive doorman.

'Thank you,' he said. 'I'll take my chills inside.'

4

COTTON WAS at the desk he had been given in the
Chancery by 8 a.m. the following day, 12 September,
with security and bureaucracy done. The desk was empty
apart from a telephone, and was one of eight crammed into
a room with faded parquet flooring. This was the Intelligence
Room, otherwise known as the 'Snooker Hall'. It had metal
grilles on the windows and an additional door at its
entrance hung counter to the wooden door.

The Chancery itself was the business part of the Embassy
complex. It was similar to the Ambassador's mansion, if
less opulent in style, and was seriously inadequate for the
number of people working there.

To Cotton, the atmosphere had something of the hier-
archy of a public school, the leftover manners and flower
vases of the country-house Embassy with, on his floor at
least, the rush and bustle of a newspaper office combined
with a police station.

As in the Embassy, there was no air conditioning. Two
sedate ceiling fans slowly stirred the air – someone had tied
a ribbon to one, which fluttered just below the height of
the blade. Cotton watched a girl twitch and ruffle the cut
flowers by the windows and grilles and then wave a per-
fume-soaked handkerchief, like a signaller who had given
up. For a few seconds he could smell lavender over stale
tobacco smoke and something like his old school gym.

On the other side of a corridor was a room for the Physical Security staff and next to it, the Communications Room. Cotton walked down to the end of the corridor to another large room, this one filled by secretaries and the clack of typewriters, the sounds fattened by keys striking layers of paper and carbon paper. Ayrtoun's office, a glass-and-wood structure was built out from one corner of this.

It was in this large room, after the secretaries were sent out, that the morning briefings took place. Today they learned, amongst other things, that Keynes was to give a press conference and be made uncomfortable by persistent, down-to-earth questions from the journalists Mrs Duquesne had called 'hardbitten'. It was intended that he would win them over.

Tibbets was wearing his yellow tie. Neither the colour nor the shape was fashionable and it made him look even younger than usual, as if he had borrowed a tie from a young version of his father.

After the briefing, Ayrtoun called the secretaries back, beckoned Cotton and Tibbets into his office and had them shut the door. Though muffled, the sound of the typewriters was constant. Ayrtoun asked them to sit and started looking for something.

On the wall behind his desk were bookshelves. Cotton picked out Gustave Le Bon's *The Crowd: A Study of the Popular Mind*, Wilfred Trotter's *Instincts of the Herd in Peace and War* and Edward Bernay's *Propaganda*. He had not heard anyone use the 'Rikki-Tikki-Tavi' nickname yet but the titles made him see where it might come from.

Right behind Ayrtoun's head were two postcards pinned to the shelves. One read ACTON and the other SCRAPPLE.

Elsewhere on the shelves were SALT and GLUE. Cotton did not ask what they meant.

Ayrtoun handed them a circular 'to read and sign'. It was the joint statement from the heads of MI5 and MI6 drawing 'urgent attention' to the differences between war and peace that Cotton had already signed in London.

'Well, there's no point in signing it again,' said Ayrtoun. 'Is there?'

'No,' said Cotton.

'I say. Is this straight down the middle?' said Tibbets.

Ayrtoun frowned. 'Of course, it is.'

'What happens if the other side are not so bound?'

'For Christ's sake man!' snapped Ayrtoun. 'Haven't you any familiarity with the Official Secrets Act?'

'Are we being issued with weapons?'

'Not as far as I know. Why on earth would you want one? This is intelligence work in the USA. What we need is patient analysis. Now, you also have to understand that the Yanks have their own incidental security system,' said Ayrtoun wryly. 'It's called lack of continuity – every time the administration changes, so does everything and everyone else. They don't have a civil service, so every time they change President, we have to learn who matters, all over again. The last President died in April and now Truman is still finding find his feet and putting in his own men.'

'All right,' said Tibbets.

'Is it?' Ayrtoun scratched the back of his neck. He shook his head. 'Now I am going to tell you why you are here. Listening?'

Cotton and Tibbets nodded.

'In just over a week's time, something quite extraordinary is going to happen. President Truman will announce that the official American secret service, the OSS, will be broken up. It will cease to exist.'

Ayrtoun smiled, though as Tibbets would remark to Cotton later, it was not really a smile – looked more like a threat in the shape of a smile.

'Now I don't have to tell you,' said Ayrtoun, 'that "Oh So Secret" always leaked with the consistency and regularity of a rose on a watering can, but it is still a remarkable decision, don't you think?'

Neither Cotton nor Tibbets expressed an opinion.

'Un-British, if you like,' said Ayrtoun. 'We rather prefer discretion as the better part of law. Faced with a similar problem – a lack of co-ordination – we simply pulled in the SOE. The Americans are more public.'

Ayrtoun picked up his tin of cigarettes and turned it upside down.

Cotton frowned. 'If they disband the OSS, who is going to . . .'

'Its responsibilities will be divided mainly between the Department of State and the Department of War,' said Ayrtoun. 'The State Department will be handling Research and Analysis, now to be called IRIS – Got that? That's *Interim* Research and Analysis – and the War Department will be taking over Secret Intelligence and Counter-Espionage or X2. That will now be the SSU – the Strategic Services Unit. All right?'

Tibbets looked incredulous. 'How do you know this?'

'Because it is my job and this is Washington DC.'

'I mean how do you break up the OSS? Is that even feasible?'

'Feasible? Of course it is fucking feasible. It doesn't mean the split is going to last, of course. The word "Interim" before Research and Analysis gives us a little clue on that, wouldn't you say? But this is America. A decision is made before a plan for the future is quite settled. The most likely thing is that Truman's people want to clear the place out and get rid of bad habits and worse personnel. They will then, I am sure, set up another agency as a central co-ordinated source of intelligence. What nobody knows is how long they are going to take. Are you with me?'

'Yes,' they said.

'OK,' said Ayrtoun. He stood up, walked round and sat on the edge of his desk, facing them. 'Now,' he said, 'you have to understand a few things. At the beginning of the war, President Roosevelt sent Wild Bill Donovan over to Britain. His brief was to find out whether the British would be French – or whether they'd really put up a fight against the Germans.'

'I say!' said Tibbets again. Ayrtoun shot a look at him.

'As a reward for getting it right,' he went on, 'Roosevelt allowed Donovan to set up the OSS. Its aim was to co-ordinate American intelligence services.' Ayrtoun paused. 'At the beginning, the Anglo-American relationship was so close that Donovan simply took over the MI6 office in the Rockefeller Center in New York. We were fighting for survival and we needed help.

'The Americans, of course, were not fighting for survival. We weren't sure the Channel would be enough, but they had the Atlantic – they knew that was more than enough. So they set about fighting amongst themselves. You have to understand that, apart from the OSS, each of the armed forces also has its own intelligence service – and there were other agencies involved, like the FBI.'

'Right,' said Cotton.

'They were all fighting each other for power and control. Donovan found his efforts to co-ordinate things frustrated, and he was more or less limited to Europe. For example, MacArthur refused to let the OSS anywhere near the Philippines. He wanted complete control of his area. This was a truly expensive mistake – but it was not overruled. And the FBI wouldn't let him near South America. That was – and still is – completely under their control.'

'So where does Donovan stand now?' asked Cotton.

'Well, Roosevelt liked Donovan,' said Ayrtoun. 'But Truman loathes him. There has been a press campaign against him by what were the pro-German newspapers. They called the OSS "an American Gestapo", of course. The FBI has been feeding the press and Hoover has been bending Truman's ear. Donovan is over. But there is no real successor. Now that it is peacetime, the various agencies are going to fight it out while the rest of the world waits. That's why you are here. We need to keep track of what's going on.'

Ayrtoun turned to Cotton. He gave him a file.

'Right. This is on Mullins,' he said. 'I've told him to come in to see you. Have a word with him and then come back. I'll be . . . chatting to Tibbets in the meantime.'

Cotton took the file. 'And Mullins is . . .?'

'Personal Security Operative,' said Ayrtoun, and turned his attention to Tibbets.

Cotton went back to his desk. It had already gathered three distinct stacks of files, coloured buff, green and pinkish – and a pile of official news messages. The top one read: 'September 12. Singapore. Mountbatten accepts Japanese surrender from General Itagaki.'

A couple of lines further down was the information that

42

the Japanese had had to wait for a week for Mountbatten to arrive.

Cotton turned his attention to the buff pile. The top file was on John Maynard Keynes, Lord Keynes of Tilton. He began to skim-read to fill himself in on some background while waiting for Mullins.

Cotton had seen Keynes in the late thirties, dropping in on Cambridge with the likes of George Bernard Shaw to attend dinners and deliver a few lectures, but he only knew of the public man with his very high reputation made, all brilliance and amiability.

He was vaguely aware that the younger Keynes had been friendly with the Bloomsbury Group – Virginia Woolf and Lytton Strachey were mentioned as close friends – but Cotton had not known of Keynes' long affair with the painter Duncan Grant. Regarded in the report's words as 'a confirmed bachelor', there had been some 'mirth and in-credulity' amongst his family and friends when, in 1925, Keynes had married Lydia Lopokova, a Russian ballerina. To the 'surprise of almost all and the displeasure of not a few' the union had been 'gloriously happy'. Something of Jane Austen in the report writer's style, thought Cotton. He continued reading.

As well as being a professor, Keynes played the financial markets, wrote newspaper articles and books, was a patron of the arts and a government adviser. For the war years he had been lead negotiator for the British with the Americans, especially in regard to the post-war economic set-up – though as the report put it, 'while he talked for hours, power was elsewhere at Bretton Woods.' The arrangements in the end had been largely to the design of Harry Dexter

White, though he had allowed Keynes to give the International Monetary Fund its name.

Cotton turned over the pages. Keynes was not a security risk in any of the terms they were talking about. The risks listed here were his health (he had a 'viral heart condition'), his temper and 'the Americans' view of him'. He was well respected in the US for his intellect and perception, but his atheism and 'past life' made the Americans suspicious of his 'moral fibre'. They admired him, but they did not trust him.

From Keynes' point of view, his 'rationality' made it difficult for him to appreciate politics anywhere, let alone US politics. This meant that he could become frustrated, then cutting – and then extremely rude.

Cotton considered this briefly. Keynes was a very sick man. While he was here, in whatever time was left to him when not attending meetings or press conferences, Keynes would be ensconced, with Lydia, in a suite high up in the same Statler Hotel Cotton had been given a room in, often flat on his back with a bag of ice pressed over his heart and a supply of sodium amytal on the table beside him.

A shadow fell across his desk. Cotton looked up. Standing in front of him was about six foot three and sixteen stones of very large, very impassive man.

'Robert Mullins?' said Cotton, opening the file Ayrtoun had given him.

'Sir.'

'Good. Please sit down, then.'

'Prefer to stand, sir.'

During the war Cotton had been outranked and underranked. He decided to be peremptorily peaceful. 'No,' he said, 'you sit down.'

Mullins sat. Though dressed in a civilian suit, he still had about him all the creases of a uniform and spit and polish on his shoes, but more sergeant than sergeant major. His hair was not so much cut as chopped. Clipped almost bare above his ears and at the sides of his head, the hair permitted on top of his skull resembled something like hedgehog bristles that had been coated in hair oil and then flattened. His knuckles were boxer-big but he looked half a beat away from the coordination and hand speed required of a fast heavyweight. Apart from having suffered at some time a broken nose, Mullins had had years of draining his long face of all expression.

'Good,' said Cotton. Mullins' file showed he had been born in Crewe in 1909, seventh child of a railway worker, had 'entered service' at the age of thirteen in 1922 and risen first to 'footman' and then to 'under-butler' by 1931 when the titled owner of the big house he had worked in had been obliged to let a lot of staff go. He had then got a job in a slaughterhouse. In 1933, he had started work in a butcher's shop and married Beryl Roberts, the owner's daughter, in December 1935. They had no children. Cotton saw that Mullins had served in North Africa as bodyguard to one of the summarily relieved generals there. He was a crack shot.

'How long have you been in Washington?'

'Since July '44, sir. I was sent to the US for Bretton Woods and kept on here.'

Anyone showing less obvious adaptation to the US would have been hard to imagine. Cotton tried. 'What do you have for lunch, Mullins?'

'Sir? Usually pastrami on rye.'

Cotton smiled. 'Good,' he said. He was not sure what pastrami was. Some sort of salt-cured beef? But definitely – even if via Romania or somewhere – it was American. 'What were you doing at Bretton Woods?'

'Sit and watch, sir.'

'What were you watching?'

'For interruptions, sir. And also the delegates. I had a list of signs to take notice of. Inebriation, fatigue, tics . . .'

'Tics?'

'Signs of stress, sir, involuntary twitching.'

'Right. So you have experience of delegations.'

'Yes, sir. Though the cases are different. At Bretton Woods there were seven hundred and thirty delegates from forty-four allied countries. The British delegation was relatively small and I had help, sir. We were also in a big hotel tucked away in New Hampshire, sir.'

'Right. So how would you characterize this task?'

'Less removed from the world, sir, just us and the Americans.'

'OK. And what's your main worry?'

'Numbers, sir. The main people are here but a lot more will be arriving as the negotiations become particular and more meeting places are used.'

That was the first Cotton had heard of that. 'What help have you got?'

'Just one man, sir. Good man. Corporal Edwards.'

'Right,' said Cotton. 'What problems did you have at Bretton Woods?'

Mullins shook his head. 'Nothing beyond helping some of the gentlemen to bed, sir. They work very long hours and eat, drink and smoke – sometimes too much. Oh, one of the female secretaries was ill-advised, sir.'

'Who by?'

'A French sort of Canadian, sir.'

Cotton smiled. He got out the list of delegates accompanying Keynes. 'How many do you know here?'

Mullins looked. 'Most of them, sir. They'll be no trouble. Too busy.'

'Mark the ones you don't know.'

Mullins marked two out of the eight. 'May I make a suggestion, sir?'

'Yes.'

'That we call this group "The Mission".'

Cotton raised his eyebrows.

'It's what they call themselves, sir. The delegates . . .'

Cotton nodded. '. . . will be those arriving later. I understand. Now tell me. What have you been doing since Bretton?'

'Providing personal protection when required. Getting my bearings. Establishing contacts with the locals. And I have done another firearms course, sir. Revolver. And I've had some advanced driving lessons.'

Cotton nodded. There was a British kind of sense to Mullins' career: footman, under-butler, slaughterhouse man, butcher's assistant, bodyguard – and now a combination of things that had sharpened these experiences and talents.

'You've made contacts with Americans?'

'Yes, sir.'

'Do you like them?'

'Yes, sir.'

'Any particular thing?'

'They are less formal than we are, sir. More accessible. More direct.'

Cotton smiled. 'Yes. I can imagine. Any drawbacks?'

Mullins thought. 'Well, sir, I suppose it's the other side of the same coin. They are very open but the openness doesn't mean as much as it would with us. Yes, and they talk about money all the time.'

'Ah. And do Americans like you?'

'In general, sir, they seem to. At a professional level they say I am easier to talk to than some other people here.'

Cotton could believe that. He wrote down his telephone numbers and gave them to Mullins.

'Do you have a telephone at home?'

'I do.' Mullins looked momentarily reluctant but wrote it down for Cotton.

'This is your day off? Thanks for coming in. According to the schedule, Lord Keynes is giving a press conference over at the Embassy today and the first meeting will be at the Federal Reserve tomorrow. Are you on that?'

'No, sir.'

'You report to Mr Ayrtoun?'

'Yes, sir.'

'Anyone else?'

The large, impassive face froze for a moment, then nodded.

'You, sir?' ventured Mullins.

Behind him a girl pointed towards Ayrtoun's office. Cotton nodded.

'Very good,' said Cotton and got up. 'Thanks again.'

The big man looked a little alarmed as he got up.

'It's all right, I have to see Mr Ayrtoun now. The arrangement for this at present is quite inadequate. I'll see to it.'

'Thank you, sir.'

Cotton walked back to Ayrtoun's office. Tibbets had gone. Ayrtoun unpinned the ACTON card.

'What does this mean to you?'

Cotton shrugged. 'There was a Lord Acton,' he said.

'Exactly!'

48

'Absolute power? Absolute corruption?'

'Mm, but I have another quote on the back of this card.' Ayrtoun flipped it over and read: ' "Everything secret degenerates; nothing is safe that does not show it can bear discussion and publicity." What do you think?'

'I'm not sure I understand it.'

'It's absolute horse-shit. I use the word Acton as shorthand. When I say Acton it means it is imperative to stop something getting out, that we must stifle any bad publicity. Clear?'

'I understand what you mean,' said Cotton, 'but . . .'

'So we need to keep an eye on our people and squash anything potentially embarrassing. OK? You saw Mullins?'

'Yes.' Cotton shook his head. 'We don't have enough men for delegate security.'

Ayrtoun grunted. 'We'll have to get people over then. But I want one of mine in overall charge – if anything happens that could cause difficulties. I refer particularly to Lord Acton's friends in the American press.'

Cotton paused. 'Would I get Mullins?'

'Yes.'

Cotton nodded.

'Now,' said Ayrtoun. 'IRIS.'

'Yes,' said Cotton. 'Interim Research and Analysis – now under the State Department.'

Ayrtoun nodded. 'Good. You may have gathered that you have drawn the State Department. It is your job to keep an eye on them. Not too exciting perhaps? But let's get this straight. I don't think IRIS is going to last. As I said, they'll be setting up a new organization to replace the OSS. And since you are still doing your military service, we don't know how long we've got you for. Correct?'

'Correct,' said Cotton.

'Though that's your call, of course.'

'Really?' Cotton was conscious of the difference between the career intelligence people and him. It made him more vulnerable to unpleasant jobs and he really could not see what he could do about it. Intelligence had to offer him a job or he had to apply for one, but they had as yet made no offer and he was not aware of one to apply for. The alternative was managing to comply with orders until he was demobbed.

'To spice things up a bit we're thinking of you as bait. You don't have to look too happy when you're in public, that kind of thing.'

Cotton narrowed his eyes. 'Why would I do that?' he said.

'Yes, that's about the tone,' said Ayrtoun. 'A little disaffected, let's say. It might encourage the odd approach.'

'From the State Department?'

Ayrtoun gave him a 'Now, now' look. 'We'll have to see whose interest you arouse.'

Cotton nodded without enthusiasm. But Ayrtoun had not finished.

'Now let's get your colonies cover in place. You have someone to see,' he said. 'A Dr George Samson Aforey, G. S. Aforey. He teaches, here in Washington, at Howard University. He's already been contacted and is expecting your call.'

Cotton had heard neither of Dr Aforey nor of Howard University.

'It's called the black Harvard.' Ayrtoun looked up. 'Though I suppose Howard would be more a gathering of the excluded than of those who can afford to be exclusive, mm?' He smiled. 'It's all very "Advancement of Coloured Peoples", and has the first ever Negro university president, a chap called Mordecai Wyatt Johnson. Dr Aforey is in the social sciences department but I think his doctorate was actually in theology. John the Baptist comes to mind. I am quite certain he'll be expecting your call on the future of Africa.'

'I really don't know anything about Africa. Literally,' said Cotton, 'almost nothing.'

'Good,' said Ayrtoun. 'This way you can learn something and, I can assure you, in Washington nobody is going to be crowding you in any competitive sort of way on this.'

'What am I going to discuss with him?'

'London rather wants him, if not to attend the Pan-African Congress in Manchester next month, at least to provide a voice. A different voice. Non-Marxist. We would like you to encourage that.'

'I see,' said Cotton. 'Is this in Manchester, England?'

'Yes. They are calling it the Fifth Congress but I think the Fourth was back in the twenties some time. This post-war one is being organized by' – Ayrtoun broke off and looked down – 'George Padmore, some kind of trade unionist from Trinidad and, oh Christ, I don't know how to pronounce this, Kwame Nkrumah from the Gold Coast.' Ayrtoun looked up. 'Let's say there'll be a cluster of possible future leaders there.' He looked down again at his alphabetical list. 'Awolowo, Obafemi, from Nigeria, Banda, Hastings, from Nyasaland . . . oh' – Ayrtoun had seen a name he recognized – 'W. E. B. Dubois is going from the US.'

'Right,' said Cotton. 'Let me check this then. Pan-African in this context means a congress for Negroes from Africa, the West Indies and the US, that is being held in an industrial city in the north-west of England?'

'Pretty much.'

'Would I be correct in saying that the majority of possible future African leaders are already in England so that transport is not a problem?'

Ayrtoun smiled. 'I don't think the political desk would put it quite that way, but yes. I see Dr Banda is a medical doctor practising in North Shields, Awolowo is studying at the Bar and Nkrumah, who has just apparently legally changed his name from Francis Nwia-Kofi, met with Padmore when he arrived in London last May from Philadelphia, also to study law.'

'He came when the European war ended?'

'Yes.'

Cotton nodded. 'Has Dr Aforey been invited to this congress?'

Ayrtoun shrugged. 'I've got down here he tends to be a tad contrary. He'll certainly want to see you quietly.'

'Is that why it's me doing this?'

'I did say quietly, didn't I?'

'Yes. Are we prepared to pay his fare and organize transport?'

'Oh,' said Ayrtoun. 'Do tell me you are joking.'

5

COTTON CALLED Howard University and asked for extension 21. 'Dr Aforey?'

There was a pause. Though on the telephone, Dr Aforey spoke with something of public oratory in his tone.

'This is he. To whom do I have the pleasure of speaking?'

That 'to whom' came with a slight hiss of air expelled down the nose and the doctor's version of 'pleasure' sounded startlingly similar to a drunken brigadier Cotton had heard at a mess dinner on the subject of 'Glasgow girls' – 'Utter pleasure? No! Gutta plesha!'

Cotton knew, however, from the brief notes that Dr Aforey was a stalwart of the temperance movement and disapproved of 'the swinish transcendence to be had in alcohol'.

Dr Aforey preferred not to meet 'near my place of work', suggesting instead the porch of a Baptist church, 'where I am on good, even excellent terms with the pastor'.

'My friend,' said Dr Aforey, 'shall we say within the hour?'

Cotton took a cab.

'Chocolate city?' said the driver when he gave the address. 'You sure?'

'I'm sure.'

This was Cotton's second day in Washington, and as

they drove he began to understand the extent to which there were racial contour lines in the city. As they approached U Street, he noticed that the number of whites in the street abruptly dropped away. Within a few blinks rather than blocks, the population had changed from white with an occasional black face, to crowded black with barely a white face. He saw a lot of thin girls with stiff plaits playing hop-scotch, women stout with poverty, and men with hair so oiled and scraped back that the sides of their heads resembled fresh bitumen on felt roofing. At the corner of one shabby street was a fat man wearing extravagantly wide, chalk-striped trousers, pink braces, a hat with a pink band and a tie that looked like a primary-coloured ray of lightning. The man had gold rings on all his fingers, and when he smiled he showed gold teeth.

'Washington pimp,' muttered the driver.

The church itself turned out to be a very modest building, a single-storey hall with an odd, miniature steeple, no more than six feet high, set over the angle of the roof. The church did not quite fill the plot. There were some tufts of dry grass around it.

'Well, friend, is this what you wanted?' said the driver.

Cotton checked the board outside. 'Yes, this is it. Thank you.'

He paid and got out. In the porch, Dr Aforey rose to meet him. Cotton was not sure what he had expected, but probably not a plump, rumpled little man with a pot belly and extraordinary two-toned shoes. They were black patent leather at the front and something like white suede at the heel. Cotton noticed that the heels were built up. Dr Aforey was carrying a briefcase with an umbrella strapped to it. He raised his homburg hat. Cotton saw that he wore no hair oil but had a parting cut into what was left of his hair. He wore extraordinarily thick glasses, what the Spanish call 'tumbler bottoms'.

'Welcome my friend. You, I take it, go by the name of Cotton?' Dr Aforey held out a hand. 'I have to say you have the most upright and manly bearing, sir.'

'Dr Aforey,' said Cotton.

They shook hands.

'Now,' said Dr Aforey, 'I should regard it as a very great privilege to able to offer you a soda or other non-alcoholic beverage at a conveniently situated establishment, but I am not sure we would even be served at the same table at an establishment happy to see you, or that you would feel at ease in an establishment happy to see me.'

Cotton inclined his head. Without meaning to, he found himself sliding into a version of Victorian courtliness. 'You are very kind, but conversation with you will suffice, Doctor.'

'Oh!' said Dr Aforey. It was a sound Cotton had not heard before, a sort of verbal blink. It was quite short but came back, rather like a clicking tin frog he had had as a child. 'That is a good and, if I may say so, rather convenient thing for us both. What do you say then? Shall we take refuge under the Lord's roof from the harsher elements around us?'

They turned inside the church. The interior was dark. The only unshuttered window, in the far wall above the lectern, was round and of stained glass – mostly blue, black and gold – and depicted a hooded figure at the prow of a boat holding out a hand, in blessing perhaps, or pointing out a destination.

Cotton had never been to Africa and had little experience

of Africans. Dr Aforey smelt of carbolic soap and something like sweetened limes.

'Are you a man in the shadows?' whispered Dr Aforey.

Cotton glanced down at him. Was this some spiritual reference? He took off his hat.

Dr Aforey giggled. 'Cloak and dagger,' he said. 'Cloak and dagger.'

Cotton shook his head and smiled. 'I'm a soldier who studied economics and I have been attached to Lord Keynes' delegation, to work out the implications for the colonies of any agreement.'

Dr Aforey smiled. 'Dear me,' he said, 'so you are just a dogsbody then?'

Cotton saw this was in the nature of what Dr Aforey might have called 'a pleasantry'. He smiled obligingly, but played along. 'We are understaffed, Doctor, but I assure you this meeting is not lightly undertaken.'

'You are very suitably complimentary. I salute you. What do you say to the notion of taking a pew? This one?'

'Perfect.'

Dr Aforey paused for a moment, raised his hat towards the stained-glass window and led the way. Cotton followed. They sat. Dr Aforey shut his eyes and clasped his hands for a few seconds. Then he breathed in, opened his eyes, parted his hands, took off his hat and placed it on a prayer book. Cotton followed suit, placing his hat on another prayer book.

'Now what is it,' said Dr Aforey, 'that this unworldly academic can do for you, sir?' Dr Aforey smiled but his tone was a little more businesslike.

'I am sure you are aware that next month in Manchester . . .'

'Yes, yes, yes,' said Dr Aforey. 'The Fifth Pan-African Congress. I know this thing.'

'You will also know then that the Congress will, to a degree, fix the nature of the dialogue and negotiations that will follow on the future of the British colonies.'

Dr Aforey breathed in for a long time, then sighed in a rush. 'That is possible,' he said. He sighed again. 'Indeed, it is a distinct possibility, I should say.' He looked round at Cotton. 'It may, my friend, even be too true.'

Dr Aforey was working out his choice of words for the person he was talking to.

'I think,' said Dr Aforey, 'that you, sir – or better say your masters – are victims of a crass and utter misunderstanding. The name of the Congress may be "Pan-African", the delegates may speak of "international brotherhood" and of presenting a united front against oppression but – I can assure you most categorically – that does not make them open-minded or indeed tolerant of any other opinion that is not more or less Marxist. Usually more. Do you follow what I am saying?'

'I think so,' said Cotton.

'My friend, I say these things more in sorrow than in anger. I point no quivering or accusatory finger. The delegates themselves are victims of an error of perception. Racism is not imperialism. But my colleagues have produced the concept of Pan-Africanism as a counterweight to oppression. The problem is that this concept is flawed. It is, in the most literal sense, skin deep. Worse, sir, the skin colour is in the eye of the beholder, and the beholder is white.' Dr Aforey paused. 'Oh, perhaps I am too severe with you. It is likely you know nothing about the continent that saw my birth.'

'Fair enough,' said Cotton. It had been some time since he had sat on a pew and he had forgotten how hard they were.

'Let me try again,' said Dr Aforey. 'The Pan-African movement represents widely different constituents. It is a big umbrella, but ceremonial rather than useful. There are two things that link the different peoples included under this umbrella now. The first is what the white man perceives as common skin colour. The second is taken from the ideology of a German Jew who took refuge in England, and whose teachings are used to justify the present Soviet regime. I simplify for dramatic effect.'

'You're saying that the Pan-Africans themselves have nothing in common?'

'Not outside some subsumed Marxist texts, sir. Tell me now, what does someone from Trinidad have to do with someone in the Gold Coast – or with a Negro in Washington? Their experiences and views of the world are entirely different.'

'I see,' said Cotton.

Dr Aforey nodded. 'Let me, if you are agreeable, now become personal. Do you know this man Jomo Kenyatta? It is not his real name, of course. He has taken *un nom politique,* as if he were Lenin or Stalin, but he has inserted a nationalist element.'

'Have you met Mr Kenyatta, Dr Aforey?'

'In Birmingham, England. We talked about matters literary. To cut quite to the chase, a novel called *Prester John.*'

Cotton had heard of the book, but not read it. 'By John Buchan?'

'Indeed. You are correct, sir. The late Governor-General of Canada.'

'Am I right in thinking that's an adventure story?'

'Oh. An imperialist adventure story, Mr Cotton. Published when I was fifteen years old in 1910. It was given to me as a prize for my baptism into the Christian faith a year later by the Reverend Donald Soutar of Kirriemuir in Scotland.'

'What did Mr Kenyatta think of it?'

'He liked it. Thought it was a valuable aid to understanding.'

Cotton paused. 'Understanding the imperial mind?'

'Quite.' Dr Aforey smiled very slightly and leaned towards Cotton. 'I suspect, you know, in his heart of hearts, the boy who became Kenyatta identified with Prester John. He is a very handsome, almost a strapping fellow, you know. Not at all like me. I was born misshapen and utterly ill-favoured. He, sir, was a film extra.'

Cotton glanced at Dr Aforey.

'I'm afraid I don't know the story.'

Dr Aforey nodded. '*Prester John* is a medieval European myth. Like King Arthur. Or Eldorado. It is a sort of pre-imperialism, a pre-emptive loss of innocence. Most interesting. In this case, you build up the King and a fanciful treasure. Prester John is really Presbyter John, you know. He is a Christian king. When the imperialists arrive and find no Christians they are incensed. For John's lost legacy, of course. And they sack the lands of the degenerates who have succeeded and betrayed him. It is a most profitable sort of self-deception.'

Cotton found something innocent and rather grand in Dr Aforey's eloquence,

'Do you know,' said Dr Aforey quietly, 'what the late Governor-General of Canada says about John? He says – and I quote verbatim, I assure you – "He had none of the squat and preposterous Negro lineaments". Dr Aforey rocked slightly, almost as if savouring the description. He closed his eyes a moment and took a breath before opening them again. 'But Buchan then says that, despite this, the poor fellow had been "cursed to be born amongst the children of Ham".'

Cotton waited.

'You know, Mr Cotton, when I first heard the expression "beyond the pale" I thought it referred to skin colour, not a fence. For this man Buchan, the Negro is a child who can be educated but never grow up, at best an innocent ruffian who can be turned into a junior prefect. Racism in his book is merely a justification for imperialism; the diamonds go to the white hero, who then charitably supports an agricultural college. His real contempt he saves for half-breeds, for muddying the purity of the racial scheme.'

'I thought you said racism was not imperialism,' said Cotton.

'Oh! I beg you. Pay attention, sir. Where is the imperialism in the USA?'

'Well,' said Cotton, 'you could argue it was first imported when the US was still a colony. It then became a legacy in independence, was then – partly as the result of a civil war – repudiated in law, and now carries on as a highly visible social divide, encouraged by certain legal amendments aimed at separating the races.'

Dr Aforey looked at him and nodded. 'Good,' he said. 'That is very good, sir. I am impressed.'

'Manchester,' Cotton reminded him.

Dr Aforey nodded. 'Yes. The Pan-African Conference.' He paused. 'We are mostly men of books, you know,' he said. 'We are almost all mission boys, most of whom have moved on from the Bible to Karl Marx.'

'But in a month's time, a few men will be meeting in Manchester to discuss the future of a whole continent, Dr Aforey. Of course there will be compromises and mistakes. But will you engage, let your voice be heard?'

Dr Aforey looked away for a moment and shook his head. 'You are an elegant fellow,' he said. 'But consider this. You British have come here to beg, is that not the case? But your beggary has some demand in it because you say you have borne the brunt of the recent hostilities.' He shrugged. 'My Pan-African friends are not begging. It is far worse, sir. They are optimists set free. They are buoyed up. Their minds leap ahead over the difficulties. They are drunk on myths that reach out to the future.'

Cotton tried to come in here.

'Hush,' said Dr Aforey, holding up a hand. 'And what have you shown them? These men view Marxism and English laws as a mere window-dressing of fetching ideas, to be cast aside as with a fashion. You will ask them to have a loyal opposition. But you put your foot on the neck of opposition. How can an imperialist teach democracy? Your own legality is not elected. Your justification is brute power. That is what you have taught them and it is a very easy lesson to learn. These men in Manchester are as much the children of imperialism as you are.'

Dr Aforey nodded despondently. 'There have been three or four hundred years of imperialism. Is it not reasonable to expect it to take a century to undo?'

He took out a white handkerchief and wiped his brow. 'The sin of decolonizing will be to walk away and say, "You have our lawyer's wigs, we have trained your army officers and your dentists, why don't you follow our rules? Why can't you be like us?" It is a very great hypocrisy.'

Cotton tried again. 'We are still talking of ideas, Dr Aforey, and different voices. The space for African ideas remains.'

'You flatter me,' said Dr Aforey.

Cotton cleared his throat. 'If you could set down some considerations, perhaps publish them . . .'

'Ah! Some pertinent observations on the path ahead?'

Dr Aforey looked irritated. Something had gone wrong.

'I am fifty years old,' he said. 'I have worries of my own. Where will I rest my head in my old age? What will I live on? I have been plucked from a tribe, instructed in the ways of a Saviour and awarded a PhD for ignoring Salome. I have no political talents, sir. I am a man of principle but I have no country, only what I hope can be a free mind.'

'I had understood that was why I was here, Dr Aforey. The debate is just beginning. But look around you. When the Constitution of this country was devised, different minds worked on it, some ambitious for power, some ambitious for the rule of law, for checks and balances to avoid the excesses of monarchies and absolute rulers . . . there is a struggle, but the struggle is part of the debate and the results may be worth fighting for.'

Dr Aforey rubbed his chin. He nodded.

'I understand,' he said. 'This is a capitalist country, is it not? Where the dollar is king and my research budget is low.'

'I see,' said Cotton. He paused. 'What kind of sum are we talking about?'

'Oh no, Mr Cotton, I will not have any transaction besmirched with the nefarious name of bribery. I say research, I mean research.'

'Of course. I understand that.'

'One thousand dollars,' said Dr Aforey.

Cotton nodded. 'You'd have to leave that with me for a while.'

Dr Aforey laughed. 'And I shall. What is the phrase – the ball is in your court? You arrange research funds as earnest of intent and I shall write down some considerations to offer the Congress. Is that satisfactory to you?'

He got up and Cotton did too. Cotton stepped back and Dr Aforey led the way out in silence.

Outside the church, however, Dr Aforey paused.

'Where were you before you drew this – if I may say so – short straw?'

'Briefly in Germany; before that in Spain for several months.'

'Spain?' said Dr Aforey. 'Would you know the expression Sambo?'

'Yes. I believe it may come from the word *zambo*.'

'Yes! When interbreeding was as categorized as angels used to be. Sambo is a child of an American Indian and a Negro, I believe. What does the Spanish word actually mean?'

'*Zambo* means bow-legged.'

Dr Aforey smiled. 'And is the word mulatto from Spanish too? For the child of a White and a Negro.'

'I don't really know,' said Cotton. 'It may be from the word for little mule.'

'Oh!' said Dr Aforey, 'that is very interesting. Thank you. I will make a note of these things in due course. Mr Cotton, I look forward to hearing from you shortly.'

They shook hands. Cotton watched Dr Aforey walk away. He had a cramped limp as if his shoes were too tight. Bunions but, presumably, some vanity, thought Cotton. As he turned to go, someone from a passing truck shouted at him.

'Nigger lover!'

It might have been sparked by what they had just been talking about but, in a kind of early Mexican muscle memory, Cotton reacted as fast as instinct, raising his forearm from the elbow in a gesture that itself was slow and contemptuous. There was a screech as the wheels locked and the flat-back truck pulled up about thirty yards on. Cotton rose on to his toes and began walking fast towards it. As the door opened he speeded up into a run.

Cotton saw he had raised his hands as in training to break someone's neck. Absurdly, this was the position for someone sneaking up behind a sentry, left hand up and palm forward to grip the nape of the neck, right hand up and slightly curved to seize the chin and apply the required poundage when twisting, sixty-six pounds of pressure for a woman, anything up to eighty-eight for a man. He could barely see, his eyes were so tight, and his teeth were clenched and his lips drawn back.

He was very lucky. The short, red-faced man who got out of the truck took one look at him and started scrambling back.

'Drive! Drive!' Gears grinding, the truck took off with the door still open and the man's left lower leg swaying. Cotton was near enough to see that the truck carried a few boxes of fish.

Cotton pulled up. Almost at once he felt dry-mouthed and physically drained. He blinked and licked his lips. Jesus Christ! What had he been thinking? Mostly it was his own stupidity that annoyed him. He could have been shot, had been up for a brawl without a thought of how many men he was taking on. For a moment he closed his eyes, breathed in and then out.

He opened his eyes. Across the street an old lady, wearing an extravagant floral hat, was staring at him and shaking her head.

He turned. Much further along his side of the street, Dr Aforey was peering in his direction. With a nod, Cotton turned away and began walking.

6

WITHIN A couple of blocks to the east, Cotton was able to hail a taxi. He decided not to go back to the Embassy just yet. He remembered from somewhere, probably the formal reception, someone saying the Round Robin Bar in a hotel on Pennsylvania Avenue was 'traditional, but pleasant'. Traditional did not attract, but he could remember no other name.

'Your wish is my command,' said the driver.

Was the man imitating him? Cotton squeezed his eyes shut. He knew well enough what was happening. He thought of this as his short circuit – a time shortly after arriving in and beginning to adapt to a new place, when his self-control fused. That in itself irritated. Being caught unaware was additionally irritating. By this time he should be picking up the signs and dealing with them before he did something as stupid as run at a small fish truck.

In July, when he was in Germany, he had seen a kilted corporal upbraided for giving away bars of chocolate.

'I seen a woman come out of a foxhole, sir, in the rubble! And do you know what? She had two bairns with her. Turned out neat as two pins, sir. In the rubble! I have to respect a people like that, sir. Those children were clean, their hair was combed, their shoes polished. They were awful well-behaved. What's a bar of chocolate to me, sir, under those circumstances?' The man was not so much shaking as vibrating with resentment and rage at being questioned.

The young officer had tried to explain that there had been complaints from Britain, 'largely from our own womenfolk, Corporal, attempting to feed their own children in very trying times'.

'Is that so, sir?' The corporal, already very stiffly at attention, leaned forward a degree or two as if braving a gale. 'But where's the damned chocolate? Here? Or there?'

'That's enough, Corporal,' murmured the officer.

Cotton recognized the rage. And he had to admit he recognized the resentment. He had just been sent to interview someone on a subject he knew next to nothing about. As a cover? He was a little amused to be reacting almost like a Spaniard fed up with pompous, pernickety, perfidious Albion. British manners and management in Washington, the myths and attitudes, were irritating him very much. Those braying British voices, the dismissive superiority based on nothing very much, certainly in the present. The incessant droning on about English modesty, apparently unaware that this contradicted 'showing them our medals' or the demand for unparalleled gratitude.

On a personal level, the muddle and incompetence was trying him. It had passed seamlessly from war- to peacetime. Cotton had, for no apparent reason, been abruptly pulled out of Madrid in May and sent to Germany in June. When someone had seen that he was neither a professional soldier nor a qualified civil servant there had been a small hiatus, and then – perhaps because of his economics degree – he had been allowed to join a team set to examine 'the inflation pertaining in Germany at present'.

There was no mystery. The Soviets had begun flooding the

place with Allied banknotes. Since the notes were not forger-
ies, it only remained to find out how the Soviets had obtained
the plates needed to print the money in the first place. The
choices were, as someone else put it, that the Soviets had stolen
them or been given them. The British had then reassured themselves with an internal declaration that it was none of their
responsibility. None of their plates were missing and there was
no record of any being given to the Soviet Army. Who exactly
had been responsible hadn't been clear at the time.

'This is it, sir.' Cotton paid the cab driver.

The Round Robin Bar at the Willard Hotel was indeed
very traditional but also very polished and far too large for
the room, reminding him of one of those elaborate foun-
tains at spas, here for alcohol. Cotton ordered an iced tea.
He barely drank any of it. He was feeling calmer and cooler,
his temper tired. 'Never be afraid of admitting to yourself
that you've been stupid.' Parental advice when he had gone
to school. It was advice he had tried to take. He looked up.
A young woman smiled politely at him. Smiling, he shook
his head and got up. But something made him pause.

When Cotton had been in Spain, he had been followed
whenever he went out. There was no pretence at secrecy by
the followers. In fact, the whole point was that he knew he
was being watched – and so did anyone he might speak to.
He had thought of the men as gooseberries or state-run
chaperones, of the arrangement being a preventative kind
of trailing.

Now, here in Washington, it was a sensation he had, an
inkling. It made him wonder if he were imagining things.
He looked around. He saw nothing out of the ordinary.
The young woman was smiling politely at another man.
The man was mouthing something. Cotton lip-read, 'I'm

68

happily married.' But then the young woman smiled again and sat down.

Cotton went to a telephone booth in the hotel lobby and asked the operator for Robert Mullins' address. When he had it, he walked outside and got into a taxi.

Mullins lived in a fourth-floor apartment in Foggy Bottom, a rusty industrial area that had started being cleaned up but still had a long way to go. There were some empty lots, an abandoned factory, some industry still producing smoke. Mullins' apartment block was on a corner. Cotton waited a little until someone used the door, then moved in.

Mullins opened the door himself, dressed in trousers and a singlet. He looked briefly surprised but then put on a fair-cop face.

'I want you to tell me if I am being followed,' said Cotton.

Mullins considered. 'All right.' He was still cautious. 'You'd better come in, sir.'

There was a long, narrow corridor, then a small hall with a kitchen in an alcove. From it led two large rooms and a small bathroom to the right. From the left-hand room a young woman looked round the doorway.

'Very pleased to meet you,' said Cotton. 'Robert here is helping me out with something.'

'Bobbie?' said the girl.

'It's OK,' said Mullins.

They moved through to the living room. It had a window in the far wall and two on their right side. The room was dark because the windows had slatted blinds. Mullins moved past a sofa towards the far-right window. He lifted a slat and beckoned Cotton. Cotton approached; Mullins beckoned him again.

'Beryl found the intimacy of marriage a problem,' he whispered. 'Told me she had never quite got used to another toothbrush in the glass.' Cotton did not know if he had just been privy to delicacy or fact. 'Two o'clock. Third vehicle. A '42 Buick.'

Cotton peered out. He could see the parked car and the passenger, a man in a suit. The man took off his hat and used it briefly as a fan.

'Do you know who they are?'

Mullins was silent a while. Then cleared his throat. 'FBI,' he said.

'Any other possibilities?'

Mullins shook his head. 'No. They're just watching you. Probably to see how discreet you are, sir.'

Cotton smiled. 'Good. That's all this visit was, do you understand?'

'Very well,' said Mullins, without any sign that it was.

Cotton nodded. He thought he had just broken several British rules to do with rank, privacy and security but did not mind at all.

'Have you eaten?' he asked. 'I'm talking about lunch. You are both very welcome.'

'Sir?'

'I'm new in America. Eat something with me. I'm finding the food a little difficult. You must know places to eat.'

From behind him the girl spoke. 'Do you like Italian?' she said.

Cotton turned. 'Peter Cotton,' he said.

Her name was Gina Esposito. She was wearing a blue maternity dress, was six or seven months' pregnant.

*

70

They ate at a scrubbed wood table in a small restaurant a block away, belonging to one of Gina's cousins. They took a little time to get there. Gina said her ankles tended to swell but a slow walk did them good. She asked Cotton if he were married and did he have children. He said no to both. Cotton ate linguini with clams, they ate veal. He and Mullins had a glass of wine, Gina drank tomato juice. He learned that Gina's family had lived in the area for some time but were gradually moving out, 'North-west, you know, just short of Chevy Chase.' Her father had started in ice cream in 1910 when he had arrived from the Abruzzi, but now had a coffee shop, a delicatessen, a grocer's shop and was thinking about starting a restaurant.

'He's done very well.'

'It hasn't been easy.'

'No,' said Cotton.

As he lifted his coffee cup, he saw Gina glance at Mullins. Mullins cleared his throat and excused himself.

Gina leaned forward. 'Will Bobbie leave his wife?'

'Surely he's done that already?'

The girl shook her head. 'She doesn't even reply to his letters. I know. I am posting them. Can you help us out?'

Cotton made a face. 'I can enquire but I can't really be sure of offering much help, you know.'

'I have her address,' said Gina. 'The baby's due in December. My parents are . . . they rent us the apartment. I mean they're not . . . they like Bobbie. They know he's a good man and that his first marriage wasn't Catholic.'

Cotton nodded and Mullins came back. He did not sit down.

'Definitely the Buick, sir. They'll tag along for a few days. They'll want to see your patterns. They know who I am.'

71

'Thanks,' said Cotton. 'I'm sorry to have disturbed your day off.'

'No,' said Gina, 'the meal was nice.'

Cotton got up as she stood.

'You know about American tipping, sir?' said Mullins.

'Enough. You go home and I'll get back to the Chancery.'

'Well,' said Ayrtoun, 'did Dr Aforey give you a lecture?'

'He certainly talked a lot.'

'Useful?'

'I found it interesting. He's not a politician, of course, but he did make the point that the delegates in Manchester are not politicians either, not yet anyway.'

'What did you get out of him?'

'Contingent on a thousand dollars for research, he may write an article or paper for the Congress.'

'What? Reflections on an African future?'

Cotton shrugged. 'Something along those lines.'

Ayrtoun worried his cigarette tin. 'I suppose the money is not really that much. Not that we have it, of course. You could always try the Americans.' He stopped fiddling. 'What is he? A preacher? A populist? Ambitious for influence? Do you think he'd write well?'

'I've only heard him speak,' said Cotton, 'and I'm not his usual audience. But I think he would like to influence things. He's an academic and something of a pessimist, I'd say. He'd want to be an honest broker.'

Ayrtoun inverted his tin of Senior Service. Cotton began to think of it as a private sort of egg timer. Ayrtoun turned the tin the right way up.

'Try Mrs Duquesne,' he said. 'I think she might help. You'll be seeing her soon, won't you?'

Cotton was surprised. 'Yes I will. She's invited me to a supper at her house.'

'Right,' said Ayrtoun. 'Try her. Now, have we done what we were asked? Can we leave it at that?'

'No. I think I am going to get to know Dr Aforey better. I suspect he was a little coy about his connections. We need a little time for good faith between us.'

Ayrtoun considered, then grunted.

'Fine,' he said. 'A brief report will do.'

7

THE ONLY person in Washington that Cotton had met
before was Jim Gowar. They had done two courses
together during their army training, including a rain-
soaked fortnight in Colchester, in which they had had to go
for a run every morning. 'I'm guessing,' Jim Gowar had
said, 'the idea is that physical exhaustion encourages the
mind to be keen.' Cotton was very pleased to meet him
again.

They were almost exactly the same height of six foot
one, and born a day apart in 1919, though in Colombia and
Singapore. Jim Gowar had studied physics – 'Theory, I have
to say. I have no idea how to undo wet shoelaces' – and was
amiable, quiet, self-deprecating and quick.

They shook hands.

'Welcome to not much ease but quite a lot of plenty,' said
Jim Gowar. 'How long have you been here?'

'A couple of days.'

'You've joined us, have you?'

'Temporarily,' said Cotton. 'I'm still waiting . . .'

'Oh shit,' said Jim Gowar. 'That's not so good. Mind
you, there is shit everywhere. I'm in love.'

Cotton laughed. 'Odd way of putting it but congratulations.'

Jim Gowar leaned closer. 'Jewish widow.'

'Is that a problem?'

'Rather rich by our standards, awfully left wing by theirs. I'm smitten.' Jim Gowar smiled. 'Your desk looks rather top-heavy.'

Cotton's desk had acquired so many files there wasn't enough space left for him to write and the telephone was perched on top of the biggest pile.

'Just pass them on,' said Jim Gowar.

For most of Thursday Cotton handled papers. There was a lot of 'read and sign' and quantities of stuff on the colonies. The British Empire consisted of places he knew only by name. A few, some of the islands in particular, he had missed altogether. He found he knew pretty well where India, Ceylon, Malaya, Singapore, Borneo were in the East, but there were huge tracts of Africa he knew nothing about, either in terms of size or quite where they were. He found that one of the smaller colonies, the Gold Coast, was the same size as Britain, Kenya was two and half times as big and Nigeria double that. And then there were the languages. The evening news in the Gold Coast was read in six languages: English, Ga, Fante, Twi, Hausa and Dagbani.

At the end of the day Jim Gowar came to say goodbye.

'Ah, you're looking happy,' he said, 'in an unconvincing sort of way.'

Cotton laughed. 'Thanks.'

Cotton packed up and went back to the Statler to get ready for the supper Mrs Duquesne had invited him to when they had met at the reception.

Mrs Duquesne lived in a mansion on Dupont Circle almost as ugly as the State Department building. It was vaguely French, had a Mansard roof, a couple of Loire valley turrets and then some bits apparently borrowed from the Natural History Museum in London. The entrance was like a Romanesque church.

Off a very dark, wood-clad vaulted hall, Cotton was shown into a 'cabinet' about ten feet by ten. This was panelled in walnut and contained a small Renoir pastel of a rosy girl looking back over her shoulder on one side, and a tiny, very early Italian crucifixion scene on the other.

A young man came in and introduced himself as Harold, Mrs Duquesne's secretary.

'Are we quite ready?' he said.

Cotton raised an eyebrow and abruptly caught on. 'Not quite,' he said.

Harold nodded. 'I'll be back shortly.'

Cotton tried the other door. Behind it there was what Americans call a rest room, all mirrors and marble. Cotton checked himself in the mirror and washed his hands. Mrs Duquesne was evidently a most attentive hostess, anxious that her guests could be confident they were looking their best.

What she had called her 'little supper' involved a party of twenty-three guests, on a scale only a little short of the eighteenth century. The party had been arranged over three interconnecting rooms, there were several tables and each guest had been separately catered for. If the Senior Senator from Colorado preferred T-bone steak and fries, that was what he got. If a Mrs Douglas wanted to eat a tiny piece of striped bass at one table and a profiterole at another, that was what she did. Cotton was given consommé, quails and almond tart and at each course a sommelier recommended a wine.

Amongst the guests was the Hon. Penelope Ayrtoun, who had been given smoked salmon followed by chocolate mousse. She was an extraordinarily slight, very thin lady, whose hair looked the bulkiest thing about her. She was dressed in nubbed black silk and was drinking champagne from a crystal flute the size of an unforgiving bouquet.

'Penny, darling,' said Mrs Duquesne, 'this is Colonel Peter Cotton. He's just arrived at the British Embassy.'

Mrs Ayrtoun squinted at him or at least had a try at focusing on him. She gave up. 'God, I do so prefer Americans,' she announced. 'You know where you are with them.'

'Delighted to meet you,' said Cotton.

Years before he had learned that 'some women' – in his mother's words – 'will behave, even in soft light, as if faces glare like light bulbs. The stage past that is called "blotto". Have nothing to do with them. It's not romantic to save an alcoholic.' That had been in the summer of 1935, when Cotton was sixteen. His parents had been home from Mexico on one of their three-yearly leaves. On their second visit to him at school that June, they had brought him a razor, 'a good badger-hair brush' and some shaving soap in a sort of mug.

Mrs Ayrtoun looked surprised that he should have spoken. She blinked. 'Are you BSI?'

Cotton took this to mean Baker Street Irregulars, a Holmesian take on the SOE, who had been based at Number 64 and had now been closed down, the rump filleted, and included in MI6.

'No. I was part of the Economic War Unit.'

Mrs Ayrtoun winced and frowned as at some sudden earache. 'EWU?' she said. She looked unimpressed. 'I get freckles when I ski,' she announced. 'I can't abide freckles but I love skiing.' She blinked again. 'What were we talking about?'

'Skiing and freckles,' said Cotton. Underneath the powder on her face he could see she did have freckles, some blonde fuzz on her face but only at the sides; the rest, particularly her tiny nose, looked as taut as a stretched tent.

'Did I ever meet you at Sun Valley?' asked Mrs Ayrtoun. She then had some problem working out which hand her champagne flute was in and looked alarmed.

'Penny, dear,' said Mrs Duquesne, handling glass and elbow, 'there's someone I want you to meet.' Her place was immediately taken by Katherine Ward, discreetly encased in dark green velvet.

'Miss Ward. Lovely to see you again.'

She smiled. 'Colonel. Finding your way around Washington?'

'Apart from not knowing who anybody is and unwisely expecting a smaller party, fine.'

'Mrs Duquesne's larger suppers are for sixty – or more.'

Mrs Duquesne came back.

'Penny is having a little rest,' she said. 'Katherine, dear, you are looking luscious.'

Cotton cleared his throat. Mrs Duquesne smiled.

'Now who was the other boy?' she said. 'At the reception on Tuesday. The one who looks like a pretty horse.'

'Tibbets?'

'What does he do?'

'Something extraordinary and mathematical, I understand,' said Cotton.

'He didn't look that cryptic to me.' Mrs Duquesne smiled again. 'And how about you? What have you been doing?'

'Listening mostly. I saw a Dr Aforey of Howard University.'

'Really? What did he want?'

'A thousand dollars for research.'

He had pulled her up. She blinked. 'A worthwhile cause?'

'Undoubtedly. But we don't have the money.'

'I see.' She paused and looked across the room. 'Forgive me, I must circulate. It is what the hostess has to do.'

Katherine Ward leaned towards him. 'What are you doing exactly?' she asked.

Cotton looked at her. 'Asking for money, I hope.'

'I think Mrs Duquesne likes a little more style.'

'So do I. But I don't have much time to get him the money and I took my cue from the way she handled Mrs Ayrtoun.'

Katherine Ward smiled. 'This could be interesting,' she said. She leaned even closer. 'If she invites you back, you should let her know what you like to eat. Or let her know she got you right.'

Cotton nodded. 'Perfectly fair.'

Katherine Ward straightened up. 'You see that large lady with the flower in her hair? And the sort of Empire-line gown?' she said.

'Yes?'

'Talk to her.'

Cotton frowned. 'Really?''

She smiled. 'Go,' she said, and slid away.

So Cotton walked over.

'Ah!' said the lady with the flower, as soon as she saw him. 'Mrs Duquesne took up social cudgels for you Brits. Her neighbour is Cissy Patterson, you know, and I guess she wanted to even things up.'

'Who is Cissy Patterson?' asked Cotton.

'My goodness. How long have you been here?'

'This is my third day.'

'Oh, OK. She's Evelyn Duquesne's neighbour. Lives next door at Number 15. Isolationist, pro-German. She and her family own the *Washington Times-Herald, New York Daily News* and the *Chicago Tribune*.'

Cotton nodded.

'Cissy's at that interesting stage,' said the lady with the flower in her hair.

'That is?' enquired Cotton.

The lady winked. 'Bigger mouth than pockets.'

A man close by was telling a story about someone he called 'The Bride of Clyde' and Cotton felt his arm being taken.

'Let's listen in.'

'Who's Clyde?'

'You've heard of Bonnie and Clyde?'

'Gangsters?'

'You·said it. But Clyde here refers to Clyde Tolson.'

Cotton nodded. 'I am sorry. Who is he?'

'Bonnie Hoover's companion.'

'Are you talking about . . . ?'

'Yes. The two top men in the FBI eat together, play together and go to nightclubs together. The rumour that Edgar wears a dress has no foundation, corset or suspender of disbelief.'

Cotton was removed by Mrs Duquesne asking him to look at some of her paintings 'in the gallery'. He had not seen her eat or drink but she put her arm through his and looked wistful as she took him away.

'I never had children,' she said.

'Was that a disappointment?'

'Not really,' she said and laughed.

At the far end of a dark and, after the party slightly chilly version of a medieval hall, in a corner, were a Murillo and a Zurbarán on either side of a Spanish suit of armour.

'My late husband started work at eleven years old, when his father died. He had no education, you see, but he longed to learn. What do you think?'

'It's very impressive,' said Cotton.

Mrs Duquesne laughed. 'You British have a remarkable talent for making the polite override any emotion.'

'No, I am genuinely impressed. Did your husband go to Spain for these?'

'No, darling, he had dealers for that kind of thing. You say you're impressed. Do you actually like them?'

Cotton decided to be honest. 'The Murillo, no, I've seen a lot of Virgins like that. And, in theory anyway, I can appreciate why Zurbarán is famous for his abilities with cloth and shadows.'

Mrs Duquesne beamed. 'Which Spaniards do you really like?'

Cotton shook his head. 'I am not at all original. There's Velázquez, Goya and now Picasso.'

'One painting you'd like to live with.'

'Velázquez. A small painting of an Italian garden.'

Mrs Duquesne nodded. 'So you're a place person as opposed to a person person.'

Cotton laughed. 'If you say so, Mrs Duquesne.'

She smiled. 'I have to attend to my guests.'

'Of course.' Cotton offered her his arm again.

Later, Harold, her secretary, came up to Cotton and whispered, 'Mrs Duquesne will take care of Dr Aforey's research.'

'Tell her I am eternally grateful and can only hope Dr Aforey will be so too.'

It was not part of Harold's remit to show any reaction. 'OK,' he said.

And at the end of the evening, Mrs Duquesne beckoned Cotton and they approached Katherine Ward who was talking to the lady with a flower in her hair.

'Katherine, darling. Go with the Colonel. Drop him off or have yourself dropped off, whichever is more convenient.'

'Thank you, Mrs Duquesne, for a lovely evening,' said Cotton.

They went downstairs and got into the automobile.

'I think,' said Katherine Ward, 'I may be beginning to share your view of Mrs Duquesne's subtlety..'

'I'm sure our being transported together is an economy measure,' said Cotton.

'Thank you. Statler,' she said to the driver.

'Is this really on your way?'

She smiled. 'I hope you don't mind me saying, but there were times there you were looking a little lost.'

'No, no,' said Cotton. 'Completely lost. Sorry.'

'Why? Gossip's always local. I don't know anyone in London. Besides, you had a productive evening.'

'Yes. Money. And I got to know there was a Mrs Ayrtoun and that she was here.'

'Nobody had told you? You see, Mrs Duquesne can be very useful and is obviously braver than your colleagues.'

They pulled up at the Statler Hotel.

'I'll be seeing you at other functions,' she said.

'I certainly hope so.'

She laughed. 'Goodnight, Colonel Cotton.'

'Goodnight, Miss Ward. Oh, who was the lady with the flower in her hair?'

She smiled. 'I do like a mystery,' she said. 'Oh, all right. She's married to one of the Armed Forces' intelligence chiefs. Goodnight.'

8

A T THE Friday morning briefing, though Keynes was a long way from finishing his introductory presentation at the Federal Reserve building, Cotton learned that the Americans had already turned down the British plan for the organization and structure of the negotiations. They were insisting on a separate commercial round of talks. The Board of Trade would be sending delegates from London.

Ayrtoun called Cotton into his office afterwards.

'You've had an invitation,' he said, 'from someone at the Soviet Embassy.' He looked up. 'Dear Christ!' Ayrtoun tore out from behind his desk, dashed to the door and jerked it open. 'Quietly!' he bawled. 'How the hell can I think with your clatter?'

Cotton was grateful for the small delay. 'What kind of invitation?' he asked when Ayrtoun came back.

'To a chaperoned stroll in the park. You'll be meeting a man called Aleksandr Slonim – that's a Jewish surname. Apparently he's responsible for what the French call *Négritude*.'

Cotton stared. 'Blackness? Negro matters?'

'Quite. You can tell just how little we have on him by our belle-lettriste researcher's recourse to French. Been here since July, apparently. Came in through Mexico. I think he wants to find out if you are his equivalent. In his area.'

'Of Blackness?' said Cotton. 'What's this about? My cover? The Pan-African thing? Or what you call bait? '

Ayrtoun smiled briefly and, with the nail of his middle finger, traced the strip of very smooth skin between beard-line and right ear. 'You'll be able to find out. The meeting is at eleven this morning. We've told the Americans, of course.'

Cotton sighed. 'Anyone else?'

'Just Mullins. He'll cover your back from an indiscreet distance. Take a few photographs.'

'And where is this going to happen?'

'On the steps of the Lincoln Memorial.'

'As if we were tourists?' said Cotton.

'The photographers will have no difficulty keeping the Father of Emancipation in frame, will they now? We didn't think their choice of an easily recognizable place as a back-drop warranted a counter-proposal. It may even have been a gesture of goodwill on their part. Besides,' said Ayrtoun, 'as you yourself say, tourists take snaps there.'

The index card on Slonim was barely marked, and what was there was largely made up of 'possibles' – ranging from unknown, to guesses, to facts to be checked.

His date of birth was given as 9 May 1909, place St Petersburg/Leningrad, father a schoolteacher, mother 'daughter of a furrier'. But there was a mark against even this – meaning they were not sure they had the right person. The best information they had dated only from 1939: a Major Slonim had been mentioned in dispatches at the Battle of Khalkin Gol in August that year, when the Soviets had defeated the 6th Japanese Army.

In pencil, right at the bottom of the card, someone had written 'July/August 1945. Subject saw African Masks in

85

private collection in San Francisco and African artefacts in gallery in New York – possible exhibition?' Cotton supposed that might have given the report writer the notion of 'Négritude'.

Cotton went along to see Herbert Butterworth, the Chancery's excellent archivist, part librarian, part historian, who sat in a cubbyhole. Herbert was pear-shaped with a small face like that of a wrinkled child, and narrow shoulders that gave no idea of the bulk lower down. He had an unlikely quantity of straw-coloured hair.

'If you ever need to know anything, always try Herbert first,' Ayrtoun had said. 'He's a one-man Brains Trust.'

So Cotton tried Herbert on Négritude.

Herbert scratched his chin. 'Yes. It's about solidarity in common black identity – a socio-cultural movement really. Oh, and I think there's some connection with cubism,' he said. 'Yes, if I remember, the cubists, Picasso and Braque in particular were rather keen on Négritude. And on boxing. I think it was all regarded as rather elemental and savage, getting rid of too much civilization and prissy intellectual stuff. And in their case, of course, landing a few punches on the Renaissance view of perspective.' He paused and thought again. 'Picasso has a painting with women starting off one side as rather heavy classical nudes and shifting over into an African sort of mask at the right. Do you want any more?'

'No, I don't think so. Not for now. Thanks a lot, Herbert. That's extremely helpful.'

Common black identity, thought Cotton as he walked back to his desk. He remembered what Dr Aforey had thought about that.

*

Mullins drove Cotton to the meeting in a green MG from the car pool, an open-topped two-seater British sports car dating from about 1937.

Wind noise, road noise, the burble of the engine and the noise from a patched-up exhaust discouraged conversation. The suspension had not been adjusted for American roads. Cornering, even at low speeds, made Cotton grip whatever he could that was not the door. From time to time there was a back-draught of petrol. Mullins said something, then shouted. Apparently the MG found American gas 'a bit tricky!'

A lot of trees in Washington streets had either been cut down entirely or had most of their branches sawn off to allow room for storage sheds. They obscured the sidewalks. Even so, the MG made enough noise for people to turn and glance at the obviously foreign vehicle.

Cotton was relieved to get to the Lincoln Memorial. Whether it was the petrol fumes or the ride, he was beginning to feel queasy. Mullins parked and turned off the engine. There was a quick ticking noise from under the bonnet though nothing was running. Mullins pulled a leather-covered camera from under the seat.

'Good German camera,' he said, 'a Leica and some nice fast Agfa film. You can look through the viewfinder and keep the other eye free.'

'I understood the Russians were good at removing people from photographs,' said Cotton.

'They'll want you in, sir – for reference purposes.' Mullins permitted himself a small jerk at the sides of his mouth. 'I don't know about their man.' Cotton turned to look. The FBI car following them had pulled up about twenty yards away. Two shadowing agents got out and moved off.

The British got out of their MG. Mullins hung the camera round his neck. Cotton turned towards the tidal basin, breathed in and tried to blow out. Though the air was warm, he felt slightly better.

'All right,' he said.

They started walking towards the Lincoln Memorial, a white Doric temple with the footprint of a small football pitch, massive granite columns and a statue of Abraham Lincoln inside, seated like a canny, craggy, democratically elevated version of Zeus.

Cotton saw that the Lincoln Memorial constituted one end of a grand vista that went all the way to the Capitol. Immediately in front of the Memorial was the Reflecting Pool stretching away towards the Washington Monument, a large obelisk punctuating the view. The Pool itself was shallow but very long. Cotton shut one eye.

'Six hundred and seventy-five yards,' said Mullins the crack shot. 'Width fifty-five.'

Set back from it were stately lines of trees, mostly American elms. But the war had cluttered the plan. Some way down on the left-hand side from the Memorial, adjacent to the main Navy and Munitions buildings put up in the First World War, were two very large, white, two-storey blocks facing the pool. On the right side was an invasion of some twenty-five 'tempos' or long white, single-storey stucco huts sideways on to the water. And across the pool itself, about five hundred yards down, was a covered footbridge on piles in the water. Utilitarian Japanese it looked like.

At the bottom of the three flights of steps up to the Memorial was a man wearing a double-breasted suit the colour of unbleached sailcloth. His hat matched. As Cotton approached he was aware that Mullins was stepping away, and that two men were putting some distance between themselves and Slonim. Two Americans by the Reflecting Pool straightened up. He concentrated on Slonim.

The Russian was burly, barrel-chested, with powerful legs. By contrast his hands and feet were small, almost delicate, and Cotton was struck first by how lightly the man shifted as he waited for him to approach. Slonim did not offer his hand, but instead showed his palm in a gesture as much to halt as to acknowledge him. With his other hand Slonim briefly raised his hat to show a little fringe of fine blond hair round a wide, bald head. He had a round, plumpish face, a snub nose and blue, almost violet eyes.

'I prefer to walk,' he announced. Those eyes and his bass rumble removed any notion that he was young.

'I'm happy to join you,' said Cotton.

He watched Slonim climb two steps. The Russian was then a head taller than Cotton. He turned round.

'Prefer to be in public. Recorded contact.'

'All right.' Since Cotton had almost no Russian at all, he could hardly complain about Slonim's English — the vowels very brief interludes, slippery as oysters, between the plosions and the rolls.

They turned and walked parallel to the steps.

'I understand you are in the Cultural Department at your Embassy,' said Cotton.

Aleksandr Slonim turned with an expression of such startled disbelief that Cotton almost laughed. Slonim frowned.

'Not your main interest,' said Cotton.

It took Slonim a second to reassure himself, grunt and nod.

'That is other,' he said.

'Yes. How can I help you?'

'No, no, no,' said Slonim. 'No help. Make contact. Relation. Peers.' It sounded like 'pierce'. 'You know Russian literature, Colonel?'

Cotton took this as having more to do with acknowledging rank than with culture. 'Only in translation, Colonel, and not a lot of that.'

'Full colonel,' said Slonim, prodding his own chest.

Cotton shrugged. 'I'm possibly rather younger,' he replied.

They turned and started walking back the way they had come. A child of about three trotted towards them. The child's mother, a few paces behind, was pushing a pram.

'Sweetie!' the mother called. 'Don't get too far ahead now. Mommy can't walk fast when she's pushing Harry.'

Cotton stepped out to allow the sulking sweetie, his complacent mother and the bundled-up Harry to pass between the meeting of foreign colonels. He hoped Mullins had a snap of that.

Slonim nodded and pointed up at the steps. 'What Russian writers do you know?' he asked when they had started climbing. 'Give me names.'

'Really?' said Cotton. He shrugged. 'Pushkin. *Eugene . . .*'

'. . . *Onegin*, yes. Do you know Lermontov?'

Cotton thought. 'Yes, *A Hero of our Time . . .*'

'Tolstoy? *War and Peace?*'

'No. *Anna . . .*'

'Yes, yes, yes.'

'Then, I seem to remember there's a story about someone only needing six feet of earth,' said Cotton. 'A variation on Lord Keynes' "We're all dead in the long run".'

90

Slonim's lips twitched. It was, thought Cotton, a remarkably small smile. 'Dostoevsky?' countered the Russian.

Cotton shrugged. '*Crime and Punishment*.' They walked up a couple of steps more. 'Oh, and Chekhov,' added Cotton. 'I saw an amateur production of *Uncle Vanya* in Surrey a couple of years ago.'

They had climbed the first flight.

Slonim stopped and turned. 'No Gogol?' he asked, as if he could not believe it.

Cotton shook his head. 'None.'

'But you must! *Dead Souls*! A truly great book.' He paused. 'All these men are pre-revolutionary.'

'Indeed?' said Cotton. 'How are you on English literature?'

Slonim jerked his head at the second flight. Cotton nodded.

'Oh, Dickens,' said Slonim. He gave a name every other step. 'And Robert Burns. And H. G. Wells.' He looked round. 'You play chess, Colonel?'

'No.' And then, in response to Slonim's glance, 'Too much framework, not enough colours.'

Slonim liked that. 'Black and white, yes? Ha! You can, of course, have red and white.'

'Occasionally red and black.'

Aleksandr Slonim looked pleased. 'The world is not a chess board, no?'

'No.'

'But you have a big black square, yes? Africa.'

They had reached the second platform.

Cotton paused. 'Well, I have talked to an African academic. He said there was a difference between racism and imperialism.'

Slonim made a dismissive gesture. 'Intellectual,' he said as if excusing an unfortunate affliction. 'In his terms, the Soviet people are xenophobic or pre-racist. But he knows the Soviet state is not imperialist and not racist.'

'Really?' Cotton had read the reports on Stalin. Amongst his many qualities listed was 'elementary, thorough-going racism'. 'How would you define imperialism?' asked Cotton.

'Physical occupation and material exploitation.'

'Right. And where would ideology fit in?'

'Where it can,' said Slonim. 'Where it offers structure to hope.'

Cotton had heard that the Russian Lady Keynes had a considerable talent for using her apparent struggle with the English language to make points. 'Structure to hope' he thought was quite effective.

'You drive people towards us,' said Slonim. He spread his arms. 'All we have to do is open our fold.'

'But you're not calling them sheep?'

Slonim looked disapproving, and then compassionate. 'Sincerity makes sheep. Injustice makes solidarity,' he said.

'In Africa?' said Cotton.

Slonim shrugged. 'Ideology is cheaper than money.'

'You're as ruined as we are. At least as ruined,' said Cotton.

'Ha! We're strong.' Slonim clenched his fist to show how strong.

Cotton smiled. Then Slonim switched from Soviet strength to British weakness.

'The British Empire will crack. It's inevitable.' Slonim looked round. 'I've heard the expression "managed decline"

92

for your empire.' He laughed. 'Decline yes. Managed . . .? Well.' He shook his head.

Cotton had read the phrase 'managed decline' in a paper written pre-war, in 1937. Evidently Slonim had read the same paper – and was happy to reveal that he had.

'Fair enough,' said Cotton.

'Good man!' said Slonim approvingly. 'You are a realist! Comrade Stalin has been undermining you for some time.'

'Really?' said Cotton. 'You don't mean in Egypt, do you?'

Slonim's lips twitched. 'Not fertile ground, perhaps. But Palestine . . . there are possibilities there. The Jews, you know. And then in the Far East, the Annamese are fighting a war of liberation already under Comrade Ho Chi Minh.'

Cotton smiled. 'You have everything mapped out.'

'We will win on the ground,' said the Russian.

'Why?'

Slonim thought for a moment. 'No debate,' he decided. 'We have a direct chain of command. Resolute decisions. You British have given up independence. You live in the shadow of the Americans – anti-colonial racists. And in London you have debate – stupid imperialists, left wing and so forth.'

'That's possible,' said Cotton. 'What will you do about nationalism?'

'What is your sense?' asked Slonim.

'In Africa you have . . . what, at best nascent nationalism?'

'Yes!' Slonim smiled. 'Just beginning. We invite them to Moscow. Education. Literacy campaigns. We will have an army of progress.'

Cotton shook his head. He remembered his mother's pride in the Scots education system, begun she said by bigots in the Reformation, aimed at having everyone able to read the Bible, but 'leading to so much more'.

'It would be easier for you to cause problems,' said Cotton. 'You attack, we defend. But we will offer independence, and you will find money counts for a lot — more than you can probably afford. Right now, you have hopes for the Pan-African Congress. But it's trying to do too many things and unite too many interests.'

'It is a platform,' said Slonim.

'Quite,' said Cotton. 'But what do the American Negroes bring, apart from being able to afford to pay for their own travel arrangements?'

Slonim frowned. 'Their sense of injustice,' he said. He stopped. 'There,' he said, pointing towards a spot a little to the side of the front of the Memorial, 'sang Marian Anderson.'

Cotton shook his head to show that he did not know who Marian Anderson was.

'But she is a wonderful singer! Easter Sunday 1939. Here because the Daughters of the American Revolution — hah! — refused permission for her to sing in Constitution Hall. Liberals bring her here.' He shrugged. 'And Paul Robeson! What do you say about Paul Robeson? Naughty dog? He bites when you kick him?' Slonim waggled his finger. 'Robeson never bites! He asks for dignity with dignity. So they call him a traitor and a dog. What do they say . . . "Coon? Uppity nigger"?'

Cotton nodded. 'I have heard that.'

Slonim smiled and held up a finger. 'And then,' he almost crooned, 'I have Pushkin.'

94

Cotton narrowed his eyes. 'What help is he exactly?'

'His great-grandfather was black! Great story! Pushkin had more than one drop of black blood. He was an Octoroon – one-eighth black. But he remains Russia's greatest poet. Revered, my friend, revered. Pushkin here? Would have been just a black man. There is no Jim Crow in Russia.'

'But no Negroes either,' said Cotton. 'You are forgetting "Strange Fruit",' he said, remembering.

'What is that?'

'It's a song by Billie Holliday. A jazz singer. About lynchings, I think.'

Slonim made a face. 'Oh, not jazz,' he said.

'Then I think you have to be more realistic,' said Cotton. 'You can get some propaganda out of this situation but there is nothing else here for you. Negroes in the US can't afford it. They'll use religion, not Marx.'

Slonim sucked his teeth and wagged a finger. 'Advancement of Coloured Peoples? Timid. Ridiculous. An enemy of real progress. Sometimes you have to crash.' He brought his knuckles together.

'Negroes are a minority here,' said Cotton. 'They are looking for equal opportunities and for "separate" to stop meaning inferior. They are not talking of changing the political system, but of being accepted into it.'

Cotton expected a comeback. But Slonim shook his head to show disagreement and moved on. 'In Africa,' he said, 'we will have black communists.'

'You may have Marxist variations, but there are a lot of other variables,' said Cotton. 'We'll take that.'

Slonim nodded. He thought. 'Interesting talk,' he said finally. 'We can agree that *Négritude* does not exist, not in the way Marxist ideology exists.'

Cotton nodded. He had noted Slonim's mention of *Négritude*. He did not think it was due to the Russian aristocratic taste for French over their own language. He also thought it unlikely that Slonim had visited the African continent either, certainly not the Sub-Sahara.

'I understand *Négritude* as a cultural term more than a political umbrella,' said Cotton. 'The French liked African masks and black boxers.'

Slonim smiled. 'And banana girls,' he said.

'Banana girls?' said Cotton.

'Josephine Baker.'

Slonim raised his hat and backed away a little.

'Colonel,' he said.

'Colonel,' said Cotton.

Slonim turned and started down the steps. Cotton waited for him to join his colleagues and depart.

Looking out over the Reflecting Pool towards the Capitol building, it struck him what a strange conceit it was, a vista planned to allow for future historical monuments. He glanced back at Abraham Lincoln, sitting in his nineteenth-century clothes in the model of an Ancient Greek temple.

More than ten years before, at school, they had had to make papier-mâché masks in Greek class, Ancient Greek theatre having used static types and caricatures to represent characters. Presumably they put a great deal into the voice. He had disliked the feel of the crude mask and the difficulty of speaking clearly in it, his voice muffled to the listeners, but reverberating in his ears. And an unpleasant dampness caused by his own breath coming back at his face.

Mullins reached the top of the steps.

'They had a movie camera as well, sir. Also German.'

96

'Right,' said Cotton.

'The FBI are waiting, sir.'

Cotton nodded. He took one last look at the vista. As he did so, he frowned, closed one eye, then the other. The huge obelisk of the Washington Monument was not quite aligned, was too far to the west.

'Three times the size of Nelson's Column in Trafalgar Square,' said Mullins.

'I'm sure it is,' said Cotton as they began trotting down the steps.

9

'WELL,' said Ayrtoun, 'what did you think of him?'
'I don't know,' said Cotton. 'I will say that if Slonim really is a tank commander, he has had time for a little reading and is now pretending, not very hard, to puzzle at the limitations of chess without shells.'

Ayrtoun paused, then let out one of his startling laughs.

'Good. I've been banging heads. Have you heard of Kursk?'

'No.'

'Battle in the Soviet Union in July 1943. Huge affair over an area as big as Wales with more tanks than ever before. And the Russians walloped the Germans. Oh, with help and armament from the Americans, of course. But quite a thing. How hard do you think Slonim is?'

Cotton shrugged. 'Pretty hard.'

Ayrtoun picked up his cigarette tin and inverted it.

'You haven't met many Russians before?'

'No.'

Ayrtoun nodded. 'Mm,' he said. 'In the First World War the head of British Naval Intelligence was called "Blinker" Hall, nicknamed because of a chronic facial tic. A very cold, very clever fellow, described, by an American I think, as able to remove a man's heart, chew on it and hand it back to him. A bit of a hero of mine. Helped get the Americans into the First War.'

'All right,' said Cotton. He did not know where Ayrtoun was going with this.

'Marshal Zhukov, who commanded the Soviets and Colonel Slonim at Kursk, earned a nickname from his own troops. They called him "the cannibal".' Ayrtoun shook his head. 'No comparison. Zhukov makes Hall look like a cutie-pie. He wouldn't bother to chew or to hand the heart back. Has a billboard of a chest entirely covered in medals now.'

Cotton said nothing. He had heard people more than impressed with just how hard Soviets could be, but he did not find this convincing.

'The Soviets won Kursk, not so much because of their tanks apparently, but because of air power and artillery – they rigged up a kind of web and caught the Germans broadside, literally. They drove the German Tiger tanks back and partisans blew up railways and made the German supply lines sitting ducks from the air.'

'Where is Marshal Zhukov now?' asked Cotton.

'Organizing Russian Germany.'

'You're suggesting the man I met was with Zhukov at Kursk, but has now been sent here via Mexico?'

'London thinks it is a possibility. What would worry you about that?'

'I suppose if Slonim's talent was organizing partisans.'

'On the lines that he could do that in Africa?' Ayrtoun shook his head. 'No,' he decided. 'We have a problem with that in the Far East because we trained guerrillas there. We didn't do that anywhere in Africa.'

Ayrtoun picked up his tin of cigarettes and rolled it between his hands.

'Anything else occur to you?'

Cotton shrugged. 'Only a couple of things. One would be Economic Warfare stuff. The card on him mentions African masks and galleries here. It occurred to me that, since the Soviets are as broke as us but determined not to take any money from the Americans in peacetime, they might be thinking of releasing what they call decadent art, and raising something that way. They do have a bank in Switzerland and they must have picked more stuff up from the Nazis.'

Ayrtoun nodded. 'It's possible, I suppose. I'll make a note of it. What's the other thing?'

Cotton hesitated.

'Go on, man!'

'I didn't believe a word of it,' said Cotton.

Ayrtoun raised his eyebrows. 'What do you mean?'

'We could have been sparring a bit at some diplomatic function. We skated over a few literary Russian names, had some quick chat about African and American Negroes but it was clear neither of us knew much.'

'What are you suggesting?'

'That he was covering my cover. Something like that? Impressing on me how confident they are in the new world.'

Ayrtoun grunted. 'London thinks he is genuinely Red.'

'Meaning?'

'That he is political, not intelligence. He won't know *quite* how many leaks we have.'

'He gave me "managed decline",' said Cotton, 'as well as *Négritude*.'

Ayrtoun shrugged. Whatever he was thinking he was not passing it on.

'I take it we have as many leaks as the OSS,' said Cotton.

'Absolutely.'

'So Slonim is . . .?'

'We were thinking he's strategy. Perhaps even security, in the internal political sense. He may even be checking out the Soviet Embassy here. Supervising the move from New York to Washington. But I don't think he's intelligence.' Ayrtoun looked up. 'He'll have picked up that you are not for them and told his own people.'

'Why?'

Ayrtoun looked annoyed. 'The Americans use the acronym MICE. M for money, I for ideology, C for coercion and E for excitement – the four reasons a traitor becomes a traitor.'

Cotton wondered about that. MICE sounded more contemptuous than accurate. But he was used to that British mix of dismissal and praise, as grudging as the measure for spirits in pubs. He waited.

Ayrtoun leaned forward and slid a note across the table. It was a handwritten complaint to him about threatening and upsetting 'valued members of staff' and the consequent detriment to the 'smooth running of the Embassy and its dependencies'. It was from the First Secretary, D. D. MacLean, who had taken over from Isaiah Berlin. Cotton knew little about MacLean except for having seen him drunk at the initial reception and he had been told he had installed his wife and children in New York and visited them from time to time. Evidently the P & Q had been complaining.

'Dependencies?'

'Us. In our place. I think the Americans use the word "dependencies" for the bakery and the laundry and the outhouses.' Ayrtoun paused. 'In a day or two you'll probably be warned off seeing Slonim again.'

Cotton waited.

'By whom?'

Ayrtoun shrugged. 'Well, it won't be coming from me. It'll be some diplomatic johnnie in the Embassy. We were a bit slow getting started on the infighting for the post-war. Now our people are fighting for control of departments and policies too, that's all. You shouldn't read anything more into it. Not yet anyway.'

'So will I be getting instructions to see Slonim again from someone else?'

Ayrtoun smiled. 'Always keep a record,' he said, 'a private logbook if you like. For me, think over the meeting and write me a report. Don't leave anything out. Let me worry about editing, put down anything that occurs to you.'

'Right.'

Cotton, in fact, was already keeping notes.

'Anything else before I call Tibbets in?' asked Ayrtoun.

Cotton thought and decided there was. 'Yes. Are we in a position to help Mullins?'

'In what way?'

'He has a wife in Britain who won't reply to his letters, let alone give him a divorce. And he'll shortly have a child here.'

Ayrtoun raised his eyes heavenwards as if very put-upon. 'Dear God,' he groaned. 'That's his own private mess. Why in God's name should we help?'

'So he is not distracted.'

'He's a professional!'

'I never suggested different,' said Cotton.

Ayrtoun shook his head. Then something occurred to him. 'How do you know this?'

'If somebody is supposed to be watching my back, I want to make sure they really are.'

There was another pause. 'Bloody pain,' he said, but for Ayrtoun, almost pleasantly. 'I'll see what I can do. But no promises, mind.' He waved for Tibbets to come in.

When Tibbets had sat down Ayrtoun moved briskly on.

'Cotton here has just seen someone from the Soviet Embassy with enough cameras on them not to disgrace a couple of publicity-hungry starlets. Am I clear? Nobody sees anyone with even a half-Russian granny without witnesses and a record of the meeting, preferably in a public place. The reason for this is that things have changed. This is peace not war. Have we got that? That means that what was good, even commendable, a year or so ago is now strictly off-limits.

'Stalin is no longer Uncle Joe. He's becoming the madman from Georgia who raises statues to someone simply called Mother. The winged boots of evil are passing from Adolf to Joe. Do I have your attention?'

Tibbets stirred uncomfortably but nodded.

'Yes,' said Cotton.

'Good.' Ayrtoun's tone became quieter and less cutting. 'In the second half of August this year Harry Dexter White, yes, the ex-Assistant Secretary to their Treasury, top American man and begetter of Bretton Woods – still with us but in a rather reduced capacity – was identified as a Soviet tittle-tattle.'

'But that's just not possible,' said Tibbets.

'Oh, do shut up,' said Ayrtoun. 'He is walking around now because no one – or at least very few people – know of this. Indeed, even Harry Dexter White himself may not know he is a Soviet agent.'

Tibbets looked shocked.

'As far as we know, the evidence is based on certain

contacts he had with Soviet staff when this was regarded as not only advisable for someone in his position but actually part of his duty.'

'I don't understand,' said Tibbets.

'Unfortunate,' said Ayrtoun, 'since you are, in part, now involved. What happened was that a youngish woman recently turned herself in to the FBI in New Haven, Connecticut and, amongst other shows of good faith while she tries to negotiate her transformation from traitor to heroine, she has named Mr White as a Soviet spy. Since she is a . . . what shall I say – a drunk needy of male attention but prone to dislike being ordered about – great care is being taken to check the information she has given.'

'Ah,' said Tibbets.

'This lady, daughter of a prosperous dry goods merchant, went to Vassar. She flirted, possibly insincerely, with fascism in Italy, but then certainly acquired a Russian communist lover and a job spying for the Soviets. When the first lover died she took a second lover, and a promotion to managing the spy ring she had been part of. All this time, she was managing and sometimes failing to manage a drink problem. So far, however, her information on Dexter White checks out.

'This is so secret that neither President Truman nor Secretary of State Byrnes can bring themselves to believe it. The British government doesn't know anything, of course, Lord Keynes doesn't know – and indeed he still thinks Harry Dexter White is a man to deal with.

'More to the point, it is just possible the Soviets still think their network is recoverable.'

Ayrtoun looked round at Cotton.

'This is not simply confidential. You will never mention this outside this room unless I say so. Is that clear to you?'

'Yes.'

'Good. Now, do you remember what you were doing in Germany?'

'Of course.'

Ayrtoun smiled. 'May I introduce you again, then, to Mr Harry Dexter White? This woman is the third source that identifies him as having handed over or arranged to have handed over a series of printing plates for Allied money. The other two sources also describe him as timid, but I'm sure Mr Tibbets will agree that three separate sources make a pretty convincing case.

'We don't know whether or not he received orders; we suspect he saw it as part of his remit. He was doing his job and following policy that has turned out . . . well, a little differently than he expected.'

He looked up.

'Right. Cotton, let's imagine London have this Slonim man wrong. Mm? Work on it.'

Cotton nodded.

'I have to talk to Tibbets now. Oh, just one more thing – jot down an idiot's guide to what Keynes' strategy is, would you? For us non-economists.'

Cotton got up and left. On his way back to his own office he looked in on Mullins. He told him he was likely to get bawled out but that Ayrtoun had said he would try to do something for him. There was the briefest movement in Mullins' face before it resumed normal passivity.

'Thank you, sir.'

Back at his desk, Cotton thought, trying to read some

kind of sense into what he knew and what Ayrtoun had said. Then he remembered something D had told him: 'Do bear in mind, there is not adding up, but there is also you not understanding a damn thing.'

Cotton went to the Communications Room and sent D a message. It was returned immediately: 'This avenue is no longer open.' He had expected this, in one way found the confirmation a comfort, but it did mean that he had no contact in London and was stuck with Ayrtoun.

He went back to his desk, took a piece of paper and wrote the numbers 1 to 10, but left it otherwise blank while he thought.

After a while he decided he needed something else, to clear his mind. He got out a report on Henry Morgenthau Jr and his attitude to Germany. Morgenthau had been Secretary to the Treasury from 1934 until earlier that year. Unfortunately, it appeared he had never really understood finance. During the war years, he had relied on and been heavily influenced by Harry Dexter White. At the end of the war in Europe, truly appalled by what he heard and the photographs he saw of the concentration camps, he could not see anything wrong in the Soviet plan to reduce Germany to a pre-industrial state, 'a pastoral symphony', in the report's phrase, 'led by large horses and wooden ploughs, that would never threaten anyone again'. Morgenthau had both proposed and signed the policy, but had lost out to the War Department who had seen no reason to gratify the Soviets.

Cotton felt a little better. He looked up. Jim Gowar was smiling at him.

'Ah,' said Jim, pointing at his paper with nothing on it except 1 to 10, 'I see you're in favour of the decimal system of nothing. You really must tell me when you are free of an evening.'

'Hello, Jim,' said Cotton. 'I am on a social roster. I get a note from the P & Q in the morning telling me which Embassy to go to in the evening. Apparently this will build up my contacts.'

Jim laughed. 'Only amongst people who knot their ties rather small. I'm off. Try to get a free evening. I've told Miriam I can now actually introduce her to a work colleague. In our situation, it's no small thing.'

Cotton smiled and as soon as Jim Gowar had left, filled in his ten points.

If Slonim were a tank commander, he was very probably a real colonel in a way Cotton did not consider himself to be. That made Slonim a professional soldier, an experienced and skilled man of action. Cotton wondered, then, why he would have been put on to the Pan-African case. It seemed to him unlikely, a kind of not very serious, even arrogant, cover.

Assuming Slonim was a colonel, what else could he be doing in the US? The Russians had their quota of German scientists as the Americans had theirs. All information pointed to the Soviets already having, or about to have, the atomic bomb.

It was always possible, he thought, that a professional soldier might be organizing a shopping list of other armaments and, now that restrictions had been lifted, the factories could be more easily identified and agents reinforced or placed.

Then there was the lady spy Ayrtoun had mentioned as defecting, and his remark that the Soviets might still think their network could be saved. Could Slonim be checking that out? In that case, why would he walk about the Lincoln Memorial talking of Gogol and Marian Anderson?

None of this convinced him. So he went back to simple things.

Had Slonim already known some English or was he learning? He made a note to himself to check whether Slonim was receiving tuition. Possibly from a Negro.

He should also check how long Slonim had been in Mexico.

Finally, he closed his eyes and considered his meeting earlier that day. He thought of Ayrtoun asking him how hard Slonim was. It had seemed to him a strange, not very useful question, but in those terms the hardest man the Soviets had was Stalin.

If the Soviets had heard of his cover, what Katherine Ward had called 'Trustee to the Colonies', an eager servant, Slonim say, might have been anxious to check that the British were not going to spoil Comrade Stalin's message of fraternal greetings to the delegates attending the Fifth Pan-African Congress.

Cotton put his sheet of paper in a drawer and locked it. He looked at where that evening's diplomatic reception was. Then he went back to the Statler to eat something and dress up again.

AMERICAN MENUS involved many forms of meat and the food came in huge portions. Salad dressings tended to be rich and sweet and, for a European, cheese kept appearing in unexpected places, in blue mottled crumbs beside walnuts, melted on croutons beside cubes of bacon or heaped into stalk-like shavings that turned out to be fat and soft.

Cotton asked for half a steak and a simple salad of lettuce, tomato and onion.

He got a very thick, rare-done steak, cut into two, and a salad dish that included cheese, walnuts, croutons, palm hearts and corn. There was also a side dish of French fries. Everybody was very pleasant.

Cotton had already seen that Americans cut their steaks up before putting down the knife and eating with a fork, as opposed to the British method of cutting as you ate, with the knife in one hand and the fork in the other.

He went halfway. He cut up some meat and then picked a piece of tomato out of the salad dish with his fork.

Tibbets used his fingers as he sat down and took a French fry. He was in complaining mood.

'This is intolerable,' he said. 'Oh, these are quite good.'

'What is?'

'The man's manner! I mean it's almost as if we were

shop-floor apprentices in some manufacturing enterprise. As if we were being processed or tested.'

'Yes,' said Cotton. 'That's about it.'

Tibbets shrugged and picked out another fry.

'Mind you,' he said, 'I understand his wife is . . . well . . . regimental fodder was the expression used.'

Cotton sighed and tapped a finger on the tablecloth.

'Well, you know what I mean,' said Tibbets.

Cotton looked up and paid attention. Tibbets moved his head and concentrated on another French fry. Cotton saw his parents in him: the father, a believer in male superiority through mathematics and science, the mother a powerful snob and gossip. A difficult mix to manage. Cotton asked, 'How do you know this?'

'It's no secret, apparently. Unhappy marriage doesn't quite do the arrangement justice.' Tibbets managed a sniff.

Cotton looked down at his plate and tried another piece of steak. He remembered something D had said about Ayrtoun. 'He might behave like a frenetic but not very effective squash player, thrashing furiously about after a much better opponent. Don't be taken in.'

'She's not often in Washington,' said Tibbets. 'Very fond of little breaks.'

Cotton looked up. He saw there was sweat on Tibbets' upper lip. The cryptologist was rattled and scared.

'What is it?'

Tibbets shook his head. 'I'm just no good at all this sneaking and skulking about. I solve things. I don't see through people. I don't guess. I'm not a cryptologist, I'm a mathematician.'

Cotton nodded. He thought Tibbets had put it rather well.

The waiter came for Tibbets' order. 'Just a steak,' he said. 'Well done. I'll eat his fries.'

'I take it you are spending time at Arlington Hall?'

'Yes.' Arlington Hall was the US Army cryptology headquarters across the Potomac in Virginia, in what had once been a girls' school.

'What's it like?'

'Lots of girls in jumpers.'

Cotton put another piece of steak in his mouth.

Tibbets leaned forward. 'Ayrtoun wants me to check that the Americans aren't cheating, you know, or holding stuff back from us,' he said.

'Well,' said Cotton, 'I can see that he might be interested in that. Does he want more than an indication?'

Tibbets frowned. 'What do you mean?'

'Does he want meticulous proof? Or just your best guess – that we are missing out on something?'

Tibbets went into what looked like a little sulk. After a while he nodded.

'Thanks,' he said. 'That was helpful. But you see – he just doesn't seem to appreciate what I do!'

'It's all right,' said Cotton. 'That's not really his job. He has to put things together instead. We gather things for him.'

Tibbets blinked. 'Do you really know what you are doing? I mean, do you know how to do it?'

Cotton sighed. 'Not really. We have to play it by ear, don't you think? Find out where we have to go. I'd guess Ayrtoun also wants you to tell him if you find anything before you share it with the Americans. Check it out with him first.'

Tibbets frowned. 'Yes, I see,' he said. But then he shook his head. 'That damnable manner of his!'

Damnable? Tibbets' left hand was trembling and Cotton understood he was intimidated, or an odd mix of indignant and exalted. There was a physical element in this. He had allowed himself to be bullied into loathing. Cotton wondered whether or not Tibbets would now try to avoid Ayrtoun, keep out of his way.

'Have you written to Joyce?'

'What? No. I don't want to talk about that any more.'

'OK. I have to attend a reception shortly. Are you doing that?'

'No. I have to think.'

Tibbets gave the word 'think' a rather po-faced reverence. The waiter brought his steak – and another side order of French fries.

Cotton grunted. He had begun to think of Katherine Ward as very attractive relief.

On Saturday the 15th Cotton received a long letter from his sister Joan, shorter letters from Emily and Halliday and a drawing from Foster who had signed his name with the 's' and the 'r' reversed. His sister repeated the suggestion of what she called 'Columbus Day plus' in October for his visit and wondered whether Cotton would prefer them to invite friends or keep it family. He was welcome to bring anybody he liked, 'lost Brits, strays, anybody'.

At breakfast, Tibbets told him that he had to go to Arlington Hall.

'I really feel I should,' he said. 'They work extraordinarily long hours.'

Cotton was relieved to have the morning free of Tibbets. He ordered more coffee, sat down in a lounge and replied to the letters – he said he didn't mind what kind of party it was. Foster's drawing possibly included a tree, at least some green fuzz on a blue line and to one side something brown, possibly, from the shape and what might have been a spout, a whale. Cotton used print-style writing in his reply:

Dear Foster,
What a wonderful drawing! I am very pleased you have sent it to me. I am looking forward very much to meeting you.

Later he went out to the Scottish Rites Temple further along 16th Street between R and S Streets. Cotton had heard of the tomb of Mausolus at Halicarnassus on which it was modelled but had never seen an illustration. It was white and prettily elegant, certainly against some of the other neoclassical buildings in DC. It had been voted the fifth-most beautiful building in the world by American architects, the original, in modern-day Turkey, having been one of the Seven Wonders of the World and giving us the word mausoleum. Cotton had been intrigued by the name, did not know what Scottish Rites might be. He found out that the temple had been built by Freemasons and contained a library, rather than a corpse or a church.

Having done a little formal tourism Cotton strolled on. In S Street he stopped for lunch. He ordered a sandwich and coffee and watched. He was impressed by the owner coaching a new employee – 'You can do this, Horace', 'Are you happy?', 'Check it all out.' 'That's it,' 'OK, now present to the client' – in what he thought of as a curiously tender piece of good business practice. The other clients were various. A mother and son – 'No salt! No salt!' – a very old lady who left her dog outside and kept checking on the pooch's welfare, four young soldiers who asked for more ketchup, and two young women who brushed off the soldiers – 'Get lost!' – and who talked stockings. The sandwich wasn't bad, the coffee good and strong.

Cotton walked back to the Statler. It felt a long way in that heat. He was offered a petition to sign and politely declined, as a foreigner. The petition-gatherer looked suspicious, as if he might be lying. When he got back, Cotton stripped off, showered and, for the first time in several months, went to bed for a siesta.

He woke about three. He put on the bathrobe provided, got paper and pencil, sat down and responded to Ayrtoun's request for an idiot guide to Keynes' negotiations:

Earlier this year, before the end of the European war and the American termination of lend-lease in the European theatre, Lord Keynes had already addressed himself to Britain's coming financial crisis. In a memorandum to British civil servants, he foresaw the present negotiations and, in civil service terms, identified three possible negotiating positions.

He called these Justice, Austerity (or Starvation Corner) and Temptation.

Justice would be an outright gift from the Americans as recompense for British war expenses prior to lend-lease, and our unparalleled contribution to the triumph of civilization. This represents the ideal.

Austerity – Britain having to go it alone without any help from the Americans – is the opposite.

The third possibility, with very ample space between the extremes, is Temptation – a loan on more com-

mercial terms. This allows him and his team considerable leeway in the negotiations.

His plan is to present the first argument to the
Americans, stifle any suggestion of British support for
the second – and work on the third.

The problems he faces are a) the Americans b) the
optimism he has created in London and c) (as far as I
know) no agreed fall-back position with either HMG
or the Treasury.

Cotton considered whether he should put down Keynes'
apparent faith in 'bamboozling' the Americans, and his
description of people he did not respect on either side as
'baboons'. He decided against that.

He added notes on the sterling area and imperial prefer-
ence, both of which were less bargaining chips than necessary renunciations to get anything from the Americans.
Britain's bargaining position was very weak. Any threatened delay, for example, in ratifying the Bretton Woods
Agreement, would be far more expensive for Britain than
the US.

Cotton put the paper away and for a time sat, listening to
music on the radio, enjoying the air conditioning. Then
he ordered and ate an ice cream and got ready for the
evening.

16th Street was the original Embassy Row, chosen for prox-
imity to the White House. The Soviet Embassy was one of
many there. As was the French Embassy, the venue for this
evening's event.

This Embassy also had eighteenth-century décor, but
French. There was a lot of wood panelling, unpainted, and

the lighting was particularly weak. Cotton presumed they were pushing intellect rather than medals but the diplomats had an unfortunate manner, as if raising their noses above the recent war. Within a minute Cotton had heard someone remark on Racine (the playwright) and '*trop de racine*', a remark on roots and getting rid of the past, used by an artist, Cotton thought. Henri Matisse? Georges Braque?

'Not too many blacks here,' said someone behind him in French.

Cotton turned. Slonim, dressed in uniform that showed discreet gold leaves at the sleeves and a kind of epaulette substitute, was showing his wide, bald head that evening.

'The French have the only bourgeois communists in the world,' he added, 'and want to wrap their colonies in culture.'

Cotton smiled. 'Really? And the other French?'

Slonim almost grinned. 'What happens if you open the oven door too quickly?'

'The soufflé collapses?'

'Exactly. *Au revoir, mon ami.*'

'Are you leaving already?'

'I'm needed somewhere else,' said Slonim, 'and I have paid my respects to liberty, fraternity and . . .' He pretended to be doubtful.

'Equality?'

'Exactly,' he said.

Cotton had not expected to see Slonim again so soon. A coincidence? He doubted it. And yet the conversation had, if in French, been pretty much more of the same.

'Colonel.'

He turned. 'Miss Ward.'

'Katherine.'

'Thank you. My name's Peter.'

She nodded. 'I didn't know you would be here,' she said. 'But I am interested that you have come for a harpsichord recital.'

Cotton did not quite manage to suppress a start. 'I don't think I've heard one before.'

She smiled. 'You're trying new things?'

'And some old. I was hoping for some wine.'

'The canapés are delicious but very small. You speak French?'

'It's been some time. It sounds . . .'

'. . . a little unctuous? But you were not here for Jean-Paul Sartre's visit a few months ago. I can assure you, that had flutter and flattery as well.'

He grimaced. He got a glass of wine and a canapé, and for some reason he was then monopolized by a *soignée* French lady with pearls and neck veins who talked to him of Molière and who sat with him and admired his steadfast reaction to the harpsichord recital.

'I knew you would be moved,' she confided, as if he had gained entry to a club for the sensitive. Because of the Spanish he knew not to kiss her hand but to bow over it, something, she said, 'these Americans can never get right'.

Katherine caught up with him at the end.

'Well done!' she said. 'I enjoyed watching you. What are you doing next weekend?'

'God knows. Is it always this dreary?'

'No. Not if you get out of Washington. Why don't you do that next weekend? There's a bunch of us, a cabin in the forest. You'll meet people. It should be fun.'

'I'd be delighted.'
'OK. Round four thirty at your hotel on Friday?'
'Yes.'

On Sunday, Tibbets went off to Arlington Hall again. Partly because he remembered it was Mexico's Independence Day, Cotton wrote a long letter to his father. After that he tried to have a walk but gave up. The humid heat, mixed with a blustery wind, made it too unpleasant.

He got some newspapers – 'Florida braces for 150-mile Hurricane' – read a *New York Times Magazine* story on General MacArthur who had entered Tokyo only a week before, listened to some Fats Waller music he found on the radio – 'My Very Good Friend the Milkman says', 'Liverlip Jones' and 'The Jitterbug Waltz' – had a drink, went on his own to the movies and saw *Dorian Gray*, for the experience rather than the film, but mostly he thought about Katherine Ward and, occasionally, about Slonim. He did wonder whether or not the two of them had spoken at the French Embassy but was really more interested in just what her invitation for the next weekend might mean.

11

ON MONDAY, everyone in the Intelligence Room found a note from Protocol waiting for them. 'The mastication of chewing gum and similar products is herewith discouraged. It is forbidden in the public areas of His Majesty's Embassy.'

Cotton put it to one side.

The custom, when calling out for information from others in the room, was to start with the country.

'Mexico!' called Cotton.

'Hamilton's in charge of that,' whispered Jim Gowar. 'He's a bit hung-over from yesterday.'

Cotton went over to Hamilton's desk.

'I need a contact in Mexico City,' he said quietly.

Hamilton grunted. 'What would they be doing?'

'Watching the Soviets.'

Hamilton made a face. 'Uh,' he groaned. 'There's a sublime idiot there who is writing a book on Tolstoy.' He paused and frowned. 'Did I just say Tolstoy?'

'Yes.'

'I meant Trotsky.'

'Someone with two eyes for detail.'

Hamilton thought, waggled a finger, rethought. 'Wait a minute,' he said. 'There's a woman there now, not quite in the Embassy, if you know what I mean. A Catalan lady called Gil. Might she do?'

'Montserrat Gil? She brought me up to date in Spanish last year.'

'No. This one is called Margarita – the sister, I think. She's married. Doing something in publishing.'

'Thanks.'

Cotton decided to ask Margarita Gil de Wilkins to help him with Slonim. He drafted a letter. How long had he stayed in Mexico? Did she know anything of his activities there?

Ayrtoun asked, 'What do you think she can do?'

'Her sister is efficient and tough. If she is anything like her, I imagine quite a lot.'

Ayrtoun looked doubtful, then shrugged, sat back and put his hands behind his head. 'Let me ask you something. When is a tough woman not better described as resilient?'

Cotton narrowed his eyes. Ayrtoun appeared to have some sort of Mohs scale of hardness but for humans. 'When she's investigating something.'

Ayrtoun grunted. 'Go on then, send it.'

In his mail Cotton had received a note from Dr Aforey. It thanked him 'for a recent great kindness promised and delivered' – Cotton took this to mean Mrs Duquesne's donation – and suggested 'opening up a strictly private correspondence'. Dr Aforey suggested that Cotton assume a pseudonym for this purpose, 'so that my professional reputation does not suffer from improper or mischievous interpretation of the facts. I leave the choice of name to you.'

Cotton took two sheets of unmarked paper. On one he wrote to Dr Aforey. He gave his pseudonym as Moses Campbell, after the porter at Penn Station, and arranged a PO Box as an address.

On the other, he wrote to Mrs Duquesne to thank her for her help. He used words like prompt, gratitude and true friend.

Later, Ayrtoun asked him for his idiot guide to Keynes' negotiations.

'So,' said Ayrtoun when he had read it. ' "Temptation" is just the usual bugger's muddle then. Basically we are pretending to negotiate and the Yanks are allowing us to pretend we are. Is that right?'

'Not quite, not in the detail, but in general, yes, that's about it,' said Cotton.

At the morning briefing on Tuesday, Ayrtoun informed them that, the day before, after three working days, Lord Keynes had finished his exposition of the British situation to his American counterparts. Indications were that the American response would be neither prompt nor generous. Fred Vinson had privately expressed disappointment that he was 'none the wiser' after listening to Keynes. Will Clayton had wondered aloud when they would ever get down to business.

Cotton had already had to attend a number of diplomatic receptions. That evening he had two, the first with the Canadians, the second with the Brazilians. He liked them both, though for rather different reasons. The Canadians were straight, amiable and politely practical. The Brazilians were charming and sly, and had music to cover their dictator's difficulties. Somebody's seventeen-year-old daughter scandalized the French lady he had met at the harpsichord recital with her extraordinarily relaxed and rapid pelvic twitching as she danced.

He missed Katherine Ward — she was at the Argentine

reception. So he returned to the Statler about ten, wanting to eat something and go to bed.

'Peter! I say, Peter!'

Tibbets was in the bar. He spread his arms. There was something of the crucifixion in his stance. Then Cotton understood that Tibbets was showing off the lines of his new Brooks Brothers suit. The suit looked good, though perhaps slightly baggy at the hips. Tibbets had combined it with his new yellow tie and what he called 'desert boots', in brown suede. Cotton knew the boots as 'brothel creepers', though, despite his efforts, Tibbets did not look particularly rakish.

'Drinkies?' said Tibbets.

'What have you been drinking?'

'Something called a Manhattan?'

'Right. I'm pretty well done in and you're looking pretty cheerful without me.'

'Are you in town from Boston?'

Tibbets turned. Two young women, neatly differentiated into blonde and dark, had taken up position.

'Let's say that I am,' said Tibbets.

The blonde laughed. 'You're not from Boston.'

'But let's say that I am, shall we?' said Tibbets.

The blonde laughed again. 'Have you heard this guy speak?' she asked her companion. 'It's like the King of England.'

The dark girl lowered her lashes at Cotton. He smiled and shook his head. He leaned towards Tibbets.

'You're on your own,' he murmured. 'All right?'

'Fine by me, old boy!' said Tibbets. 'The more the merrier.'

Cotton turned and walked out of the bar towards the elevator. He pushed the button. He had to wait a little. Just as the lift arrived and the doors began to open, Tibbets tapped his shoulder.

'You wouldn't have any money on you, old boy, would you?' Tibbets looked around as if someone might be listening. 'Apparently the Statler frowns on this kind of thing, but frowns can be greased.'

'How much are we talking about?'

'I say,' said Tibbets. 'It is about to be my birthday, you know.'

'Really? Congratulations then. Against that, are you quite sure what you are doing?'

'Absolutely! I clock up a quarter of a century in about an hour and a half.' Tibbets squinted at his watch. 'An hour and twenty minutes actually.'

'I meant the girls. You don't know who they are.'

'Come off it, they're not a security risk. I've made some calculations.'

'And?'

'They're just after some remunerated fun. Don't be such a prig.'

Cotton grunted and opened his wallet. For a drunk man Tibbets extracted the notes very fast.

Cotton went up to his room. He turned up the air conditioning, showered, got into bed and made use of the earplugs provided.

Around 3 a.m. he was woken by thumping on his door. He removed the earplugs. He got out of bed and went to the door.

'Who is it?'

'It's me, old boy. Jeremy . . . Tibbets.'

Cotton cleared his throat and opened the door. 'What do you want?'

Tibbets, immune to bad temper, was insecurely wrapped in his dressing gown and was swaying a little. 'Fabulous,' he groaned, 'absolutely fabulous. Quite the best opening movement to a birthday I've ever had.'

Cotton winced. 'Wonderful. But what is it you want now?'

'Well, I may just oversleep, you see. I'm quite fucked out.'

'All right.'

Tibbets blinked. 'They made me wear what they called a mac. A French letter! Hell of a job getting it on. I'm rather big, you see.'

'If you say so. I'm thrilled for you. Now go to bed.'

'Are you sure?'

'Yes. I can always say you're feeling a little peaky this morning. All right?'

Tibbets smiled. 'Good man,' he said. 'That's the spirit.'

He smiled again but gave no indication of moving. Instead he closed his eyes. ' I heard from Joyce, you know. She's getting married to some old man. Hasn't even got a leg.'

'What?'

'He lost it. First War casualty. Local doctor. At least fifty years old. I never did get round to writing to her.' Tibbets managed a sort of leer. 'Have you ever been with two girls?'

Cotton shook his head. 'No, I haven't,' he said. 'I am delighted for you, I really am. Now do piss off.'

'Haha. I'm one up, old boy, one up.'

The next day Ayrtoun wanted to know where the hell Tibbets was.

'He's feeling peaky. The girl he thought of marrying

decided on someone else, apparently an elderly fellow with one leg.'

'Ah,' said Ayrtoun. 'She went for security, did she? Pity.' He looked sympathetic. 'All right. Take him out for a drink or something. Get his mind off it.'

Dr Aforey's reply was by return. 'Dear Moses, I like your choice of name exceedingly. I should be most happy to assist you in your studies and with your interests in the upcoming Pan-African Congress. Sincerely, G. S. Aforey.'

As befitted an academic, Dr Aforey had enclosed 'a small reading list' (twenty-four books) and made the suggestion that Cotton study with attention an 'ethnic map of the Sub-Sahara prepared by someone in Whitehall in 1936'. 'Though this is not entirely accurate, indeed, in some areas, notoriously wrong, it will be of benefit to you in consider-ing the diversity of peoples in the concept that is Africa.'

An hour or so later, then, Cotton was surprised to receive an open telephone call from Dr Aforey.

'Is that Mr Peter Cotton of the British Embassy?'

'Speaking.'

'I am Dr Aforey from Howard University. I wonder if you are in a position to help me by bearing witness to a very distressing occurrence that affects us all?'

From which Cotton immediately gathered Dr Aforey had other people in the room.

'Dr Aforey, I shall, of course, do everything I can.'

A few minutes later Cotton was in a cab going along Florida Avenue on his way to Howard University Hospital. It took some time. There had been an accident on Georgia Avenue involving a truck and a Packard. A committee of three, Dr Aforey, a young medical doctor called Lionel

Cusworth, and Miles Codling, an attorney-at-law, were patiently waiting for him. Cotton shook hands with them and they began walking.

'Mr Cotton, this was originally called Freedman's Hospital, you know, when it was established after the abolishment of slavery,' said Dr Aforey. 'Later, it was judged convenient that the university become involved in the training of Negro doctors as well, so that Negro patients elsewhere would find no barriers to treatment.'

Cotton nodded. They walked down corridors and reached a room off the trauma department.

'Dr Cusworth here is keeping the room in the dark. Your eyes will gradually become accustomed.'

They went in. There was a shape in the bed and for a moment Cotton wondered what he was looking at, then his eyes focused. The person's head did not look real; it looked like one of those games in which children use a big cabbage or a ball rolled in a towel as part of an apparent shape in a bed and then escape through the window. Cotton peered, but the features of the face did not become clearer. The face was too swollen. He picked out the lines of the eyelids, the smashed nose, lips the size of fingers . . . then flinched. He felt a wave of nausea.

Behind him Dr Cusworth began reading. 'Cracked skull, concussion, probably detached retina in left eye, broken nose, five front teeth missing, a broken collarbone, a broken arm, four broken ribs . . .'

Cotton held up a hand. 'Who . . . is this?'

'A citizen of the British colonies,' said Dr Aforey, 'concretely a Nigerian. His name is Austin Ojukwu. And he is a graduate student at Howard in the field of sociology. He is something of a Durkheimite, I understand.'

'Who has done this to him?'

Dr Aforey shook his head. 'Oh,' he said. 'That is a moot point, I feel.'

'Really?'

'A more interesting question would be *why* these things have been done to him.'

'Very well,' said Cotton.

'You see, sir, Austin here obtained gainful employment by giving some classes in the English language to a diplomatic personage of military rank. Austin, you understand, has some basic knowledge of the Russian language, gleaned I gather from an elderly Ibo-speaking Russian-German priest and subsequently improved by reading. I also understand he has been an enthusiastic student of American social mores since his arrival here.'

Cotton nodded. 'So, he could give this particular Russian phrases like "coon" or "uppity nigger"?'

'Oh,' said Dr Aforey. 'You are in a colloquial mood today, sir. But you are most likely correct in your summation.' He smiled. 'In one sense Austin should consider himself most fortunate. He could have been deported on any trumped-up charge. This way combines — how shall I put this — crippling contempt and a definitive warning?

'He was taken into an alley by two men, Mr Cotton, and used as a punchbag. They warned him repeatedly as they were beating him of the dangers of being mistaken for a subversive element.' He looked up. 'Do you want an example of a Washington tautology, Mr Cotton? Negro and subversive. They are the same thing for a certain Federal organization. Austin is far too poorly and we are far too intelligent to bring a complaint against any of its agents.'

Cotton nodded. 'I take it the Soviet Embassy has kept out of this?'

'A most deafening silence from that quarter, Mr Cotton.'

'All right.' Cotton looked round at the lawyer. 'And what is Mr Codling's role in this meeting?'

'He is here for testimonial purposes only.'

'Why have you called me? Do you wish to communicate formally with the British Embassy?'

Dr Aforey shook his head. 'This is a private matter,' he said quietly. 'I wanted you to see. We will leave it to you, Mr Cotton, as food for thought.'

Dr Aforey and the lawyer accompanied Cotton out.

When Cotton got back to his office, he found another circular from the P & Q on his desk. It concerned the consumption of 'colas, sodas and other so-called soft drinks'. He crumpled it up and tossed it into a waste-paper basket, then went to see Ayrtoun about Austin.

Ayrtoun listened, then nodded. 'Was Aforey threatening you?'

'Recording and testing, I think,' said Cotton.

'Testing? You got him a thousand dollars, for God's sake!'

'Testing my interest, I think, possibly in things I can't do much about.'

Ayrtoun nodded. 'All right,' he said. He turned his tin of cigarettes upside down. 'When Roosevelt had a heart attack, J. Edgar Hoover kept it out of the press. Roosevelt didn't ask him to do any such thing, of course, but I think we can say he was grateful Hoover did not shy from doing the dirty work for him. Think about it. He got one hundred per cent of American newsmen to shut up.'

'Surely the same thing was done for Churchill?'

Ayrtoun shook his head. 'It's not the same. We gag the press, we slap an order on them. There was nothing official here. The American press is not nearly as forthright as it pretends. There are various sorts of fear applied. The fear of not getting access, of being cut out, works wonders. There is also the fear of a personal indiscretion being exposed. But I can assure you a journalist called Hartman ended up brain-damaged after a run-in with some ruffians in neat suits. Hoover does not mind having people roughed up. In fact, that is part of his offer.'

Ayrtoun righted his tin of cigarettes and turned the palms of his hands up.

'For practical purposes the FBI treats the US as an isolation hospital. They wage war against criminal infection, moral contagion and communistic viruses. They decide what is a risk to the US, and they do so without supervision or restraint. They supervise and restrain themselves. Clear?'

Cotton nodded.

'Actually,' said Ayrtoun, 'this is quite interesting. As far as I can tell, the FBI appear to be the only American agency to have studied Nazi and Soviet techniques properly.'

'What does that mean?' said Cotton.

'That intimidation is its own reason. It doesn't need anything else. While people wonder why, the intimidation spreads.'

Ayrtoun looked up.

'So you should speak to them,' he said.

'The FBI?' said Cotton.

'Yes. I'll handle the request.'

The reply was prompt. Ayrtoun called Cotton back to his office within an hour.

'They suggest a meeting at the Lansburgh department store on 7th and E Street.' Ayrtoun shook his head. 'Lansburgh's caters for people at or below the pay grade of the lowly agent they'll send. Go. We want to impress on them that we are taking this seriously. So outrank him, give him stuff that is beyond him. We want to move up the scale.'

They ran over what Cotton should say and how he should say it.

'Keep plugging away at the communist threat to the US from the colonies if we get out too quickly,' said Ayrtoun.

Cotton was a few minutes early. The Lansburgh Department Store was what he called Victorian, brick-built in the nineteenth century with arched windows on the upper floors and a huge Stars and Stripes flying from the roof flagpole. It had the old-fashioned shell of an emporium but had been somewhat modernized on the inside. It had a 'Whites Only' soda fountain and cafeteria.

He went outside again. The FBI man was late. Cotton watched a father and two young daughters get out of an automobile. Doors opened, closed, reopened as the girls put things back in the car and took other things out. Then, as it were on the final closure, one of the girls reacted as if the tips of her fingers had been caught in the door. From Cotton's angle she was a good six inches short of any damage. The girl spun round, shook off her sister's concern and commandeered her alarmed, pink-faced father's attention and apologies for being such a clumsy old dad.

From Cotton's left, a large, round-faced man in a brown suit shambled towards him. He was just finishing eating something that left a fleck of coconut at the side of one of his lips.

'Fred Warwick,' said the agent.

'Peter Cotton.'

'Pete, right?'

They shook hands.

'We gotta wait. Jim is parking. He'll be along any minute. Then we'll go to the men's department.'

Cotton looked round at him.

'Tie section they leave you alone.'

Cotton nodded. Jim appeared, indicated Fred wipe his lips, but did not really join them.

'Jim's riding shotgun today.'

'All right,' said Cotton, though he did not understand.

They went into the store and all three took the elevator.

'We have to wear sober ties,' said the agent. 'And white shirts.'

Cotton nodded. They got out. Jim went to the bright ties for today's man; Fred told the assistant they were just looking.

'OK. Floor's yours.'

'Thank you. This morning,' said Cotton, 'I went to Howard University Hospital. I saw a patient called Austin Ojukwu, a Nigerian. He was in a bad way. There is the related possibility that he had been giving English conversation classes to someone in the Soviet Embassy.'

Fred Warwick blinked. 'Yeah?'

'What I am here for is to encourage better channels of communication. You will be aware that the person Mr Ojukwu was assisting asked to see me on the steps of the Lincoln Memorial. As agreed with your agency, some of your people took photographs of that meeting.'

Fred Warwick cleared his throat and lifted a tie on the rack.

'What you may not be aware of,' said Cotton, 'is that we had hopes of Mr Ojukwu, information that we would certainly have passed on had it amounted to anything.'

Warwick nodded. 'OK,' he said, 'I can see that.'

'Of course, our main interest is in the man he was teaching, and who was with me when two of your agents took photographs of us.'

Warwick thought. 'Maybe someone was thinking of containment,' he said.

'Yes,' said Cotton. 'But that is only half of it, as I am sure you know. It's not possible to stop a high-level diplomat from extending international friendship and brotherhood, and speaking at suitable events in this country, possibly causing embarrassment.'

'Right,' said Fred Warwick.

'We want to know what Slonim is doing here. He talked to me of Africa and possible future communist influence there. My superiors think it's a strange thing for an ex-tank commander of his rank and reputation to be doing. Unless, of course, the Soviets have upgraded Africa.'

He paused.

'You know the Soviets are backing the upcoming Pan-African Congress to be held in England? My understanding is that only Marxists and fellow travellers will be allowed to speak.'

Fred Warwick lifted another tie. 'Right,' he said.

'A lot of the conference will concern industrialization and raw materials. Against that, my superiors think that the Africa business is a bluff. Slonim may be here for something else – and that something, I don't have to tell you, could be of great interest to your agency.'

There was a pause before Fred Warwick spoke. 'You're saying this "Niggerian" might have told you?'

'No. But he might have told us how important Africa really was to them.'

'I've got to take notes,' said Fred Warwick.

Cotton spelt out Ojukwu and Slonim.

Warwick said he'd get back to him. He said he'd buy a tie first. They shook hands and Cotton left the Lansburgh department store. On his way out he saw the two small girls eating huge ice-cream concoctions.

12

IN THE Embassy compound, the P & Q had moved up a gear. A fairly lengthy production arrived in the Intelligence Room. It concerned 'general etiquette in the United States of America' and included a list of recommendations on what was 'proper' and what 'improper'. Amongst the improper was included 'comments on the Race Question that may offend the Host Country'.

It arrived with a letter from Dr Aforey.

Dear Moses

Do you know why Thomas Carlyle called economics 'the dismal science'? It was because classical economists persisted in stating that a market wage set by supply and demand was superior to slavery. What Carlyle considered 'dismal', was market forces when opposed to what he termed 'the beneficent whip' of slavery.

Someone interrupted him. 'Are you Cotton?'

Cotton looked up at a man in a chalk-striped suit wearing a rose in his buttonhole 'Yes. Who are you?'

'Patrick Whickham. I resent having to come here.'

Cotton said nothing. Mr Whickham had scraped-back hair and had recently had a manicure.

'Who said you should meet Dr Aforey? And on what grounds?'

'His interest. And this is part of my cover.'

'Cover for what?'

'Mm,' said Cotton. 'What's your clearance level?'

'You bloody people! You have no idea what you are getting mixed up in.'

'Are you going to tell me? Won't you take a seat?'

'I don't suppose you've heard of the Pan-African Congress.'

'Of course I have. That's initially why I met Dr Aforey.'

'Well, you know he's anti, don't you?'

'I don't think that quite represents his position.'

'That's not your judgement to make.'

'Really?' said Cotton. 'Then whose is it and on what are they basing it?'

'HMG are not encouraging the Congress but are keeping a close eye on developments.'

'That's not a judgement,' said Cotton. 'In any case, Dr Aforey is not attending the Congress.'

'I'm saying it's not your pigeon.'

'I'm not attending it either. But I will keep my contact with Dr Aforey here for another reason. If you want to make any further representations, I suggest you contact Geoffrey Ayrtoun.'

'He told me I should see you.'

'And you have.'

'You haven't heard the last of this.'

'I'm sure.'

Cotton looked round.

'What a very silly man,' said Jim Gowar.

'Who is he?'

'He is a diplomat. One of Halifax's boys. First-class berk.'

*

135

Tibbets had not been much in view for some days. When he appeared he told Cotton he'd had 'considerable success with an encryption algorithm. I think the Yanks were pretty impressed.'

Cotton smiled politely. 'Good.'

Tibbets sighed. The cheerfulness seeped out of him, quickly and thoroughly.

'I don't suppose you know what I do,' said Tibbets gloomily.

'I am not supposed to, am I?'

'Oh, I am not giving out secrets.'

'Good.'

Tibbets blinked. 'You have a number of possibilities when you want to choose and use a code. The Soviets use two, a conventional coding system as a first step and then what is called a one-time-pad system.'

Cotton waited. 'OK. What's the problem?'

Tibbets sighed. 'The problem is I'm a mathematician, you see.'

'I had understood that.'

'No,' said Tibbets, 'you don't understand. The one-pad system is *not* mathematics. This is not what I do.'

'All right.'

'At Arlington Hall the main star is a linguist, another an archaeologist, and there's a girl there with the patience of Job who gets amazing results from almost nothing.'

'What are you saying?'

Tibbets dropped his voice. 'It's *not* mathematics! It's more like deciphering the Rosetta stone. That's not my field at all. My Russian isn't even very good. But Ayrtoun doesn't seem to think it's of any importance.'

'Arlington Hall works for all the intelligence agencies?'

'Yes, but it is still the Army and I suppose it does more for some than for others. The FBI seem, well, very protective in a piecemeal sort of way of what they have. But I am pretty sure the Army is keeping something from them as well.'

Cotton shook his head. 'You mean all the agencies have their own secrets?'

'Well, I suppose there's power in them. And there is the security issue.'

'Leaks,' said Cotton.

'Mm. But not to me,' said Tibbets. He looked up and shook his head. 'My main work was on random numbers, you know,' he said. He sounded very wistful. 'What's an algorithm after all?'

Margarita Gil was as prompt and as efficient as Cotton hoped. On one sheet of paper she had written:

Subject arrived in Mexico 29 May 1945. Full honours at Soviet Embassy where he stayed as Ambassador's guest.

Throughout June he received nine hours of English classes every day for the 30 days. Classes were of the so-called immersion type, with much use of a tape recorder. He had three teachers, one woman and two men. The woman, light-skinned mixed race, has an American passport in the name Grace Simmonds, born Baltimore MD 12 February 1910. Arrived Mexico 1940. Lives with Slovenian cameraman, also teaches private classes. No children.

She listed learning problems normal at his age and rank – rapid progress in basics, particularly vocabulary, but his grammar is relatively poor and his Russian accent remains strong.

Subject certainly ate listening to English-language radio. Saw several American films, including the silent *Birth of a Nation, Gone with the Wind* and *Pennies from Heaven.* Also saw a number of US wartime newsreels that mentioned the Soviet struggle.

The other two teachers are more problematic. Maximilano Rodriguez, age 52, Mexican passport, despite name had an English mother and attended Haberdashers' Aske's School in England. Described as a journalist, was a stringer, based in New York, for anti-American newspapers from 1932–37 when deported for pimping.

Francisco (Curro) Simone does not appear to be third teacher's real name. Best guess is Italian-speaking Albanian who appears in Argentina in late thirties. Very possibly double agent spying for Soviets on pro-Nazis. Has been in Mexico for several months and the Argentinians have a contract out on him. Not known as an English speaker, let alone a fluent one.

During stay, subject left Embassy twice, once to go to a dentist, once to visit National Monument where he was photographed with the Ambassador and a Mexican minister. He was heard there to speak slightly stilted but competent Spanish.

Visitors to the Embassy during his stay included delegations (trade unionists, journalists, academics, etc.) from Bolivia, Columbia, Cuba, Chile, Paraguay, Peru and Argentina.

Along with this there was a personal note to say that Houghton and Marie in Madrid, the couple who had looked after Cotton when he had first arrived there, had lost the child they were expecting.

Cotton took what Margarita Gil had written to Ayrtoun. He read it.

'Shit.' He looked up. 'This woman is an associate?'

'Part-time apparently.'

'Right. I'll get this Grace Simmonds to the Americans.' He frowned. 'What was *Pennies from Heaven* by the way?'

'No idea.'

Ayrton used the internal phone.

'Herbert says it's a film with Bing Crosby and Louis Armstrong.'

'A musical?'

Ayrtoun shrugged.

When Cotton got back to his desk, he found amongst the pile of news updates that President Truman had, earlier that day, formally announced the break-up and dissolution of the OSS, its responsibilities to be divided between the War Department and the Department of State. The hand-over would be completed by 1 October. The people of the United States should rest assured that government vigilance on their behalf was constant and unceasing.

13

O N T H E morning of the 21st at the daily briefing,
Ayrtoun appeared with a card that he had unpinned
from his bookshelves. It bore the word SCRAPPLE.

'Good morning, gentlemen. Let me sum up our situation
for you in simple terms.

'We are working in a new-found world in which both
the Americans and the Soviets are far better funded,
better equipped and with many more operatives than we
have.

'To put it bluntly, we're broke, and likely to remain so.
While the Americans and the Soviets are expanding their
intelligence networks, we – and I suggest you all get used to
this – are retrenching.

'Our priority is quite clear. We are dependent, and will
become increasingly dependent on the USA for information. That means that our contribution, our worth to them
and ourselves in the Western alliance, must be in analysis.
Have you all got that?

'This is not a grand position. The reverse.'

Ayrtoun held up his card. 'Now the Americans have a
delectable morsel called scrapple. Some of you may have
tasted it. It consists of scraps of pork that are boiled with
cornmeal, strained, made into a kind of loaf which is then
sliced and fried for consumption.

'It is an example of doing what you can with leftovers.

Are you following me? Making the best use of what you have got is what I recommend to you.

'Some of you may think I am exaggerating, others that I am belittling the importance of our task. Believe me, I am not. It will be a lot of work, it will be painstaking and it is necessary you learn very quickly.

'Now, we have possibilities and advantages. In general the Soviets are poor at analysis. They have too much information and some of it is deeply unreliable. Their analysts are bound by the regime and ideology. On the other hand, they are excellent strategists. They were very quick pre-war to get people in place and have obtained extraordinary advantages. These advantages will gradually decrease with time.

'The Americans plan to listen in on the world. They are in some disarray at present, but have at least appreciated they need to reorganize.

'Perhaps you think I am belittling the Americans – giving you the intelligence version of "They have the money and we have the brains." Incorrect. We must offer them the very best analysis we can, so that we have access to as much as possible of the information their money will bring. Understood?

'Under no circumstances feel superior. The Americans at least have started to clear out their Soviet agents. That will be a political problem in a country like this and one of the terms of the debate. We, on the other hand, have done absolutely nothing about Soviet agents with us, except prosecute the occasional usually low-level operative – often on American say-so.

'I am not preaching humility. I prefer to call it scrapple for short. If I say "scrapple" you will know it means fighting to get every scrap we can and to make it count to our advantage.

'Finally, a few numbers. I am talking to just nine people in this room. The present estimate of Soviet agents in New York alone is between two hundred and fifty and three hundred, though recently they have decided to shift the bulk of their operations to Washington. The American agencies are also well supplied. The FBI, for example, has doubled in size even in the last couple of years. Its counter-intelligence operation in Washington employs five hundred. There is also the War Department and now a State Department that has just swallowed another thirteen hundred people working exclusively on Latin America.

'Gentlemen?' He held up the card. 'Scrapple,' he said.

The briefing was over. Everyone started murmuring among themselves as they left the briefing room. Cotton had been sitting next to Jim Gowar.

'He gives these "we blessed few" harangues periodically,' said Jim. 'Though they tend more to the sardonic than ra-ra, chaps. I don't think they're meant to shake us up but to accelerate our brain waves. I'm not sure whether they do any good. He calls it team building, I believe. I think the idea is we cluster fruitfully around a point or an angle.'

Cotton was struck that Ayrtoun had again mentioned the recent shift of Soviet operations from New York to Washington. That was, surely, at the very least, a possible job for Slonim. He looked again at Margarita Gil's message on Slonim in Mexico, and the note about Houghton and Marie. He decided to send a message to Houghton in Madrid.

He went directly to the Communications Room. He picked out one of Mullins' better snaps of Slonim, but then had a wrangle about the expense of sending it. He got Ayrtoun's signature, then had to reduce his written message. He kept it to – 'Do you know this man?' He added a personal message about Marie's miscarriage to take it up to twenty words.

When Cotton was back at his desk, he received a call from Dr Aforey.

'I am calling you directly,' he said, 'on behalf of Austin Ojukwu, whose case is familiar to you.'

They agreed to meet at the Euclid St. Noir side of Meridian Hill Park.

'Mr Cotton,' said Dr Aforey, 'I approve of your humility. You do not bluster. You do not behave as if you know everything.'

'Well, I don't,' said Cotton.

Dr Aforey smiled. 'And you turned like a lion, sir, on those ruffians who insulted me outside the church.'

Cotton did not correct him. He remembered something vague from Sunday school to do with lambs lying down with lions.

'It wasn't the cleverest thing to do,' he said.

Dr Aforey slid him a piece of paper. It contained a name and an address. 'Austin knows her. You will note her address is in Anacostia.'

'What does that tell me?'

'It is not a Negro area and that is her parents' house.'

Dr Aforey held out his hand.

'You want this back?' said Cotton.

'Yes. Should you agree to see her, contact me and I will contact her.'

Cotton paused.

'I'm concerned about her,' said Dr Aforey.

Cotton nodded. He gave the slip of paper back and said he would be in touch.

*

Despite Dr Aforey's concern, Cotton was worried that if he saw the girl he might cause her problems.

He asked Ayrtoun's advice.

'Balls!' said Ayrtoun. 'We'll tell the FBI.'

So Cotton met her where instructed, outside a café called Peabody's, by Farragut Square on 17th St. NW. Dorothy Feiner was a heavy-set girl with curly, slightly reddish hair and very pale skin.

'There's a fair chance our conversation will be recorded,' said Cotton.

'Only fair?' she said. 'Please.' She shook her head.

They went inside. He ordered coffee, she chocolate.

'How's Austin?'

She shook her head. The movement was almost a shudder. 'Dreadfully beat up. The doctor says he may be blind in one eye.'

'I'm sorry,' said Cotton.

She shook her head

'They've done nothing, Mr Cotton. No solidarity, no protest, no interest. Nothing!'

Cotton noted her resentment was not against the Americans but the Soviets.

'Yes,' he said. 'I know.'

'It's not in the least fair.'

She was, he thought, frightened but indignant.

'He was simply giving classes?'

'Yes! The man wanted modern idioms, that's all. What meant good, what meant bad, that kind of thing.' She looked up. 'I think it's because of him.'

'What do you mean?'

'I don't know. Austin said the other Soviets kind of resented him; some were maybe frightened of him.'

'In what way?'

'They sort of didn't want to be near him. Austin said someone came in once and froze and then started to back away. And this man said something about roll, little apple, roll.'

'You have a name for this man?'

'Yes. Slonim.'

'What about Austin? I'm sorry to be blunt, but . . .'

He did not have to ask the question. 'It's nothing like that,' Dorothy Feiner said quietly. 'We're friends. I know you're going to say that girls can't have friends who are men. Least of all with Austin's skin colour.'

'What does Austin say?'

The girl stiffened. 'He's asked me to marry him.'

'What did you say?'

She shook her head.

Cotton leaned forward. 'I'm sorry,' he said. 'This awful thing has made you lose a friend.'

'Yes,' she said. 'That's what's happened. I . . . I don't want to see Austin again but . . . I feel disloyal.'

'Write him a note.'

'Do you think he'll understand?'

'He has good friends at Howard. They want to be fair to you because Austin is too vulnerable to be fair for himself.'

He heard back from Houghton about the photo he had sent of Slonim.

'Subject in Spain in 1936. Involved in purges of Spanish Communist Party. Code name then Aristophanes, aka The Clouds, more colloquially known as 'La Criba'. 'Real' name given then as Arkady Musin. Possible

145

he had passports with surnames Druznhikov and Goncharov. *Lagarto, lagarto.*

On little Houghtons we are resigned to trying again. Or perhaps adopting.

He took the note to Ayrtoun.

'What does the Spanish mean?' said Ayrtoun.

'*Criba* means sieve in the sense of sift.'

'Do you mean "sift" as the Elizabethans sometimes used it to mean search?'

Cotton considered. 'It's possible. The other is *lizard, lizard.* What they say to ward off the evil eye.'

'Fuck,' said Ayrtoun. He sighed. 'A few passports in different names and we're baffled.'

'Do you know who Slonim might be now?'

Ayrtoun shook his head. 'I suspect it takes us away from the brave tank commander. It's called intelligence *gathering*, for Christ's sake!'

Cotton watched the vein in Ayrtoun's neck.

'What,' said Ayrtoun, 'are you doing this weekend?'

'I've been invited to spend it with some friends.'

Ayrtoun looked at him and nodded. 'All right, you do that. See me first thing on Monday.'

Cotton was barely out of the office when Ayrtoun started snarling down the phone.

'What the hell is the point of sending you pinheads photographs if you fail to recognize the fucking subject?'

Someone in the Soviet section was having their weekend cancelled.

14

WHEN COTTON had visited his father before leaving for the USA, his father remembered something.

'There's a letter for you. I put it on the mantelpiece. In the drawing room.'

Cotton went through and saw that the envelope was addressed simply to 'Peter'. It took him a moment to recognize his mother's handwriting. He picked it up.

Behind him, his father spoke. 'In 1938 I was . . .'

'I know,' said Cotton.

His father blinked. 'Then I had to pack up, you see, to come back to England and the letter disappeared somehow. A complete mystery to me, I have to tell you. In 1943 I found it again in a sewing box when I thought I should learn how to darn socks. But that was the war and I didn't know what Isla might have written.' He looked up. 'These days though you're not going to be killed, not in a war, are you?' His father almost always called his mother Isla now, as if he had claimed her back entirely as his wife.

Cotton nodded. 'It's all right. Do you know what it says?'

'Of course not.'

'Do you want to read it with me?'

His father looked shocked. 'No,' he said. 'The letter is to you, old man. Of course it is.'

His father shuffled over to the French windows and

stepped outside. He had just spent some time changing his footwear. Cotton watched him cross the lawn in his carpet slippers towards the pine trees and bend to pick up fallen cones.

Cotton opened the letter that had been written to him in pencil on lined paper seven years before.

My darling Boy

You'll probably get this after I am dead. In a way, it has been my fault. I must have missed the early warning signs and now it is too late and things are moving irredeemably fast.

The purpose of this, however, is three fold. First, your father is going to require time and attention. He likes matters to be settled but this kind of certainty flummoxes him. He didn't deserve this.

The second thing is absurd but I need to wish you well. I mean I was not keen on sending you to school in England but here you are, just up to Cambridge. I am proud of you, of course, but I'd have liked some more time with you, been able to see more of you growing up.

The way things are, men look after women. It is not ideal. It can make women dependent and men despondent, unless they can both convince themselves otherwise. An illusion, possibly, but at its best an exploration of mutual need and benefit. But there is another part, that few people ever mention, a conspiracy of two I suppose, as you learn to tackle things together, without recourse to others.

It is absurd of me to look ahead and, of course, I can't help you. But I want you to think of what you want. It is not at all easy, not if you really think. Yes, I am talking about a clear view of yourself and I am talking about women. Whoever you pick, learn her and encourage her to learn you. I have to say your father always did his best. No, the dead can't impose on the future, but you have to remember their example. That's time – eternity if you are delusional, something very short if you are not.

Te mando muchos besos y muchísima suerte.

Cotton's mother had always been taken for someone forthright to the point of eccentricity, at least in the staider business and banking circles of Mexico City. It was what he remembered her for. And her use of Spanish to express love. She had been a voracious if sometimes violent reader, would throw a book she disliked out of the window into the garden. It looked more violent than it was. The book would always land on a particular bush. The gardener would collect it and put it beside others in a wheelbarrow in an outhouse.

One of the things Cotton liked about her was her occasional forays into the outhouse when, some days later, she thought she might have been 'too hasty'.

Cotton had left for the US directly from his father's house and had taken the letter with him. He had been struck both by looking up and seeing his father in his garden with an armful of pine cones and by his mother being unable or perhaps forgetting to sign the letter. Later, in mid-Atlantic, he had dreamt of a shadowy girl playing hopscotch on a pavement, but there was something strange about the chalk numbers. He awoke irritated. He had never played hopscotch.

149

Tidying up prior to Katherine Ward taking him away for the weekend, for some reason he remembered his mother's letter again. He took it out and re-read it, then put it away and went down to the foyer to wait for Katherine. There was a magazine on a table. The cover told him that velvet was this season's fabric and that 'shades for the fall' were 'vivid gold, russet, red and bright blue'.

Cotton had never seen her in anything but formal evening gowns and a tailored suit. Now she was casually, if expensively, dressed in a matching skirt and collared knit and her manner had changed too, felt less pre-scribed.

'Isn't it bliss to kick off and relax?' she said. 'We'll be at the cabin in two hours, maybe less, way above mosquito level.'

Cotton nodded. He had not found mosquitoes any sort of problem in the Statler.

'Did you bring a sweater? It's high enough,' she asked when he was putting his case into what she called 'the trunk'.

'It's lightweight clothes for here that have been our problem.'

She smiled. She was a confident if casual driver. She told him her automobile was a Chrysler Royal Coupé. It was black and the tyres were white-walled. The seats were covered in plaid material not so different from his dress trousers. Her father had given it to her on her graduation in 1941. It had Fluid Drive or 'clutchless shifting' and the gear shift was on the column. She handled that with the easy air of someone flicking ash off a cigarette.

'Dad thought it apt for a graduate. Before this I had a small undergraduate Dodge. Oh, this has a Spitfire engine with a 7.2:1 compression. You could call that a compliment to the British.'

Cotton could drive but had never owned a car, nor ever had much interest in engines. He was surprised she should make him feel so unmechanical.

'Do you want to listen to the radio? It's only factory. Or are you a talker?'

'I'll talk.'

'Not fond of music?'

'Only sometimes.'

She smiled. 'What kind of music do you like then?'

'Piano jazz mostly. Art Tatum.'

'I'm impressed,' she said. 'Or are you just being polite?'

'No, no. I went to see Tatum perform in London in 1938. Ciro's Club in Orange Street.'

'Wow!' she said. 'How old were you?'

'Nineteen.'

'Well, look at you! I wouldn't have guessed. I thought your piano would be Beethoven, maybe a ripple of Debussy for lighter moods.'

Cotton laughed. 'No, it was my sister who took the formal piano lessons and my mother who introduced me to jazz.'

Whatever material the girl was wearing, some kind of very close knit, the new arrangement was pleasantly outgoing when compared to the stiff dresses he had previously seen. Katherine Ward was euphoric. Cotton doubted that this was due entirely to him or to the prospect of a weekend away with friends.

They pulled up at a crossroads. He looked out of the automobile.

The peculiarities of American billboards weren't so

much in the number of them as in what they advertised. Here, staring down at him, he saw an ecstatic bovine with round eyes, huge eyelashes and a smile, cutting thick, red steaks from its own legless rump with a cleaver. There was something in the pose that reminded him of a centaur. Beneath the billboard on a bench a very young couple were necking with some of the skill he had been told trumpeters used in 'circular breathing'. Their legs were loosely intertwined.. They broke off and, chewing gum, looked around to see if anything interesting was passing, then got back to it.

'That's called necking, I believe?'

'Oh, yes. Very important subject and skill at high school,' said Katherine.

'The difference with kissing?'

'Ooh, that's a tough one. For them I guess kissing would be just too gooey a word and I think parents like to think it is puppy love.'

'I see.'

'You're shocked?'

'No, I'm learning America. I've heard of something called "the tingle test" when chewing gum is advertised.'

She laughed. 'You've got it. Look ahead.'

She pointed and used her pointing finger to flick the gear lever. Strung under an upstairs window was a cotton sheet on which someone had painted BRING DADDY BACK.

'I almost got saddled with that at work.'

'What do you mean?'

'The President is getting about a thousand letters a day from troops' families, and the Congress a lot more. Bring Back Daddy clubs are quite the thing.'

'How did you get out of it?'

She smiled. 'First there is the why. This is only going to get bigger. And I had already been working on Debunk.'

'What's that?'

'There was a radio station called Debunk, pro-Axis. It started broadcasting stuff about the Waacs, you know, women military personnel. They were adjudged as sapping morale. It turned out most of the stories were coming from us, our troops, male, and believed by married women back home. The result was that fathers were not allowing their daughters to enlist. And we needed them. If you are a woman you tend to get girl stuff, family, education, health physical and moral. Do you want to light me a cigarette? In my purse.'

She meant her handbag. Cotton was surprised; he could not remember ever having been invited to open an English handbag. He obliged, breathed in perfume when he opened the clasp, tasted menthol in her absurdly long cigarette.

His mother had used the word 'bursting' to express things just contained, from urine to pride and pleasure.

He handed her the cigarette. 'New job?' he asked.

'Mm,' she said. 'Thanks. Don't you ever feel the need to smoke, Colonel?'

He smiled. 'Like the piano, I missed those lessons.'

'My mother taught me as a minor but necessary social accomplishment, like dancing. My little sister took over the piano until she got the non-wallflower treatment.'

'Brothers?'

'No. Just two girls.'

They were heading north-west out of Washington.

'Where are we going exactly?'

'Frederick County in Maryland. The cabin is on the Catoctin Mountain ridge. It's not too far from Shangri-la, you know, where the President has a camp. Didi Johnson's parents hire it every third weekend. Didi and I were at Vassar together. There'll be a bunch of people there. Should be fun. Do you play tennis?'

'Not very well,' said Cotton, 'and it's been years.'

'Nooo,' she said, smiling. 'It's most definitely not that kind of weekend. Let's see. Do you serve underarm or overarm?'

'What? Oh, I can do over.'

'You'll be just fine then. Damn, do you want to keep an eye out for a packet store?'

'Of course,' said Cotton. 'What's a packet store?'

'A packet store? I just missed one. For liquor. What do you say in England?'

'Off-licence.'

'There you go. Doesn't make much sense to me.' She smiled. 'It's not formal and it is a good idea to take something.'

Twenty miles on, they stopped at a packet store like a low barn. It was still more than warm, perhaps 80 degrees; the slightly sweet smell of tree-sap and liquor and the sound of rubbing insect legs and vibrating wings contributed to a feel almost as if the air was thick. Cotton looked for wine to take but did not see that the store had any. He bought some representative malt whisky and she bought gin, and they consulted.

She wrinkled her nose. 'Get some bourbon too,' she said.

They also bought Coca-Cola and what Katherine called soda.

'The idea is you bring what you'll drink yourself – and then some.'

As they drove on, what struck Cotton was how different the landscape was from Britain. There were miles of country with no sign of houses, and where there were settlements, there was a scruffy, makeshift feel to them, individual plots but some, almost stagey, coherence from commercial patterns. He enjoyed the drive, particularly the roads cut through the forest as they climbed. The green was dense and close. Cotton knew nothing of American trees but enjoyed whizzing past those with an almost white underside to the leaves.

Higher up, the trees thinned with the thinner soil and the green faded off or became waxed dark in conifers as they turned off the road down a track that went on for a mile. They arrived around six thirty into a clearing with a number of automobiles parked and the accommodation above them. Cotton had to turn his head to take in the extent of the roof lines.

'This . . . is a log cabin.'

She smiled. 'Is that British? When you begin as if you were going to ask a question and then don't? And I didn't say anything about logs, you know.'

From quite near, as Cotton got their bags out of the trunk, came a querulous, high-pitched sound with something of a sneezing rodent about it that increased in speed to a rapid peeping of complaint. There was a brief pause and then the tattattat of a beak drill. He looked round. A bird about the size of a crow, with a red crest and a white-and-black-striped head and black body, adjusted its footing and showed a flutter of white underwing.

'Those things are everywhere,' she said.

'I'm guessing it's a woodpecker.'

'Yup. Pileated woodpecker. They make square holes in

hardwood trees. Oh, there is wildlife here. We have rattlers too and . . . you have ever experienced skunk, Colonel?'

'I can't say I have.'

'Then you have something powerful to look forward to.'

'Potent?'

'An entirely new take on how odour can cling and persist.'

They had to climb steps to get on to cabin level. The 'cabin' was a complex. Years before, Cotton had seen an illustration of a tenth-century Japanese palace, an extensive arrangement of covered walkways and buildings. This was an updated, New Deal, frontier version, set into the hill, spreading out over steps and levels, without formal gardens but with a tennis court on one of the lower levels.

As Katherine had said, there was a bunch of people, the large Johnson family, each generation of which had brought friends. He found the guests polite, even careful with him, but quite insistent. Mrs Johnson asked him if he thought the chestnut tree replacement policy was working; Mr Johnson told him something about a Parks Committee of which he was a member; Mrs Johnson's father talked of his experiences nearly half a century previously in the Philippines 'in the brewery business'; he admitted to never having tasted Coca-Cola to a fifteen-year-old called Buddy – no, nor eaten a Hershey bar – and was listening to Didi Johnson's younger sister, April, on the concept of IQ – 'Do you think there is something in it, accurate I mean – not some awful determinism?' – when he was offered a glass of Coca-Cola to try. He tasted it. The drink reminded him of the fizz of sherbet with a touch of cinnamon and then something cloying, like coffee drowned in sugar syrup.

They were in a long room, all wood, stone and ironmongery. Cotton was not sure whether the reddish colour of the planked walls and ceiling was natural or stained. The floor was crazy-paved and the stone fireplace hugely over-scaled. The chairs were massive, simple and of wood, the soft furnishings lime green, raw linen and a pale grey and red thread. The whole was a mix of Arts and Crafts with a nubbed streak of American Indian allusion in a couple of wall hangings. He'd seen similar in Mexico where rich people had employed national motifs and modernism together.

Cotton met Katherine Ward's friend, Didi, a slim, sallow girl wearing a very similar but different-coloured outfit, a young man with her she introduced as 'my beau, Joe', an air-force navigator and another young man called Brian Kirkland who bore, from one angle at least, a resemblance to an actor in one of the films shown on the Atlantic crossing, John Dall in *The Corn is Green*. At the time, Cotton had been surprised at the respect the troops had shown for the film. Others they had hooted at mercilessly. The resemblance was in the hair, long face and the full, slack lower lip. He was dressed in baggy trousers and a very tight jersey top. Brian Kirkland winked at him.

'Grand to meet you, suh, Colonel.'

Cotton understood Brian was already past what Americans called 'primed' and on to 'stewed' and that the accent was not permanent.

'And it's grand to meet you too, Brian, finally.'

From down the room came a shout.

'Who Jew? Who Catholic?'

Cotton saw a tiny, elderly Chinese man.

'The call of the wild,' said Brian Kirkland. 'Or supper-time in the Catoctin Mountains.'

On Friday evening, at a long table in a long dining room cum cabin, they were given pork chops and invited to choose from a lot of bowls containing a kind of pineapple salad, corn on the cob, creamed spinach, potatoes mashed, hashed and fried.

Mrs Johnson indicated Cotton sit beside her and asked him question after question, about the Royal princesses, Laurence Olivier, Robert Donat, Churchill's drinking and Oliver Cromwell's refusal to declare himself King. Cotton did not know much about any of these subjects but did his best and scraped up that one of the princesses was called Margaret Rose, that Olivier had made a film of *Henry V*, that Robert Donat had been in a film version of *The Thirty-nine Steps*, based on a book by the late Governor-General of Canada, that Churchill very likely started the day with a glass of champagne and that Cromwell, having been influential in arranging for the Lord's Anointed to lose his head, may have been anxious to show due deference to the one and only Lord Protector he acknowledged.

'He's saying,' said Brian Kirkland, 'that getting people to bow isn't power, chopping off their heads is.'

Mrs Johnson blinked at him and turned back to Cotton.

'Katherine told me you spent some time in Spain. Last year, was it?'

'Yes. And part of this one.'

'Tell me about Leslie Howard.'

Cotton could think of nothing at all to do with Leslie Howard except that he was an actor.

'Well, they say, you know, that he was working for Churchill himself and was sent to warn . . . what's the Spanish dictator's name?'

'Franco.'

'Yes, to warn that man off joining the war on the German side.'

'Really? I hadn't heard that.'

She put her head on one side and gave him a look. It combined puzzlement and great wonderment.

'But Colonel,' she said, 'Leslie Howard *died* doing that. His plane was shot down by the Germans. There is a story they thought Churchill was on it. Their bodyguards looked the same.'

Cotton had not even registered that Howard was dead.

'I get him confused with Glenn Miller,' said Brian. 'I never quite know who went down where.'

Mrs Johnson leaned across and patted Brian's hand. 'Brian dear, I know you're dying for a smoke.'

'Bless you, Mrs J,' said Brian. He got up and left.

'More chop?' bawled the elderly Chinese cook. Cotton found he was called Cookie and was noisily assisted by an elderly woman called Ma. Cookie later told Cotton the woman was 'not my sister, not my wife. She Hokkien, I Cantonese.' Liquids and ice were handled by another elderly man, a Negro in a white coat, called Chester.

The weekend was a well-off American variation of 'muck-in' – with servants. Guests did some things – 'usually to cushions' as Brian would put it – but some guests did more than others and Cotton certainly helped clear the table and take dishes down a small corridor to the cook-house. In this he was helped by April.

Around 9 p.m. he managed to step outside on to the deck. Brian, Katherine, Didi and Joe were stretched out on loungers, smoking.

'Oh, you poor mother's boy,' said Brian. 'Smoke?'

'Brian!' said Didi.

'No, thank you,' said Cotton.

'I did not mean *that* kind of mother's boy,' said Brian. 'I'm saying mothers like this man. They get that look, as if they had suddenly thought it might really be possible to replace toothpaste into a tube. You know?' He shushed a groan from the others. 'They look at him but they are looking at themselves in the past. He makes them reflective. They consider themselves in a mirror but after a time they catch sight of a daughter over there, down on the right, and then begin to think . . . marriageable.'

'I have Joe,' said Didi.

'But April?'

They laughed.

'How do you know mothers don't see a threat?' said Katherine. 'A threat to their daughters.'

'As opposed to themselves?'

'Brian!' said Didi.

'Oh, my dear, I regret I have heard of such awful things. In Washington DC, for example, I've witnessed the most awful catfights and . . .'

'Brian likes to appear sophisticated,' said Didi, 'but that's only because he uses that tired old line of wanting a woman to save him and mend his ways.'

'You have no idea,' said Brian. 'But the last time I got close, it turned out it was her mother who was more interested, poor thing, in having a drinking companion. An impotent symphony of ice cubes.'

They laughed again, a comfortable reflex. Cotton looked up at the sky. There were very few stars out but that was due to the moon and a gleam that moved from dull gold to something silvery just above the treetops. He closed his eyes. The air was by no means cold but certainly fresh and clean, a relief after Washington.

He was given a room to himself, entirely of wood, with a small, Swiss chalet-type window that gave on to a rock face about fifteen feet away. He lay on the bed, breathed deeply, inhaling the night air, and slept more soundly than he had since arriving in the US.

15

AT BREAKFAST on Saturday morning Katherine smiled at him over a table containing waffles, pancakes, muffins, bagels, fruit salad, fruit juices, bacon, maple syrup, chilled water, pots of coffee, butter, conserves and toast racks.

'I give you eggs benedict,' said Cookie. 'You want bacon too?'

'No, no bacon thanks.'

'Brian described you as a decidedly polished diamond.'

Cotton wasn't really thinking. 'Don't tell me,' he replied. 'He's a social jeweller?'

'Ow,' she said. She smiled. 'We think of him as someone who drinks a lot and can sometimes be amusing. He loved the film *The Four Feathers*. He's something of an Anglophile and used to tuck a white feather into his top pocket but complained it was too fluffy.'

'What does he want to do after his war service?'

'He says he's not sure, though he is thinking of writing pulp fiction or hard-boiled fiction, whichever is easier. Oh, and perhaps studying interior design, in case neither works out.'

'A raw egg, please,' said Brian as he came in, 'a little tomato juice and some clear spirit. In a glass.'

Later a group of them went for a walk. The air felt thin, it was another hot day and Cotton, the only one not to have sunglasses, squinted against the bright light. Even when he squeezed his eyes shut there were still traces of resin red behind his lids.

'My favourite tree. The chestnut oak.'

'What? This one?' Cotton tried to focus on the irregular bark, found his eyes were watering. The bark of the chestnut or rock oak looks like layers of irregular shingle.

He felt a tug on both his sleeves and she kissed him with the expression of someone trying out a new, potentially pleasant flavour. For Cotton, she tasted fleetingly of mint and a tremor behind the lipstick. It was all rather unexpected and welcome, but part of the unexpected was her natural, almost casual air of experiment.

'Oh, that'll do,' she said, though she wagged a finger at him. 'I wanted to see how you tasted.'

'On the principle of what? '

'I was just curious. I had guessed you didn't slobber. And I know you are a gentleman. I guess that's kind of exotic in an old-world kind of way.'

'Right.' Cotton wondered what on earth she was thinking.

'Stop that, you two! Come on,' called Didi.

Cotton was not at all sure what this public kiss was about. Lip shopping? A declaration of an independent woman?

A few steps later, still climbing the hill, Katherine in front of him, Brian Kirkland caught up with Cotton.

'She's interested,' he said.

'In what?'

Brian laughed. 'Perhaps you'd like a game of tennis later?'

163

Cotton shrugged. 'I'm not much good.'

'I was a champion. But only until I was thirteen. I've had almost another thirteen going downhill so. . .'

'We're about even?'

They came to a kind of flat-topped knoll, a clearing fringed with trees. Cookie was already there.

'You people late!'

In the event, having been dragged out on the tennis court, he found Brian played with more of an eye on not spilling his drink than on the ball. This made the game a one-man show. Cotton served as amiably as lack of practice and some effort at control allowed. The ball got over the net and passed an entirely static Brian on a leisurely bounce.

'I say, old pip,' Brian said in his most British voice, 'if you are going to take this seriously . . .'

That evening Cotton felt tired. The relentless niceness and noise was getting to him. Joe and Didi were showing off a dance, the jitterbug, for Grandpa Johnson. Cotton slipped outside and found a seat by the tennis court. A few minutes later Brian stumbled down the steps and sat himself down. There was some stagger and slump.

'I used to be able to play tennis, you know, but I acquired certain addictions,' he said and belched. 'Booze, pills, but my most serious vice is . . . I'm sorry, I am forgetting my manners.' He got out a silver pillbox.

'No, thank you.'

'No?' Brian blinked. He put the pillbox back in his pocket. He smiled. Nothing followed. Lapse time. From fuddle, he roused himself to fumble for a cigarette.

'I love her, you do know that? I really do love her.'

'Katherine?'

'Yes, of course. Who else?'

'Of course.'

There was a pause. 'As a sister, naturally — the sister I never had.'

'Yes, I had understood that.'

Brian blinked. 'You did? Brownie points to you, asshole.'

Cotton looked across at him. Brian was smiling slightly. Then his lips began to quiver.

'His name is Calvin,' he said. 'Hell.'

Cotton waited. 'What has happened?'

Brian mumbled. 'He has to get married.'

Cotton said nothing. Brian put out a finger and jabbed it towards Cotton.

'You've got to get married. We've all got to get married.'

'Come on, Brian. Nobody has to get married. I thought you were saying Calvin had got someone pregnant.'

'You have a cruel mind, do you know that?'

'You just say you haven't met the right girl yet. If you want to, you can say you're really enjoying looking. That will put the mothers off.'

Brian frowned. 'What kind of a pervert are you?' He lowered his chin and tried to focus on Cotton. 'Know what it is?'

'What?'

Brian sighed. 'I am so tired. You've no idea how tired I am. I am so tired of hiding.'

Cotton was still nodding when he heard Brian begin to snore. After a while he tried shaking him but got nothing conscious in return. He was fairly sure Brian was used to this. He went back to the deck, took a rug, went down again and placed it over Brian. Then he decided to go to bed.

'Are you OK?' mouthed Katherine.

He nodded and smiled. 'See you in the morning.'

On Sunday, at breakfast, Brian said nothing about their conversation but chose something more grandiose.

'The recuperative powers of the drinker, Colonel. I will outlive you all.'

It reminded Cotton of Prince Harry's 'I know you all, / and will awhile uphold / The unyok'd humour of your idleness: /Yet herein will I imitate the sun, / Who doth permit the base contagious clouds / to smother up his beauty from the world . . .'

Katherine had just come in on this. 'Not again, Brian,' she said. 'Not sunny on Sunday after saturnine on Saturday. Did you sleep well, Colonel?'

'I did, thank you. And you?'

'Fine. ' She smiled at him.

'You two make me sick,' said Brian.

'Then take your Bloody Mary outside. Add an egg, Brian.'

Brian laughed

'Sorry,' said Katherine when Brian had gone off to look for Cookie.

'Why should you be?'

'He gets a little possessive sometimes.' She drank some orange juice. 'When we were about five, our mothers thought it would be awfully nice if we got married. Didn't last.'

'Do you know someone called Calvin?' asked Cotton.

'No. Oh, wait a minute. Brian works with him. Big guy. April would call him hubba-hubba.'

'Meaning?'

'A hunk. *Très chaud.* You know, good looking.'

'Are you talking about me?' said April. 'Hey, don't look at me. It's not fair. I'm a fright this morning.'

'We were talking about Calvin.'

'Yeah? He's a rat. He's getting married to some mousey little thing on fifty thou a year from Newport. All us girls are heartbroken. Isn't there any pineapple juice?'

April shuffled towards the kitchen.

'Do mousey and Newport go together?'

'I don't know. Fifty thou, though, must be attractive.'

'In a Groucho Marx sort of way.'

'Why, Colonel, I hadn't thought of you as a romantic.'

Sunday the 23rd was even hotter, about 85 degrees. Katherine asked him if he would mind getting back to Washington because she had an early start the next day.

'Not at all.'

They got back by 4 p.m. She was friendly and polite. She was back in Washington.

'Thank you very much,' he said. 'You've been very kind.'

'It wasn't entirely selfless.'

'Good. Can I be boring?' he said. 'And ask for help? I have to buy some presents for three children, my niece and nephews, and I must admit I'm finding it tricky. There wasn't anything I could bring with me and I am at a loss here.'

'How urgent is this?'

167

'Well, I have to see them in three weeks' time.'

'Where?'

'A place called Centre Island. It's on . . .'

'Long Island. Who are you talking about?'

'My sister. She is married to an American.'

'I didn't know that.'

'You know now.'

'OK,' she said. 'Are they rich?'

'Well-off, I think.'

'Ages?'

'Girl eight, boy six, boy four.'

'I think that would be "books and".'

'Meaning?'

'Books the parents will like and something they might like.'

She opened her handbag and wrote in a little pad. She tore off a small piece of paper.

'This is my home number. Call me and I'll go shopping with you.'

'Thank you very much.'

Cotton went up to his hotel room. He showered and changed into fresh clothes. A little after five o'clock it started raining. The rain came down and bounced almost a foot high. Looking out over 16th Street Cotton watched the effect of splashback meeting falling drops in the air. It formed what looked like an understructure of trumpets to a haze of small droplets above the street and sidewalk. When Tibbets came back his trousers were soaked to the knee.

'Good weekend?'

'I went for a walk to think,' said Tibbets morosely. 'Are you hungry at all?'

168

'I've spent the weekend eating.'

Tibbets blinked. Whatever was troubling him had to come out. 'I say, old boy,' he said tragically, 'I've got rather a bad rash.'

16

ON HIS return to work on Monday 24 September Cotton found a note from the housing officer. He went along to see him and found a chubby, balding, ginger-haired army captain with a tremendous handlebar moustache, Captain Cecil Harvey-Graeme.

'Time's up at the Statler, I'm afraid. We're moving you to P Street.'

'Where's that?'

'Georgetown. Between 30 and 31st. It's not quite an efficiency. In some respects it is rather a lot better.'

'What's an efficiency?' asked Cotton.

'Good heavens. There's a housing shortage on, Colonel. An efficiency is an apartment. You get a fair-sized room, a kind of kitchen in a cupboard but, I assure you, you'll have a full-sized bathroom except you'll have to share it. Only with one other person though, chap called Tibbets.'

'Yes.'

'I think he's moved there already.'

'Are we talking about a lodging house?'

'No, no. HMG has been making some strategic investments, you see, in up-and-coming areas.'

'Georgetown is one of these?'

'Yes. The New Dealers came in a while back. They passed a slum-clearance law about ten years ago. And well, there is some way still to go, of course, before the area is quite white, but I think the investment is a good one. Bricks and mortar, you see, bricks and mortar in the right place. It's a whole house and we have a number of higher-level staff there. There's a man to look after the boiler and a maid comes in to clean the rooms once a week. Send laundry out. All OK?'

Cotton nodded. 'All right.'

'You get two keys. For the house and for the room. Rent is direct and in advance. You'll get a service bill, as well, at the end of the month.'

Cotton signed the forms and took the keys.

After work he cleared up at the Statler and took a cab to P Street. By then he already knew that he was going to the superior 'bunkhouse'. There were two others elsewhere in the area, both off Volta Place, and a dormitory for unmarried girls 'near the cement factory'. His efficiency was in a yellow-brick Federal-style house on four floors, dating from 1830, that must once have been quite grand. Now it reminded him of something shabby in Notting Hill.

A plaque – *British Embassy Staff. Strictly No Unauthorized Admittance* – was on the door.

He went in. The décor in the hall was gloomy and worn but his room, on the top floor, was reasonably light. He had a window, a small round table and two dining chairs, a single bed, a closet for clothes, a closet that contained a sink, a two-ring plate to cook on and a wall-mounted cupboard with some crockery. There was also an armchair and a side-table that doubled as a bedside table. There was not much he could do to rearrange things. The room was narrow, about nine feet wide but about nineteen long. Not quite a corridor. It struck him that Mullins lived in much more spacious accommodation. He had two rooms quite a bit larger than this.

Halfway down the non-closet wall was a door with a fanlight. That gave on to the bathroom. There was another door in the bathroom that gave on to Tibbets' room. These doors were lockable from the inside. Thus he could lock Tibbets out and Tibbets could lock him out.

Apart from the lack of a shower and air conditioning, Cotton liked it. He liked the relative privacy and lack of attention after the hotel. After unpacking his things he went for a walk to get his bearings. He particularly liked the area. Although he was not much of a cook, he decided to walk down to the shops to buy food. He liked the relaxed, uncomplicated way this was done. He wanted to buy something, the shopkeepers wanted to sell and, while pleasantly enough done, there wasn't much else to get in the way.

Things in Washington, other than housing, struck him as cheap. His Majesty's Government was treating the pound sterling as being worth about four dollars a pound. He was getting paid at a wartime rate of well over two thousand pounds a year and could claim some expenses. He found a delicatessen cum bakery, a fruit and vegetable place, and a small restaurant where he could eat if late. It was Italian, 'a Mom and Pop place'. He looked at the menu outside. He'd eat food he recognized, adapted from what he was used to in Mexico and Spain. It was pretty much *menu del dia*. On Tuesdays, there was vegetable soup, liver, *fegato*, or roast lamb, and a peach-based dessert or ice cream for 75 cents. On Fridays it was fish, in one way Catholic, in another suitably Mediterranean. He'd eat fresh tomato soup, baked white fish and tiramisu.

*

172

On the 25th Ayrtoun gave Cotton a note on IRIS – Interim Research and Intelligence Service at the Department of State.

'Colonel Alfred McCormack,' said Ayrtoun, 'is leading it. He's a New York lawyer who was in Military Intelligence Division and now Special Assistant to the Secretary of State for Research and Intelligence. I have no idea why he has taken this on.'

Cotton nodded.

'I've met him,' said Ayrtoun. 'At Bletchley Park during the war and again here more recently. He certainly has his good points.'

Cotton waited.

'But he hasn't got a hope in hell with this. He's up against every other agency anxious to control the flow of intelligence. As a politician he is nil. He can have a manner like rough sandpaper on a baby's bottom, and puts a hell of a lot of backs up – even when they are on his side. In the Department of State he has almost nobody on his side. The political desk officers – who are the real powers there – have no intention of allowing him to get between themselves and the Secretary of State and the President.' He paused and shook his head. 'I'm giving him six, perhaps nine months in all, but a lot less before he finds himself what they term here as "neutralized". I'd say neutered. End of this year, perhaps? Possibly even before.'

Ayrtoun spoke with aggressive confidence, then became dismissive. He frowned.

'There's a dreary little fellow called Ridley who is in charge of watching State. A grammar-school type, if you know what I mean. Can you keep your little beady eye on what he's got? Mm, watch over IRIS?'

What Ayrtoun meant by dreary was quiet. Cotton thought Ridley looked very efficient. He reminded him of the enthusiastic boy who had been the scorer at school cricket matches. He was small, wore spectacles, had a tweed jacket over the back of his chair and expandable bands round his shirtsleeves just below his biceps. He literally kept his head down. Rather than raise it he'd peer over the top of his glasses. But he had organization charts, names and was right up to date.

'I suppose this is low level,' he said. 'Our main sources are the kind of employees who go to Child's restaurant.'

'Administration?'

'That kind of thing. Child's is quite a good deal, you know.'

'For the meal? Or the sources?'

'The meal. You get pot roast, mash and string beans for 40 cents. It's a little military, I suppose.'

'In what sense?'

'It comes in compartments in a platter. But the platter is blue.'

But whether Child's restaurant or Scrapple, where Ridley really had done his work was in identifying who was what, where they came from, to whom they might owe the job and that person or group's agenda. He was proud of this.

'Try me,' he said. 'Anything you like.'

'Africa?'

'Fellow called Williams. A Presbyterian missionary's son. Speaks Swahili and Kikuyu. Africa is quite Christian, if you know what I mean. In the sense that there is a heavy proportion of people with a background at least of spreading the good word. Williams has the backing of a devout banker, a director of J. P. Morgan called Frederick Hailes, who has his own leper colony kind of thing. Williams also has a lot of support from New England.'

Ridley rattled off politicians' names. He could go on and on and did. It took Cotton some time to get to the names in IRIS and Katherine Ward.

'Popular girl,' said Ridley.

'What do you mean?' asked Cotton.

'Mr Ayrtoun asked about her too. She wrote this paper, you see, called "Coherence and Contradiction", about US foreign policy towards Japan in the thirties. Quite brilliant, apparently.'

'Does she have backers?'

'Oh yes. In particular Wallace Chater. He now sits on boards and has interests from oil, through steel, to car parts and insurance.'

'Politics?'

'A Democrat from North Carolina.'

'Meaning?'

'In his case I think we'd say a free trader playing to every advantage he can get. He has a reputation as a fixer and negotiator. He's often consulted by government departments.'

'So what does she do for him?'

Ridley shook his head. 'He recommended her. Family favour.'

'All right. What about her now?'

'Well, she's recently moved to IRIS. Security is a little tighter there. But our best guess is she is an analyst within the Latin American section.'

'Latin America? What languages does she speak?'

'Fluent French, can read German, has some Russian – and she's learning Spanish now.'

Cotton nodded. 'Very good. Very impressive,' he said.

'Thank you,' said Ridley.

'Thank you,' said Cotton. He had meant Katherine Ward.

That evening in P Street Cotton called Katherine Ward's home number. Didi Johnson answered first, then called Katherine. They agreed to meet that Saturday for their shopping trip.

17

A T ABOUT two in the morning of 26 September the
telephone rang. Cotton picked it up and groaned,
'Yes?'

'I need you to come with me, sir,' said Mullins. 'We need
to be discreet.'

'How long will it take you to get here?'

'Ten minutes.'

'Right.'

Cotton pulled himself out of bed, wet and wiped his
eyes, dressed and went downstairs. Mullins was already
there in a Humber Super Snipe from some way up in the car
pool.

Cotton got in. 'What's going on?' he asked.

'We're going to a roadhouse, sir,' said Mullins as he put
the car into gear.

Cotton waited. When Mullins had the car in fourth gear,
he cleared his throat.

'You were on my way, sir.'

Cotton glanced at him but Mullins said nothing more. A
little later Mullins turned a corner at enough speed for the
back to slide. Expertly he corrected the drift and put his
foot down. If they were being discreet they were also in
a hurry.

They entered a riverside area of warehouses and alleys,
very run-down, some buildings abandoned, some in ruins.

What lighting there was there was poor, but Mullins used the disused metal rails set in the cobblestone road as a guide and barely slackened speed. At the end of a derelict row he slowed and turned. Ahead of them, beside rather than overlooking the Potomac, was Mullins' 'roadhouse'. Even at night it was a clapped-out-looking place. The painted sign lit from above said 'The Flying Boat'.

They got out of the car and Mullins turned directly to their left. Cotton had not picked out the police car parked in the shadows. He saw Mullins bend to the window, saw him nod, then stand up and come back.

'I need another ten dollars, sir.'

Cotton looked in his wallet. He had precisely eleven. He gave Mullins the ten.

'Back in a minute,' said Mullins. 'Keep the dollar ready.'

Cotton nodded. He put his wallet away and slid the dollar bill into his side jacket pocket. Near him he could see the ground was scrubby and littered. When he looked up and back towards his right he could see a faint, slightly grainy glow over Washington from the lighting and the silhouette of some sort of crane nearby.

The police car door slammed and Mullins and a Washington patrolman approached him.

'You don't need to say anything, sir,' murmured Mullins, 'but you will look around, won't you? In my slaughterhouse there was a health inspector who would always scowl.'

Cotton nodded and the three of them walked to the roadhouse door. A puffy-faced bouncer opened it and stepped back.

'If I can I help, gentlemen, just call.'

They ignored him. Barely lit, the place reeked of fried food and spilt alcohol that had turned rancid. The few clients were middle-aged males, there were a couple of bar girls and, swaying on a stage as small as a podium for an orchestra conductor, lit by an overhead bulb, was a plump lady wearing white powder, shadows, fringes and tassels.

Mullins and the policeman did not pause. They walked towards the back and opened a door without knocking. The manager of the Flying Boat was sitting behind a desk in a white shirt with flaps on the shoulders. His tie had a clip of a flying boat and a name badge on his shirt pocket said *Captain Bob*. There was something wrong with his hair. It was entirely white at the side but looked dyed or as if he was wearing a toupee on top. Then Cotton saw the hair was real but that Captain Bob had mixed white powder and oil at the sides, presumably to give him a mature, rakish look.

'I am just the Master of Ceremonies,' he said.

Stretched out on a sofa the Hon. Penelope Ayrtoun frowned, opened the eye not squashed into the armrest, then closed it. She was half covered by the manager's blue pilot jacket.

'She kept showing her ass,' he complained.

Mullins turned and nodded at Cotton. Cotton gave up his last dollar. Mullins placed it on the edge of the manager's desk.

The manager shook his head. The gesture was more resignation than protest.

'Let's hear it, Captain,' said Mullins.

Captain Bob said the lady had come with a 'young navy guy, yes, an officer'. At one stage the lady had wanted to take over from 'our dancer', and her companion had tried to stop her. There had been an altercation, the navy guy had got a black eye and cut and run. A little later the lady had passed out. Worried, they had looked in her purse and, given the delicacy of the situation, decided to call patrolman Price.

The policeman shook his head. 'Bullshit,' he said. 'What you do is tell me why they came here in the first place.'

'Hell, I don't know!' said Captain Bob. 'Slumming it?'

The policeman shrugged and took a small step forward. 'Come on now. You can do better than that.'

'They say there is someone who sells stuff here. I've never caught him,' said the manager.

The policeman leaned forward and removed the dollar. 'Now there's nothing on the table,' he said.

'OK, OK. He's called Marvin,' said Captain Bob, 'but I don't know his last name.'

'What? Does he want my card?' said patrolman Price. 'You speak to him, he speaks to me – or he moves on.'

Cotton saw that the Hon. Penelope Ayrtoun had put out an arm and was waggling her fingers. He took this as *help-me-up*. He went over, removed the manager's jacket, put his arm round her but he did not grip hard enough. Whatever she was wearing slid underneath his fingers and she slumped down again on the sofa. Then he put his arm round her and cupped her ribs. He pulled her up, his smallest two fingers digging under her ribcage.

'Can you walk?'

Penelope Ayrtoun knew someone had spoken to her but not much more.

Cotton caught her under her knees and lifted. He was struck by how light she was. Six stone perhaps. Eighty-four pounds. She grunted quite loudly and, for a moment, fearing she would vomit, Cotton held her away from him. Then he saw that her head was lolling. He pulled her back and jiggled her head into the crook of his right arm.

Mullins nodded and Cotton started walking.

Behind him he heard a swishing noise and a grunt.

'You want to check that everything is in the purse,' said the patrolman. 'We don't want mishaps.'

Cotton kept going. The plump, tassel-and-powdered-flesh lady was still swaying on the drum-sized podium and the bar girls were almost asleep. Cotton walked to the entrance and stood aside. Mullins pushed the screen door, then handled the main door. The puffy bouncer stood back.

Cotton walked down the steps and paused. Behind him there was a crunching noise. It sounded a little fat and was followed by a grunt.

Cotton walked over to the Humber carrying his boss's wife in his arms. Mullins opened a rear door.

'The policeman is called Norman,' he muttered.

'Much obliged to you, Norman,' said Cotton.

The policeman nodded and gave Mrs Ayrtoun's evening bag to Mullins. 'It's part and parcel. I'll be seeing you, Bobbie,' he said.

Mullins and Cotton considered how they were going to get Mrs Ayrtoun into the Humber. Cotton saw Mullins had a blood blister on one knuckle of his right hand. He was carrying Mrs Ayrtoun's spangly evening bag in his left hand.

'Difficult to do this elegantly,' said Mullins, tossing the bag on to the front passenger seat.

'Jesus Christ!' said Cotton. 'How much did you have to pay that man?'

'That would be twenty-one in all, sir'

'What? Because that's what he needed?'

Mullins shrugged. 'Norman said blackjack.'

Irritated, Cotton adjusted his grip on Mrs Ayrtoun and failed by a whisker to hide that she was wearing stockings but not underwear. He lifted a knee to free up his arm, hefted her up and tugged at her dress. Mrs Ayrtoun started, rolled her eyes but lapsed again.

He nodded and looked at Mullins. Between them they came to a silent agreement to maintain what they could of the modesty of a drunk female while transferring her like a limp, slack-limbed package into the car.

'Better if you get in the back with her, sir.' Mullins sounded apologetic.

Cotton groaned and got in. He got her legs round on to the floor and let her slump back and to the side. Her legs felt puffy and soft, the only fleshy part of her.

'Perhaps a restraining arm at the ready, sir?'

'I've got it!' snapped Cotton. 'Can we get out of here?'

'Just one moment more, sir.'

Mullins opened the lady's bag. A little later he handed Cotton fifteen dollars.

'You'll need to get a taxi later,' he said. 'And this way we don't get into expenses.'

Cotton nodded and took the money. 'Where do we go now?'

'California Street. In the Kalorama Triangle.'

'Far?'

'Not very close,' said Mullins.

'Where is . . . '

'He's normally at the Chancery around this time. It's nearly nine a.m. in London.'

They rumbled off through night-time Washington. The Ayrtouns lived in a grand apartment building. Mullins had to wake the Negro maid and had her bring down a shawl so they could wrap it round Mrs Ayrtoun. Then with Mullins on one side and Cotton on the other they each took an arm and carried her inside, the maid handling doors. Nobody said a word in the elevator. At the door to the apartment Mullins took over and carried Mrs Ayrtoun directly to her room. Presumably this meant he had been there before.

Cotton thanked the maid. She shrugged. Mullins came back.

'I'd put some aspirin and water by her,' said Cotton.

'I normally do.'

Mullins used the hall telephone to call Cotton a cab. They went downstairs.

'You go home,' said Cotton.

'I'll wait for the cab, sir.'

They waited.

'It's a shame,' said Mullins after a while.

'Yes,' said Cotton.

Mullins cleared his throat. 'She has a private income, I believe,' he said.

'I'm sure she does,' said Cotton.

The two men waited. It was still warm. In Spain there is a kind of exhaustion to the end of summer, something like old bones. Washington was still clammy. An early-rising bird was fluting monotonously somewhere.

Mullins cleared his throat again. 'It can look raw,' he said, 'but there is a kind of honesty in America.'

'You really want to live here?'

'Yes, I do. It's more personable. It's not the Labour Party exactly but we've just got what we wanted, Norman got what he wanted and Captain Bob got a little fucked.'

Cotton smiled. 'It was a trade at any rate.'

'That's it. Look! Here's your cab, sir.'

Cotton got back to P Street a little after six in the morning. He went directly upstairs to his room but found the bathroom occupied.

'I have an early start, you know,' called Tibbets from behind the door.

'Me too, you know. Stop hogging.'

18

AFTER THE morning briefing (Lord Keynes' Mission and the Americans would be meeting for informal talks at Blair Lee House from tomorrow), Ayrtoun raised an eyebrow at Cotton.

'I say, you're looking a little rough,' he said. 'Mm? You don't want to overdo the social side, you know. I'd be happy to get the P & Q to reduce your social roster, if you want.'

'Not necessary,' said Cotton briefly. 'It was a one-off thing.'

Cotton was not sure that Ayrtoun was ever going to know about his wife's nightlife; he thought that he had probably made a decision not to. What he did know was that Mullins could surely have picked someone else to help him out at the Flying Boat. What was Mullins' unwanted wife called? Beryl.

'We have an important meeting today,' said Ayrtoun. 'Be ready at ten thirty.'

Cotton was ready and waiting.

'We're on,' said Ayrtoun at the door and kept walking. Cotton went after him. Ayrtoun was already in the car when Cotton got outside. He got in the car.

'FBI, Archie,' said Ayrtoun.

The chauffeur drove.

'I lead. I speak,' said Ayrtoun. 'You get to know them.'

'Right.'

Ayrtoun cleared his throat. 'They are a pretty humour-less bunch, actually,' he said. 'You can joke at the State Department. But you don't joke at the FBI. You'd think their policy depended on being utterly humourless.'

The car swept on down Massachussets Avenue. Ayrtoun grunted. He had thought of something else.

'Yes, they also have a curious sort of language. It's called "gobbledegook", I understand – a kind of formalized use of euphemism. As plain and as unemotional as science.'

The FBI office was included in the Department of Justice building, 950 Pennsylvania Avenue, part of the Federal Triangle. It was another pseudo-classical building given the dignity of columns – though here, at either extremity of the façade and starting two floors above ground level, with no pediment in the middle. Cotton and Ayrtoun entered the building on the Constitution Avenue side through a door fit for a tomb.

The inside was art deco, with aluminium detailing and large stretches of mural. In Mexico, murals had tended to be a mix of bright folklore and naïf nationalism. The murals in the Department of Justice – and there were a lot – were of the worthily noble, historically didactic school, meant to be inspirationally realistic. They were not quite as aspirationally muscled as those in Fascist Spain or, Cotton knew, in Soviet Russia. There were also a number of smooth, metal statues, neither classical nor art deco, but somewhere uninteresting between.

Theirs was a formal visit. They signed the guest book, were accompanied to the third floor and handed over to an FBI receiver. They had to sign again, were given visitors' passes, and then taken along a very quiet corridor and shown into a conference room, where there was a highly polished light wood table and twelve matching chairs.

On the table was one tray with coffee things and another with glasses and chilled water. On one wall below a clock was a photograph of J. Edgar Hoover. On another, a large landscape painting of American mountains in oils, and on another, a watercolour of stampeding bison. On a side-table was a framed photograph of President Truman and J. Edgar Hoover in the White House.

At eleven, a waitress came in with freshly made coffee and a selection of pastries. A minute later a young woman calling herself 'the stenographer' appeared and at five past Sam Hoberman and Bill Dawes for the FBI arrived. Ayrtoun introduced them to Cotton. They were, as Ayrtoun had said, on the serious side and, while the waitress poured coffee and water for the four men, there was not much in the way of chitchat. They were pleased to meet the Colonel. They hoped he was at home in the Federal Capital. Cotton was equally pleased to meet them and he was finding a great deal to admire and observe.

When the waitress had gone Sam Hoberman began the meeting. He told the British that his agency had code-named Slonim 'Trapezoid'. He was also in a position to say that Trapezoid had visited San Francisco and New York since his arrival.

Bill Dawes handed Ayrtoun and Cotton a piece of paper each. It was a report from the FBI's San Francisco office and began:

The incidence of fatalities amongst low-level Soviet defectors is statistically improbable.

An example of 'gobbledegook', thought Cotton. He read the report through.

'Low-level defectors' translated into 'merchant seamen and dependants', seventeen of whom had died so far in 1945 alone. This figure broke down as ten seamen, six wives and one adolescent son.

Amongst the wives, one had committed suicide by hanging herself with a washing line, another had fallen from a window, another had fallen down some stairs, one had been killed by stumbling into the road in front of a truck, one had drowned at night in a hotel swimming pool and the sixth had taken pills and been found with a bottle of vodka beside her.

The boy had committed Roman suicide, opening his veins in a warm bath after the death of his father 'in a bordello' where he had consumed 'tainted drugs'. The other men had died similarly unlucky deaths except for one, who complained 'in very bad English' that something had 'pricked' him. His death had been attributed to 'heart failure' after a very high fever.

'Trapezoid,' said Hoberman, 'was probably responsible for confirming their San Francisco man in his post. Five days ago in New York, where Trapezoid also visited, the Soviets reported that their man there was missing. He was found floating in the Hudson three days ago.' He paused. 'Miss Morgan?'

The stenographer looked up.

'Get Mr Parker, will you?'

The girl got up and left.

'Trapezoid,' continued Hoberman, 'has written a letter of complaint to the US authorities about the death in New York. He mentioned uncontrolled criminal elements and the insecurity inherent in the capitalist system.'

Ayrtoun nodded pleasantly. 'Of course he did. Gentlemen,

188

can we agree on point one? That Trapezoid is here to check on and if need be to reinforce the teams that execute the Soviet policy code-named "Barabbas"?'

Cotton had not heard this code name but took it to mean that the Soviet policy was to make an example of – or eliminate – any defectors, no matter how uninvolved in politics. In other words, the man he had met was overseeing a Soviet execution squad.

Hoberman glanced at Dawes. Dawes nodded.

'Point two,' said Ayrtoun. 'Trapezoid is probably checking the situation for himself and reporting how easy it is to operate in an open society – particularly if use can be made of diplomatic immunity. We are getting a lot of reports that the Soviets have convinced themselves that capitalism is finished, that Soviet-style communism will prevail.'

This was, evidently, much too forward at this stage for the FBI.

'Well,' said Dawes, 'that may be something to bear in mind.'

'Then I'll wait for Mr Parker, before speaking further,' said Ayrtoun.

Cotton watched. This was all rather different from his meeting with Fred Warwick in the department store. Bill Dawes cleared his throat.

'Colonel Cotton?'

'Yes?'

'Are we correct in believing that you have made personal contact with Trapezoid?'

'You are.'

'May I enquire what the nature of the conversation was?'

'Of course. During my first meeting, which took place at

the instigation of Trapezoid, he checked my familiarity with Russian literature. We then discussed, never other than superficially, the future of Africa, the West Indies and the political potential of Negroes in the United States. This was done, as far as I could tell, with a view to the upcoming Pan-African Congress to be held in England in mid-October.'

'You've had more than one meeting?' said Hoberman.

'The second was at a reception in the French Embassy. A minute or two only. He spoke in French and said France had the only bourgeois communists in the world.'

Dawes opened a file and removed two photographs. At first glance the photographs were of the same person. Any differences could easily be attributed to lighting and camera angle.

There was a knock at the door.

'Wait!' called Hoberman.

Cotton looked, then briefly closed his eyes. He had seen Slonim/Trapezoid in daylight, wearing a hat, and in artificial lighting without. Both photographs had hats, one military, the other civilian.

'Can you identify Trapezoid from these?'

Cotton opened his eyes. 'The left.'

Cotton felt Ayrtoun turn and look at him.

'Are you sure?' he murmured.

'Yes,' said Cotton. He immediately closed his eyes a moment and checked. 'Yes,' he repeated.

He was about to explain why – a slightly thicker eyebrow ridge on the right, a marginal added plumpness in the cheek-line on the left, but more than anything it was the eyes. The right-hand face was propped by determination and quite stiff patriotism, the left was sly, more arrogant. But Ayrtoun spoke first. He tapped the right-hand photograph.

'This is Aleksandr Slonim,' he said. 'Tank commander.'

He pointed at the left. 'That's Arkady Musin – among other names.'

Hoberman gathered up the photographs. 'You can come in now,' he called.

Parker and the stenographer came in.

'Mr Parker is with the SIS,' said Hoberman.

There were quite a number of questions Cotton wanted to ask but he remembered Ayrtoun's instructions. He knew, however, that the SIS was the FBI's Latin American division and that it had resisted every effort by the OSS during the war to become involved in its affairs. He was also struck that the stenographer had been absent for a large part of the meeting.

Mr Parker was more of a maître bureaucrat. He smiled politely, opened his file and distributed four copies of a memorandum. The writer was the past Assistant Secretary of State for Latin America, Nelson Rockefeller, and the date of the memorandum was April 1945.

In the memorandum, Mr Rockefeller suggested that corruption, inequality and unelected governments in Latin America could lead to 'a good breeding ground' for communism. US interests could be 'seriously compromised' if this vulnerability were exploited.

So the USA faced a quadruple challenge. The encouragement of meaningful democracy, the protection of American business interests, the defeat of Nazi ideals and the rise of Communist influence.

'Assistant Secretary Rockefeller left halfway through August this year. A new candidate will shortly commence Senate confirmation hearings,' said Bill Dawes.

'Who is that?' asked Ayrtoun.

'Mr Spruille Braden,' said Mr Parker.

Cotton looked up. He had heard the name in Spain, where he had learned that Spruille was pronounced to rhyme with 'fuel'.

'Gentlemen,' said Ayrtoun. 'Very much obliged to you.'

A short time afterwards Cotton was following Ayrtoun as he stomped along the corridor. They handed back the passes, signed out and went down to street level. As soon as they were in the car Ayrtoun groaned.

'Have you got a cigarette?'

'No,' said Cotton

'Archie? What about you?'

The driver smoked Camel.

'All right,' said Ayrtoun. He lit one and inhaled. He did not look impressed. Cotton said nothing.

'Who decided your cover was the Colonies?'

'I don't know.'

'It wasn't D?'

'He passed the order on to me.'

'How was he?'

'Well . . .'

'I had an exasperated letter from him.'

'That's about it,' said Cotton.

Ayrtoun grunted and squashed out his cigarette. 'He turned down a knighthood, you know.'

'I didn't.'

'In fact, I believe he told them where they could put it. When did you leave Spain?'

'Last May.'

'Tell me what you were doing.'

'I was part of the Economic Warfare Unit looking into smuggling. Another man got tungsten going to Germany. I

192

got the Dutch gold the Nazis stole. Even by the time I got to Spain a year ago it was clear there was an Argentinian connection. London thought the gold had gone there – in the end I preferred Switzerland.'

'Why?'

'Because there was tons of the stuff. I had one source that said Perón had four hundred tons of gold in Zurich in his own name.'

'Perón . . .?'

'. . .will be the next general to be President in Argentina, the man Spruille Braden has been contesting from the American Embassy there. Braden has actually been on the stump, holding rallies, speaking to the crowds, campaigning vigorously against Perón.

'Perón spent a lot of time in Europe before the war and then tried to put together a pro-Nazi block in South America. Argentina, Paraguay, Bolivia, Chile would be first and then they thought they could persuade Brazil. He got some incidental help from the Pope on a refugee agreement. It means Argentina will be a refuge for wanted Nazis, Italian fascists and is already a kind of Latin Switzerland, except with more space and latitude.'

'What were we doing? Anything useful?'

'Oh yes. We have huge interests in Argentina, the railways, we get our meat from them . . .'

'We depend on it.'

'Yes. Perón still wants to nationalize our interests. But our main strength was our network in South America. It was far superior to the Americans. We collaborated with Safehaven, the American operation in charge of combating Nazi efforts to refinance and regroup in Argentina and Brazil mostly. And with the Mr Rockefeller the FBI mentioned.'

Ayrtoun shook his head. 'What happened to what you were doing?'

'In May I was ordered to wind it up. The investigation had been renamed Eldorado – and I think that was about the end of it. The Treasury took the files and gave some of them to the Dutch government. The Economic Warfare Unit was already being disbanded then.'

'And is now entirely gone.'

'So I understand.'

'Jesus,' sighed Ayrtoun. 'Do you know what I was told about you?'

Cotton said nothing.

'That you had told us to look out for men in Spain with German accents and Spanish names, usually belonging to infants that had died thirty or forty years ago. That's it.'

'It's the same technique used to get Jews out,' said Cotton.

Ayrtoun grunted and shook his head.

'Trapezoid is an idiotic name, don't you think?' Ayrtoun paused. 'But at least he, Mr Trapezoid, thought we were being consistent – using the expertise we had available. In this case he was mistaken. But he had done his homework. He knew better than we did what you had been doing in Spain. He was checking you out.'

Ayrtoun looked round. 'How very humbling,' he said. 'Forget stuff about master spies. We stumble. The only people who fell for you as bait was us. Trapezoid wanted to see you because he knew what you had been doing and thought we were putting you in place for the Braden era in South America. No more Rockefeller and liberal concerns. Braden is the heavy brigade. Trapezoid wanted to know if you were a Braden man.'

They had arrived back at the British Chancery. Ayrtoun
paused before they went in. 'I want you and Jim Gowar to
come to dinner tonight at my home. Tell him. Nobody else.
Don't bring anyone.'

Cotton told Jim Gowar.

'Shit,' he said. 'I've been waiting for that.'

'Really?'

Jim Gowar nodded. 'I take it you have met the Honourable
Penelope?'

'Only briefly and not enough to make an impression, I
suspect.'

'She rather takes care of impressing others, doesn't she?
She told me British men lacked protein.'

'I got something similar.'

'I have to make a phone call,' said Jim Gowar.

Cotton called the P & Q to say he would not be able to
attend the reception for that evening and then telephoned
Katherine.

'I am very sorry. I won't be seeing you tonight. We're
having a little crisis of competence that somehow means I
have to have dinner with Mrs Ayrtoun. Mr Ayrtoun will be
there. And there will also be a nice man I work with but
without a person he calls his Jewish widow.'

'Mm,' said Katherine. 'You really know how to sell disappointment,' she said. 'Of course, it's OK. I'm sure there
will be other Embassies. Oh, Mrs Duquesne asked after
you . . . you've certainly impressed her.'

'Thank you.'

19

AT SEVEN thirty Cotton and Jim Gowar sat down to dinner with Geoffrey Ayrtoun and his wife in a dining room that had been panelled in wood as in the early eighteenth century except, of course, that they were in a block of flats. The furniture was antique, the curtains chintz and the food club British: pea soup, a white fish in white sauce, roast beef and treacle tart.

Mrs Ayrtoun was contained and polite, tasted everything except the treacle tart and made conversation.

'Where are your people from, Mr Gowar?'

'Originally from Epsom.'

'Really?'

'People usually think of the salts or the racecourse,' said Jim Gowar.

Her smile was a reflex. 'Yes, I'm sure they do.'

At the other end of the table Ayrtoun ate with gusto. When he was served potatoes, he mashed them up with his fork and poured gravy on them.

Cotton wondered if her presence was part of a deal between them, that when requested she would play the diplomat's wife, not with enthusiasm exactly but well enough. She gave no sign that she recognized him.

'Are you married, Mr Cotton?'

'No, I'm not.'

'Then you have that ahead of you, I suppose.'

It also occurred to Cotton that he was being shown that Ayrtoun did have some control over her though, as Jim Gowar said, 'with a whiff of ether about it'.

At the end of the meal, when the coffee had been brought in, she got up and brought out a box of cigars herself.

'I'll let you chaps smoke in peace,' she drawled. 'Lovely to meet you both. Goodnight, Geoffrey dear. Don't stay up too long.'

Cotton and Jim Gowar stood. She acknowledged them and left.

When Ayrtoun had his port and his cigar he began.

'Well, this is fun, isn't it?' he said and smiled.

Cotton saw Jim Gowar freeze for a second.

'It's good to relax and talk, don't you think? Away from things.'

If Ayrtoun was genuinely trying to make them feel at ease, he was failing.

'Of course, we face tough choices, mm? Intelligence always has to deal with what its masters want to hear or can hear. In our case, our political masters have been frightened by the new realities.' He puffed on his cigar. 'I heard the other day someone compare the Americans to prefects and ourselves to fags at school. Wrong. We are the elderly retainer. We know a lot of the history of the house but we're frail and frightened of being turfed out in the cold and will accept a lot of humiliation to stay on inside.'

Neither Jim Gowar nor Cotton said anything to this. Ayrtoun smiled, put down his cigar and concentrated on his port.

'I learned today that we've given up on South America,'

he said. 'It's now become Latin America. Belongs to our hosts. And to the Soviets, of course.'

He looked up, then lifted the glass and drank a little port, almost as if drinking a toast.

'Mm,' he said. 'The thing is, you see, that no one British really took a decision on this. One thing is to be powerless, another to face up to and admit it, of course. The Yanks are beginning to suspect what we have done. It hasn't even occurred to the Soviets yet and I suspect they wouldn't believe it.'

He smiled again, put down the glass and picked up his cigar. He combined exhalation and sigh. The smoke rose towards the chandelier.

'So how are you enjoying the States?' he asked.

Cotton almost answered.

'Both with American girls, I understand.'

'With is pushing it,' said Cotton.

'No, no,' said Ayrtoun. 'She is very choosy, I hear. Jim?'

'You know,' said Jim Gowar quietly.

'Miriam, isn't it?'

'Yes.'

There was a long pause.

'We are in a very weak position,' said Ayrtoun.

'But we've made it even weaker,' said Jim Gowar. 'Isn't that what you were saying before, about giving up on South America even though we have legitimate interests there?'

'Oh yes,' said Ayrtoun. 'Excellent point. But then intelligence work is always a trade-off, isn't it?'

'Absolutely,' said Jim Gowar. He paused. 'What did we get for South America? Or did we just throw it away?'

Ayrtoun smiled. However the conversation had started, it was no longer about South America.

'Who thinks I should be traded off?' said Jim Gowar.

'The FBI.' Ayrtoun parted and flipped his hands to measure an invisible sheet of A4 paper.

'Why, in particular?'

'Membership of the Communist Party.'

'She left in 1939.'

Ayrtoun shrugged. 'It's unfair, I know,' he said, 'but they do tend to treat it like being a Catholic. Once you're baptized that's it.'

'She's what a Marxist would call a rentier, for heaven's sake.'

'Quite,' agreed Ayrtoun. 'But they still don't want you.'

'On what grounds?'

'Security risk.' Ayrtoun displaced the ash at the end of his cigar. 'Why don't you take a couple of minutes and I'll just chat to Cotton here. Mm? There's some nougat in the drawing room I believe, if you've a sweet tooth.'

Poor Jim Gowar nodded, got up and left the dining room.

'Awful business,' said Ayrtoun. 'They can destroy a career just like that.' He snapped his fingers.

'I'd need to know more,' said Cotton.

'Oh, you will I'm sure. What about your girl in the State Department?'

'She's not my girl. I told you that.'

'You don't have to be coy, you know.'

It cost Cotton to smile but he did. 'Coyness has nothing to do with it,' he said.

Ayrtoun nodded. 'Oh yes, she's as bright as she is pretty. A bit academic as yet, of course.' He drew again on his cigar. 'Difficult for young women, you know. They take on more risk than we do.' He dropped the cigar into the ashtray. 'You could personalize that risk, you know, get her emotions confusing all that intelligence. It's one thing to be writing brilliant papers, quite another when a man's admiration is very close to personal boundaries. Bright as a button? Start looking as if you really would undo that button.'

Cotton bit his lip. 'Do all women we meet get vetted? Up to now my interest has been personal, if not, evidently, private.'

Ayrtoun looked at him in disbelief. 'Oh, don't be naïve, old man.'

'Me?' said Cotton. 'How innocent are you making her?'

Ayrtoun smiled. 'Her background makes her innocent.'

Cotton shook his head. 'D told me not to be a pillow-diddler.'

Ayrtoun let out one of his loud snorting laughs. 'In our business, it's diddle or be diddled, old man. And don't misunderstand what I mean by innocence. She'll have had a motor car since she was in her teens, money, education, she's seen people and seen what they do. But she'll have hopes of her own and she's had a lot of expectations placed on her. The thing to ask yourself is this – is she politically streetwise?'

'If you think Charterhouse and Cambridge and some running over Scottish moors is streetwise . . . '

Ayrtoun laughed. Whether or not genuinely, Cotton did not know, but Ayrtoun had decided he had said enough. 'Jim!' he called.

The dinner lasted very little after that. Jim Gowar was told to sleep on it. He could be got another job but that would mean leaving Washington. How would Miriam feel about that?

'She has a mother,' said Jim Gowar.

'Ah,' said Ayrtoun. 'The only other thing I can think of is her tackling the thing head-on. You know, seeing the FBI. Co-operating.'

'Lawyers?'

'Always a possibility,' said Ayrtoun with no sign he believed it was.

'I'll sleep on it then,' said Jim Gowar.

Shortly after, they thanked Ayrtoun for his hospitality and took the elevator down to the ground floor.

'Well, that's me fucked,' said Jim Gowar.

'I'm so sorry.'

'She's a liberal. Awful thing. Has even got some principles.' Jim Gowar looked round. 'I did think of resigning. But I am not sure that would help. I'd need another visa, stuff like that. What did he say to you?'

'I think he wants me to fuck some unspecified information out of a nice girl in the State Department.'

'Right,' said Jim Gowar. He nodded. 'Quite how does that work?'

'I haven't the foggiest idea.'

'All ticketyfuckingboo then,' said Jim Gowar.

They came out of the elevator and went outside.

'Will you have dinner with us some time? Sooner would be better.'

'Yes, of course. I'd be delighted.'

'It's a risk.'

'Oh, come on.'

'You think I'm joking,' said Jim Gowar. 'I'm now officially a security risk. And therefore a risk to you.'

*

But Jim Gowar did not come in to work the next day. 'Something about a spot of leave,' said someone.

'How long will he be gone?'

'I don't know. Usual, I suppose. Week maybe. Or two.'

Cotton did not know whether or not 'leave' was a euphemism for something worse and Ayrtoun made no mention of it. He did ask Cotton to write him out a report on his work in Spain. Cotton spent the day doing that, heard, at length, from Ridley about 'an enormous bust-up' between the State and War Departments over relief for refugees, then had to repay the person who had substituted for him the evening before by attending a reception given by the Siamese or Thais. Despite the P & Q's note ('Thailand is, after six years, Siam again: avoid subject') this turned out to be a quiet, almost restful affair. Later he ate at his local restaurant and strolled back along P Street to what Tibbets called 'the digs'.

Shortly after he got back his telephone rang.

'Oh,' said Dr Aforey. 'I am most severely tried, Mr Cotton. I am in a state of shock, I assure you.'

Cotton glanced at the time. It was already late.

'Mr Cotton?'

Cotton met him.

'This evening,' said Dr Aforey, 'I felt called upon to pray for guidance. When I came out of the church, I was approached by a white man who asked me how I felt able to call myself a Christian.'

Cotton raised an eyebrow. 'Go on.'

'I replied, of course, that Christian is not a name to possess but rather to strive for.'

'Dr Aforey . . .'

'I will cut to the chase. This fellow asked me if I would help a friend. Austin Ojukwu.'

'What did he mean?'

'Mr Cotton, they were strong-arming me! Not literally, but the threat was overt! And it was explicit!'

'All right,' said Cotton. 'What did they say?'

'You are with us or against us. If you live in America you stand up for America. They said I should be very public in my opposition to the Pan-African Congress, that I should stand up against the Marxists. Well, Reds. And if I did not do so, Austin would be deported. That is not only beaten, Mr Cotton, but thrown out of the country. And I myself should take care where I stepped.'

'Was this man an American? Can you describe him?'

Dr Aforey gave quite a good description of Fred Warwick and his Buick car, beginning, 'A very *beefy* man, Mr Cotton . . .'

'This is intolerable,' he went on. 'They are plumbing new depths. They are leaving no space for us. I am an academic, not a man of violence. I have been rendered nearly witless with fear.'

'It's all right, Dr Aforey, I'll do what I can.'

Dr Aforey was, in part, mollified. He shook his head. 'These are not the ways of a civilized government,' he complained.

'I would hazard that he was working to some extent on his own initiative.'

'Do you really think so?'

Cotton thought. 'Yes,' he said, 'I really do.'

On the last working day of September the morning briefing was cancelled. Ayrtoun was seeing a man called Harris, newly arrived with the Board of Trade delegates. And that caused something of a stir. A number of people in Cotton's office wanted to see him and did see, quite briefly, a sad-faced man in his forties, with a moustache more long-haired than thick, wearing a grubby trench coat. Harris was an interrogator of some fame.

'Ex-policeman,' said Ayrtoun later. 'The Yanks like him, asked for him. They think he is no-nonsense and all job. Dogged doesn't quite do him justice.' He smiled. 'I don't imagine he'll have a long career but he'll do all right for now.

'Now, I want you to see a man called Fielding. He's in charge of delegate security. Somebody's friend, maybe a relative, if you know what I mean. Very keen on paper, I understand.'

'Very keen on paper' was one way of putting it. Fielding had an otherwise admirable desire to establish timetables, rosters and responsibilities without the paper scheme ever quite matching what happened. Easily agitated, he quickly acquired a nickname – Origami Fielding. If things went wrong he looked put upon and studied what was on paper. He was not particularly young, late thirties perhaps, but called Cotton 'sir' and described the delegates as his 'charges'. The responsibility was already disabling him, and his awe when he pronounced the name Sir Percivale Liesching, with Lionel Robbins, the leader of the trade negotiations, was dispiriting.

Around noon Cotton got hold of agent Warwick of the FBI.

'I want you to lay off Dr Aforey,' he said.

'Why?'

'Because you don't have an Empire.'

'He lives here, doesn't he?'

They agreed to meet at two in the men's department at Lansburgh's department store.

Cotton went to Mullins and told him what had happened.

'Will you provide me with back-up?'

'I'll drive you,' said Mullins.

On their way there Mullins handed Cotton something. It was like a miniature muslin money-belt. 'Knuckle protection,' he said. 'That's sand inside.'

'They get violent?'

Mullins glanced over. 'You never know and it's better to be prepared.'

It turned out that Mullins did know a little better. Cotton was at first intrigued, then irritated, then disbelieving. By the men's changing rooms, Cotton and Mullins met Fred Warwick and his partner Jim. Fred stood too close and refused to give up Dr Aforey.

'He's mine,' he said.

Quite quickly Cotton confirmed to himself that there was unlikely to be any agreement. He put his hand in his pocket and while musing, covered his knuckles. He took a step back.

'Fred,' he said.

'What?'

Cotton hit him. It did not feel like a good punch. Cotton rocked on his left leg and his right arm worked on a very short arc, the top of his arm sticking hard to his body, his forearm and wrist twisting, the fist forming as a kind of last second clutch. And his aim was off. Cotton's sand-covered fist hit Fred Warwick just in front of his left ear.

Fred Warwick looked shocked, swayed a moment, then sat down on the floor.

Cotton held up a finger at the other agent. 'Don't move,' he said.

'I can drive a man's nose up into his brain,' said Mullins. 'That's because I'm a veteran. Neither of you are. Got it?'

Cotton glanced round at him. To Jim he said, 'No more bullshit. You make sure Fred understands that.'

They walked out. Cotton gave the sand-dusters back to Mullins and they started back to the Chancery.

'If you don't mind me saying so,' said Mullins, 'I thought you evaluated the risk very well, sir.'

'I'm not sure.' Cotton had been in violent situations. His blood usually felt thin afterwards. Not this time. He looked down at his knuckles: They were slightly reddened.

'I am,' said Mullins.

On Saturday 29 September Cotton met Katherine Ward in a bookshop. Katherine had brought Didi Johnson. He asked after Joe.

'Poor dear has had to fly stuff down to Florida. You know there was a small hurricane there? Right now he is suffering on a beach somewhere.'

The two girls had decided he should buy English books.

'Books written by British people, you know,' said Didi.

Cotton bought *Alice in Wonderland* for Emily.

'That's perfect,' said Didi. 'She's the same age as Alice.'

Didi suggested *Peter Pan* for Halliday.

Cotton was doubtful. He couldn't remember. 'Do you think that is all right for a boy?'

'It has a boy in it that can fly!' said Didi. 'Kids don't know the difference between fairy dust and a bomber jacket.'

Foster proved more difficult. Didi suggested *Little Black Sambo*. But, after his conversation with Dr Aforey, Cotton turned it down. Didi then picked an American book. Dr Seuss. *Horton Hatches the Egg.* An elephant called Horton goes up a tree to sit on an egg for a bird called Mayzie. Cotton did not like the illustrations and was unsure about the ending – the creature hatched takes on some of Horton's characteristics.

'At four,' said Didi, 'fantasy means more than the birds and the bees.'

'Or the birds and the elephants,' said Katherine.

Cotton thought the browsing had gone on long enough. He bought the book.

Katherine and Didi then had shopping to do and left him to choose the toys himself.

'Are you free this evening?' said Katherine.

'I certainly could be.'

'Then invite me to dinner.'

'May I . . .?'

'I'd be delighted,' she smiled.

Cotton went to buy his niece and nephews some toys. He was unsure whether or not Emily liked dolls and if so, whether she liked what he thought of as hard or soft, so he ignored them, and the assistant's suggestion of Li'l Abner's Dogpatch Band wind-up toy. Instead he bought her something called a Slinky. New on the market, it flopped like a spent spring coil but could be teased out into looping quite elegantly downstairs while making a noise between whirr and clonk.

For his nephews Cotton decided to ignore all the clunky

little military vehicles and got Halliday a glider and Foster a wheeled duck. He was not confident he had not bought something too young for Foster.

Just after he got back to P Street, the telephone rang. The caller was Harold, who identified himself as Mrs Duquesne's social secretary. He wanted to know if Cotton would come to 'a little brunch' the next day 'after church'.

'I'd be delighted,' said Cotton. 'Is after church about noon?'

'That would be on the late side,' said Harold.

Cotton would have asked Jim Gowar where to take Katherine for dinner. There was no point in asking Tibbets. And he certainly wasn't going to ask Ayrtoun. In the event he chose wrong. She was very good about it.

'Don't look so glum,' she said. 'Do you dance?'

'I can.'

'Good.'

She took him to a place with a jazz trio.

'They are playing Dorothy Fields without the lyrics this week.'

'Who's Dorothy Fields?'

'Listen.'

They danced. Cotton recognized 'The Way You Look Tonight', 'A Fine Romance' and 'I'm in the Mood for Love'.

'Hey,' said Katherine, 'you can dance OK. Maybe even more.'

Cotton had learned basic dance with his sister when dancing had mattered very much to her and she had been able to boss him around. 'You can't be a stick unless it is the tango and I am not going to be dancing tango. You have to relax and be firm. You have to guide and be flexible.'

At the end of the evening Cotton kissed her.

'I've been waiting for that,' she said.

'So have I.'

'There is fresh and there is old school.'

Cotton laughed and kissed her again.

'I like a man who is contained,' she said.

'Come with me to Long Island.'

'I'll think about it,' she said.

At 11.45 a.m. on Sunday 30 September Cotton presented himself at Mrs Duquesne's Dupont Circle mansion. In bright daylight it was even uglier than he had thought.

Mrs Duquesne lit up when she saw him at the top of the stairs.

'How lovely to see you again, young man! You're better than a cure! I do rather miss that lovely expression you had of energy contained, restrained and, well, almost baffled in those amazing pants. But this'll do.'

Cotton laughed. She took his arm and they walked.

'Darling, I never eat out if I can help it. Washington is not crowded with good restaurants. No demand, you see.'

Cotton nodded and waited.

'Washington isn't even a pond,' she said, 'it's a puddle. I'm delighted for you.'

Cotton smiled. 'So let's see. I got the restaurant wrong and our date is now public.'

'Harold will give you a list of decent places. And I thought you knew more about women. They quite like a trier, at the beginning anyway.'

As they walked Cotton became aware that the mansion was silent. They walked into the gallery and Mrs Duquesne opened a door to the side.

In a small panelled room was a round table set for a meal and three chairs. On one pushed-back chair was a tall young man, now with a layer of fat over his muscles. He had stretched out his legs and was smoking. His hair was almost centre-parted and he was wearing what Cotton thought of as the American equivalent of a country suit, a heavily flecked grey-and-brown affair. He had a dark green silk handkerchief pushed into his top pocket. He stood up at once.

'Mr David Brewster,' said Mrs Duquesne, 'Colonel Peter Cotton.'

They shook hands.

'David's in the State Department. Political. I'm not allowed to say. Oh, and I'm not allowed to say what you do either, am I? Is it something to do with the British Empire?'

A servant came in with champagne. Then there were scallops and bacon for the men, waffles for Brewster, toast and coffee for Mrs Duquesne.

'Now come on,' she said. 'I want the truth but I may settle for gossip.'

She had to settle for a lot less. Brewster was chummy, a hearty eater and the conversation was pretty much the usual Anglo-American stuff, British experience, American drive, the British class system, American naïvety, the American dislike of Empire.

At one time Mrs Duquesne interrupted Cotton when she thought he was getting too technical and said, 'Ooh, you're turning creamed chicken into something I once ate in Paris.' But later, she smiled, and asked Brewster how the State Department was dealing with IRIS.

Brewster waved a piece of toast.

'We've got McCormack corralled,' he said. 'All his efforts

are going to have to be on drawing up an acceptable budget.' He shrugged. 'He's getting support for that, all right. But when your intelligence agency's activities are limited by an amount you haven't even negotiated yet, your energies are kind of wasted.'

Mrs Duquesne was showing Cotton what she was good at.

20

ANGLO-AMERICAN Commercial Negotiations started on Monday 1 October, the same day that the OSS formally ceased to exist.

Cotton noted for Ayrtoun's information what he had picked up from David Brewster on the budgetary limitations at IRIS. Ayrtoun nodded, and responded by telling him that President Truman was already working on a plan for a genuinely co-ordinated intelligence service.

'But even though it's temporary, keep your eye on McCormack and IRIS.'

'Yes,' said Cotton.

'I've written a letter complaining about an FBI agent,' said Ayrtoun. 'I understand he may have threatened you.'

'It was only a little personal difficulty,' said Cotton, 'resolved.'

'Good,' said Ayrtoun, 'but we don't want to let that kind of behaviour pass, now do we?'

Cotton went back to his desk. He wrote a note to Dr Aforey saying his matter was apparently resolved.

In his in tray was a note that Grace Simmonds, a language teacher in Mexico City, had had her American passport rescinded and was, in consequence, in trouble with the Mexican authorities.

*

On Tuesday Jim Gowar was at his desk.

'Jim?' asked Cotton.

Jim Gowar did not look up. 'I can't talk about it,' he said. 'I mean . . . I can barely speak.'

Cotton looked at him. Jim Gowar looked lost and sorry. 'OK,' said Cotton.

Jim Gowar shook his head. 'My fault,' he said. 'I've lost her.'

Later Cotton brought up Jim Gowar with Ayrtoun.

'Is that your business?' said Ayrtoun.

Cotton nodded. 'I see. So I wasn't at the dinner with you the other night?'

Ayrtoun looked up sharply. He smiled, and shrugged. 'He chose,' he said.

On the evening of Wednesday 3 October Cotton attended a reception at the Embassy of the Bolivarian Republic of Venezuela in the United States. The atmosphere, putting on a brave face and marking time while events played out back home, was similar to that of the Brazilian Embassy a couple of weeks previously – without the dancing, but with an acting Ambassador looking as dignified as a very late substitute in a soccer match. There were some American oil-men there, not perhaps looking quite as happy as they should by the advance of AD, *Acción Democrática*.

'Democracy and oil don't mix,' said someone with a strong Russian accent behind Cotton.

Cotton turned. 'I thought communism was the ultimate democracy, Colonel.'

For a fraction Slonim froze – then laughed loudly, not like Ayrtoun; this was more from the chest than the nose, but amply loud enough to attract attention.

The Washington Soviets were not famous for relaxing when they attended diplomatic functions. Their Ambassador, Andrei Gromyko, known in the American press as 'Mr Nyet' and 'Grim-Grom', set the tone. Soviet officials were always on duty against frivolity and fraternization. They tended to operate in groups, with the result that they were collectively abstemious in a way Dr Aforey would have approved of.

Slonim did not appear to mind the attention at all. Whatever was in his glass he downed in one and then, as if it was quite natural because they were in the Venezuelan Embassy, broke into Spanish rather better than his English.

'They do half my work, these good Northern neighbours. This Rockefeller? What is the difference between a liberal Republican, Rockefeller, and a ham-fisted Democrat like Braden? The liberal has a mother who founded the Museum of Modern Art.' Slonim laughed loudly again. 'Exploitation and some paintings is now exploitation for South America's good. Look around you. Do you think these businessmen want dollars or free votes?'

The talk of neighbours Cotton took to be the so-called Good Neighbours Policy initiated by Roosevelt in 1933, in which trade and commerce with the countries of Latin America were meant to forge ties and interests stronger than political differences. The mention of Rockefeller was, Cotton presumed, just to show that the Colonel was up to date. And, of course, Slonim/Trapezoid was demonstrating that he knew Cotton would understand him in Spanish.

Slonim reverted to English. 'I understand the English say trapezium.' he said.

So he knew his own code name at the FBI. Trapezoid. Cotton smiled. A lot of Hoover's attacks on the OSS and the State Department had been because of leaks. Not that Slonim's remark meant the leak was from the FBI – they had presumably passed it around to other agencies, as they had passed it to the British.

'American billions are not British billions,' said Trapezoid, as illustration of another difference in American and British English.

'The British have no problem in accepting some things,' said Cotton. 'Have you finished what you came here to do?'

'Not quite,' said Trapezoid in Spanish again. 'There are some loose ends.' He turned a little as if about to go, but paused and looked back. 'A big, Braden man runs at you. What do you do?'

'You make use of his own weight and impetus against him,' said Cotton.

Trapezoid made a there-you-have-it gesture. His palm came up. It was beginning to become more acknowledgement of agreement than a measure of distance between them. Cotton could not gauge how drunk he was – or even if he was drunk at all.

Around half past eight Cotton left the reception and went to meet Katherine. For the first time since his arrival in Washington there was a slight chill in the air. She came directly from work dressed in a demurely expensive suit. She looked a little tired. They ate crab cakes at a small restaurant and then she asked him to come home for coffee.

'I'd be delighted.'

She smiled, almost patted his forearm. 'Didi and Joe should be there.'

'All right.'

At first Cotton was intrigued that she was going to show him, for the first time, where she lived. In the cab she explained that the apartment belonged to Didi's father, 'otherwise we couldn't afford to live there.'

'What does Didi do?' he asked.

'Mostly bride-to-be and keeping a watch on Joe. She also does something with a literacy programme.'

Cotton nodded. Katherine's clothes and manner looked to be comfortably above what she would be paid by the State Department. Presumably her parents were ensuring she did not drop out of what his mother would have called 'their set'.

But when they arrived outside a three-floor brown brick building with large bay windows, they found Didi and Joe outside, sitting on the steps up to the front door. Didi's face was tear-streaked and, despite wearing Joe's jacket around her shoulders, she was shivering.

'Burgled,' said Joe.

They had got back about forty-five minutes before. The place was a complete mess. They had called the police.

Cotton and Katherine went in and climbed to the first floor. The front door was open and inside the apartment there was a patrolman and two plain-clothes policemen, one called Doyle, the other Burns.

Katherine identified herself. The burglars had got in via the fire escape. They had used what Doyle called 'the soft window'. This did not mean a vulnerable window but a technique of breaking the glass without much sound. They had stuck a patch of adhesive cloth on the window and then 'like, you know, tapping an egg with a spoon', broken an area of glass and just pulled it away. After that

216

it was simply a question of undoing the latch and climbing in.

'Looks sort of professional,' said Doyle.

Burns, dusting the window for fingerprints, shook his head. 'It's been wiped,' he said.

Till then, Cotton had been watching Katherine concentrate on the policemen. The expression 'sort of professional' struck him as odd. Now he looked round.

Didi and Joe had said the flat was a complete mess, but this barely met the case. The place looked as if it had been attacked. The apartment took up the whole floor. There was a very large central room. Off one side were two bedrooms and a bathroom. On the other, closed off by louvred doors, was what Cotton thought of as a stretch of kitchen.

The refrigerator had been left open. The burglars had smashed eggs on the floor, dropped butter on them and added tomato juice and milk. In the central room they had ripped the cushions, scattered books and papers and punched holes in the lampshades.

The bedrooms were worse. They had disembowelled the closets and scattered the girls' clothes on the floor. They had poured bleach and perfume on Katherine's gowns – Cotton recognized that first red velvet now with whitened patches.

Doyle leaned towards Cotton and muttered, 'Can you help? They pissed on the underwear.'

Doyle was too late; Katherine had already seen it. Cotton put his arm round her.

She blinked at him and shook her head. 'Why?'

Cotton looked at the plain-clothes man.

'They may have got the wrong idea. Thought you were wealthier than you are. We'll need a list of what's missing.'

Katherine pointed. 'My jewel box is empty.'

'That's no place to keep items of value,' said Doyle.

'Not that kind of value,' said Katherine sharply.

'Sorry.'

Katherine nodded. 'Are you saying they've been watching us?' she asked.

'You have casual burglary, when the thief sees a chance. This looks more planned. I'm thinking more than one person, Miss.'

'Come on,' said Cotton, 'you need to get out of here.'

'We will need that list of what's missing,' said Doyle.

'Of course,' said Cotton.

'And a list of what's been spoiled?' said Katherine.

'The insurance company will need that too,' said the policeman.

'Neighbours?' said Cotton.

Katherine shook her head. 'Downstairs is for Didi's grandfather. He's with her parents. Upstairs is for her sister. She's at Wellesley now.'

'Have those flats been burgled?' asked Cotton.

'No,' said Burns. 'We checked. Neighbours on either side saw and heard nothing.'

They went downstairs.

'That is just so hateful,' said Didi.

Katherine considered this very briefly. 'No,' she said, 'it was revenge.'

'For what?'

'For not having enough to steal,' said Katherine. 'That's what the detective said.'

'I can't stay here,' said Didi.

'No,' said Katherine. 'We'll go to a hotel.'

'I mean here in town,' said Didi. 'I'm going to my parents.'

Katherine shook her head. 'No,' she said. 'It's late and you'll just alarm them. Come with me. We can share a room if you like. You can go to them tomorrow.'

'Joe and I can come back and clean up if you want,' said Cotton.

Joe stared but Katherine managed a smile.

'No,' she said, 'that's very sweet. But I have to work tomorrow and Didi's father will want to look at it. We need to make a list of what's missing and what's spoiled.'

Didi started sniffling again.

'Go get a taxi, Joe,' said Katherine.

'I feel' – Didi made a face – 'invaded. Smeared. I . . .'

'It's OK,' said Katherine. 'It's been a shock, OK? But just because there are scumbags doesn't mean we have to be intimidated by them.'

'She's right,' said Cotton. He put his hand to her back and felt that Katherine was trembling.

They took the girls to a hotel.

Early on the following morning, 4 October, Cotton called Katherine at the hotel but she had already left. Later he had a chat with Mullins about the break-in at Didi and Katherine's apartment.

'It could be a genuine burglary,' said Mullins. 'Mind you, it could also be a shake-down.'

'What's that?'

'It's not unheard-of. The police are not well paid. They might want to be . . . encouraged to keep a closer check on the place. You should keep an eye on whether they recover at least some of the stolen property but don't actually arrest anybody, well, nobody very convincing.'

Cotton nodded. 'They use tame burglars?'

'Something like that.'

'Right.'

But Mullins had not finished. 'I believe Miss Ward works for the State Department?'

'Yes.'

Mullins nodded. 'Check what has been broken. If they need an electrician or plaster work.'

'Tell me where to look.'

Mullins blew out. 'Where people don't clean mostly. Behind pictures, mirrors and lamps can be good. Listening devices can also be in air vents – check the screws – and check out the people who do any work.'

Cotton nodded. 'If you found something at home, what would you do?'

'I'd probably call in our people before I did anything.'

'All right,' said Cotton. 'Thanks.'

In the afternoon he got a call from Katherine. She said she had been busy at work and had had to do some shopping 'for clothes mostly'. They agreed to meet outside the burgled apartment at six. She was waiting for him.

'How are you feeling?'

She made a face. 'Worse than I thought,' she said. 'Didi was right. Having your stuff trashed makes your skin crawl.'

'Are you sure you want to go in?'

'I'm sure. The place has been cleaned and . . . all the clothes thrown out.'

'Where's Didi?' asked Cotton.

'She's gone home. She is pretty cut up and her dad insisted. He's here now. And he's asked Brian round.'

They went upstairs. Brian embraced Katherine – 'Oh,

sweetie, this is just so vile!' – and Cotton shook hands with Mr Johnson. Two Negro maids were still working, one in the bathroom and the other in the kitchen. The window had already been replaced and the main room had been cleaned up, but the lampshades had gone and the sofa cushions, though back in their places, were still ripped.

'Damnedest thing,' said Mr Johnson. 'You wonder what kind of degenerate cowards can do this.'

It was agreed that Katherine would stay in the hotel, 'for a couple more days at least', until the apartment had been properly fixed up. Mr Johnson didn't think Didi would be back any time soon.

'So how about it, Brian? Couldn't you stay here?' he asked.

Brian emitted something like a giggle. 'What? In Grandpa Johnson's place?'

Didi's father did not see anything funny. 'Or April's if you want.'

'It's OK,' said Katherine. 'The police don't think they were after us. This is unpleasant but it's not dangerous.'

'You'll be saying you are going to get a gun next,' said Brian.

Mr Johnson did not think that was such a bad idea.

'You do make me feel rather like a guard dog,' said Brian. 'But OK. I could do that for a few days. Yes.'

'You don't need to,' said Katherine.

'No, no, it's not a problem. I can help out, you know. I can be useful.'

It was agreed that Katherine would move back at the weekend and Brian move into April's apartment on Friday evening.

Cotton took her back to her hotel.

'Mr Johnson is protecting his investment,' she said. She smiled. 'He doesn't want the property value declining because of crime rates. I don't think Brian is quite thinking like that.'

'Will he be all right?

'I think he will. He might even make it an adventure. Can I ask you something?'

'Of course,' he said.

'You know you invited me to visit your sister and her family?'

'Yes? You'll come?'

'I'd love to.' She leaned over and kissed him. 'I like you in a crisis,' she said.

'Containment – wasn't that the word you used?'

On Friday he cabled his sister that he might be bringing someone and on Saturday, he helped Katherine move back in. Brian was there. He had a book but Cotton did not know if he was actually reading it or using it as a prop.

'Dashiell Hammett,' he said, holding up *Red Harvest*. 'Hammett studied Hemingway, I am studying Hammett. Then I will have a go myself.'

'How does that work?' asked Katherine.

'I think I've got the basic elements of the style. It's about excluding, you see, until there is only one possible choice of word.'

'I don't see,' said Katherine.

'Right. I don't say – "he got up". That's too ordinary. I don't say – "he rose". Too floral. So I am left with – "he stood".'

'This could take you time, Brian,' said Katherine. 'And I think Goldilocks has been done.'

Brian laughed.

'Are you writing a detective novel?' asked Cotton.

'I'm not sure,' said Brian. 'I am getting the idea that, however hard-boiled or weary they are, they are always about the same thing.'

'What's that?'

'Putting the romance back into pornography,' said Brian.

'Brian,' said Katherine. 'Go get pizza. I'll have a Coke. Do you want beer, Peter?'

But Brian ordered by telephone.

Later they went shopping for lampshades – Brian insisted he accompany them. Katherine raised her eyes.

'Brian is consistent,' she whispered when she kissed Cotton goodnight. 'When lonely and beginning to feel afraid, he turns into your shadow.' She smiled. 'I'm going to have the place looked over, swept in the parlance, for nasty devices.'

'You are?'

'You were looking worried.'

On 8 October a certain agitation spread to the Chancery from the British Embassy next door. An opinion poll suggested that the British were deeply unpopular amongst working-class Americans. In consequence they failed to see why the USA should bail the United Kingdom out at all. Middle-class Americans were 'more understanding' of foreign policy matters.

But on 9 October something startling happened. There had been a sudden breakthrough and an Anglo-American agreement had, in principle, been reached. While an interest-free loan was politically impossible for the Americans, Will Clayton suggested a $5 billion loan, repayable in fifty annual instalments to begin in five years' time. The loan would be at 2 per cent, or an extra $50 million a year. Clayton even suggested Keynes draw up a waiver clause in case there were any years Britain could not pay and, more, gave a press conference in which he announced that the sum of $5 billion had been agreed.

Cotton heard about this at the briefing on Wednesday 10 October.

'You see,' said Tibbets afterwards. 'I said six. You said three.'

Cotton remembered slightly differently, but shrugged. 'They haven't signed anything yet.'

'Didn't they teach you how to lose?' said Tibbets. 'I didn't know you were going to react like this to a little ribbing.'

'It's an agreement in principle,' said Cotton. 'Don't you see the deal is not settled yet?'

That evening he met Katherine. She told him her apartment had been 'swept' and two 'bugs' found – 'one behind my bed, for God's sake!' She added contempt to her amusement.

'Any ideas who was responsible?' he asked.

'We made the bugs, but there is a market in them.'

'There's a drawback to unfettered commerce then?'

She smiled. 'Yes.'

'Where was the other one?'

'In the base of a lamp.'

She had decided she had said enough and he did not press her. Instead he smiled and wondered how she was taking the treatment of IRIS and if she wasn't, somehow, preferring to be flattered rather than intimidated by the break-in.

'What are you thinking about?' she asked.

In fact he was thinking about candidates for the bug placers – Soviets, FBI, any number of proxies. He also wondered whether or not she had lied to him about not knowing who had placed them, the answer being probably, and what chances their relationship really had.

'I can't help feeling the toy I got for my younger nephew is a little young for him,' he lied.

She laughed. 'I want to ask you something. Will you accept an invitation to Thanksgiving with my family?'

'Of course I will.'

Katherine was very pleased. It took Cotton a second to remember that Thanksgiving was more than a month away.

'If I haven't been demobbed, of course.'

'Take me seriously,' she said.

'Oh, I do,' said Cotton.

21

WASHINGTON WAS handling its new importance in various ways. One, surprising to Cotton for how recently it had been undertaken, was the development of an adequate airport for the capital of the USA – one not bisected by a road that required police to stop the traffic when a plane was landing. He and Katherine took a cab to what she called Gravelly Point, a little over four miles south of Washington across the Potomac in Virginia. The National Airport terminal building was described as reminiscent of George and Martha Washington's Mount Vernon home but Cotton didn't see it. He did see a fairly demure cross between neoclassical and modern, with pillars instead of columns, a regular façade, all in white, of course. The runway side of the building had much more glass in it for viewing. He and Katherine sat in a waiting room with the near wing of the Dakota plane they would fly in about forty feet from the window.

The DC-3 Douglas Dakota was not a plane Cotton had ever much enjoyed. He knew all about the reliable workhorse business, but there was something about getting in near the tail and then climbing a steep slope to sit down and then feeling the weight of his body pressing backwards again down the incline, that was unsettling. And he found the clatter and rattle of the engines above their frame-shaking drone got through to his teeth when he clamped them while waiting for the tail to rise.

'Are you a good flyer?' Katherine asked.

'Resigned. At least this doesn't have bomb bays. But on this plane I worry about ... do you know what a stall angle is?'

She smiled. 'I'm OK once we are in the air. My father says it is a very expensive form of transport for the fears incurred.'

As Cotton smiled, he recognized a fellow traveller coming into the departure lounge. Trapezoid/Slonim stopped the man accompanying him simply by lifting his index finger and then, smiling and nodding, he strolled towards them.

'A couple of allies?' said Aleksandr Slonim.

Cotton glanced at Katherine. Though she smiled he had no impression she knew at all who he was. Cotton got up and shook Slonim's hand.

'Won't you join us?' he said

'Can't,' said Slonim. 'I have a travelling companion.'

'You're celebrating Colombus Day in New York?'

'Not a Soviet holiday. But I, too, am taking advantage of ... leisure time.'

'I'm sure,' said Cotton.

'But won't you introduce me?' said Slonim.

'I'm sorry. Of course. Miss Katherine Ward, distinguished member of the American State Department, this is, at least at present, Colonel Aleksandr Slonim of the Soviet Embassy.'

Slonim did not shake her offered hand. He took it and in a gesture that combined plucking and bowing he brought his lips to within about an inch of her hand, but then did not kiss it. He appeared to inhale.

'It is a very great pleasure, madam,' he intoned.

'I am delighted to meet you, Colonel,' she said.

'Are you on business, Colonel?' Slonim asked Cotton.

'No. I am going to see my sister.'

'They haven't seen each other for nine years,' said Katherine.

Slonim sighed. 'Ah, the war,' he said and shook his head. 'Too many separations. Too much heartbreak. But now, at last, we can be peace-loving peoples again, isn't that so?'

Cotton could not remember the sincerity of universal brotherhood quite so perfunctorily done. 'Yes, indeed,' he said.

'Safe trip,' said Slonim.

'And to you.'

Slonim smiled and almost retired as from royalty, walking backwards for about three steps, then bowing a little and turning away.

'Why exactly are we all smiling?' Katherine asked.

'International goodwill.'

'Who is he?'

'A Soviet patriot.'

She frowned. 'That means something? Don't you think the Soviets can be patriots?'

'Of course they can.'

'Then it is the word patriot. You have a problem with it?'

'I'm British,' said Cotton, 'brought up on Dr Johnson. He said: "Patriotism is the last refuge of a scoundrel", something like that.'

'Our Soviet well-wisher is a scoundrel?'

'I wouldn't say that.'

She thought for a moment. 'Would you describe yourself as a patriot?'

'No, I wouldn't.'

'Why not?'

'I suppose it's partly the word. I was brought up to respect the dead of the First War and was given the notion of doing my duty if called upon. Yes, sacrifice was the word used, not patriotism.'

He looked round at her.

'What kind of a patriot are you?'

She shook her head. He understood that she was a convinced patriot but he did not know what her love of country consisted of, what the foundation of it was. Something like faith?

She stayed quiet a while.

'What does your Soviet friend do?'

'We think he is a kind of Soviet Nemesis. He takes care of their traitors and defectors in foreign parts.'

She frowned. 'Are you teasing me?'

'Not really.'

But she had decided he was. She smiled. She asked him if he could read on planes.

On board the plane she couldn't stifle a flinch when the propellers cranked and the engines coughed out smoke and flames as they started up. When they began the long acceleration along the runway, bouncing quite a lot in the Washington wind towards take-off, she closed her eyes. Once in the air, however, she worked her jaw and rubbed in front of her ears and smiled.

'Hate take-offs,' she said.

The plane lurched and dropped. She smiled.

Two hours later, at La Guardia Field, Colonel Aleksandr Slonim and his travelling companion were met by a black Soviet automobile that headed off towards Manhattan. Cotton and Katherine were met by a chauffeur in uniform called Julius who drove them east out along Long Island in a black American automobile.

Centre Island in Nassau County, Long Island, New York turned out to be the name of a village with little in the way of population but a number of very large houses. From the front, Todd and Joan's country home struck Cotton as a weird congress of eighteenth-century grandeur and clapboard cottage; it had sprouted dormer windows and appendices. It was the cottage made mansion, had eleven bedrooms, not counting the nursery, and sat a little big in five acres of grounds, made up mostly of very large trees and scrupulously tended gardens and lawns. At the back, however, the house looked nothing like the front but had the appearance of an antebellum estate house with a columned double-height porch overlooking the lawn and slope down to Oyster Bay and what Todd called 'a harbour' and Cotton thought of as a jetty. In September 1944, Todd's boat had disappeared in a hurricane.

Meeting again after so long was, according to Joan, later, 'a little tense and too much tremble'.

Cotton wrapped his arms round her.

'You're down to bones,' he said. 'Are these children exhausting you?'

'No, I'm not,' said Halliday.

'I'm looking after my figure as elderly ladies do, that's all.' Joan started crying and glued herself to his cheek.

Cotton winked at Halliday. 'Tell me the sad story of your father's boat.'

'It flew!' said Emily. 'All the way to Nova Scotia.'

'Via Narragansett – and without any wings at all!' said Katherine. 'Now tell me that must have been during the great Long Island hurricane last year.'

'How did you know?' said Emily.

'I listened!' said Katherine. 'First I heard just the faintest howl . . . and then, I don't know, a kind of tugging and flapping as a sail came undone . . . and then a groan and then a creak and then a big . . . whoosh! Boats were flying, all over the North-East!' She smiled down at Emily. 'I heard one came down on a church steeple in Boston. That's the problem with wind. It can just vanish.'

Emily's eyes and mouth were open. Pink with pleasure, she buried her face in Katherine's dress and clasped her, mostly round her rear.

A moment later Cotton felt a rhythmic tug on one of his fingers. Foster was a pale little boy with huge eyes. Cotton did not say, 'Are you trying to milk my finger?' But, 'Hello there, Foster. Wonderful to meet you. Do we kiss?'

'Hug,' said Foster.

Cotton had known Todd was well-off but had not known he was quite this rich and at ease with it.

'Where do they live in New York?' Katherine had asked as they drove up the drive.

'25 Central Park West,' said Cotton. 'They have an apartment.'

She smiled.

'What does that mean?'

'That they are discreet, not showy.'

'This is hardly modest.' Cotton had pointed to the sweep of the grounds.

'Mrs Duquesne?'

'Right.'

'How's Pop?' Since she had moved to the States and had children, Joan had changed her father's name from Daddy.

'Thin. He's lost quite a bit of weight this last year, wanders about the house in an old tweed jacket and scarf even in summer.'

'You know we've asked him to come here.'

'Yes, I know, I do. He says he'll think about travelling when things have settled down.'

Joan shook her head. 'I don't understand. He left England when he was seventeen. For heaven's sake he hardly knows the place.'

'He grows vegetables, looks after the fruit trees. And collects pine cones.'

'What?' said Todd. 'As a hobby?'

'No, to bulk up the fires.'

Joan groaned. 'Oh God, is he even getting enough to eat?'

'The war is over but rationing is actually a little worse. He eats a lot of stewed apples. There is not a lot of sugar around. But I did smuggle him some cinnamon and honey back from Spain. And a cousin sent him a bag of oatmeal from Scotland.'

'Can't you persuade him to come?'

'On a purely practical level, it would actually be quite difficult now. The ships are requisitioned and they have thousands of troops to bring back.'

'He hasn't even seen his grandchildren.'

'I know. But he has photographs of them up. And he does write to them, doesn't he?'

'My, he does!' said Todd. 'And he draws for them too.'

Cotton could see a discomfort in the Americans.

'Hey,' he said. 'He is a Victorian. He doesn't want to be a special case. Or a priority. It's part of what he calls his elderly war effort.'

'The war is over,' said Todd.

'The fighting the enemy bit is. I'm here as a small part of the effort to avoid something called Starvation Corner.'

'I wrote to him!' said Todd. 'I invited him!'

'I know,' said Cotton. 'Come on, give him a few months.' He smiled. 'You know, he lives in an English version of this.' He gestured around him.

'What?'

'A sort of Marie Antoinette village and country club.'

'Peter!' said Joan.

'That's better,' smiled Cotton.

'We'll take some photographs,' said Joan. 'Lots of photographs.'

The children appeared to like the presents but were far keener on attention from their uncle. At bedtime he read them the first chapter of *Alice in Wonderland*.

'I'd never thought of you as being a diplomat, Peter,' said Joan at supper.

'I'm not, not really. I was sent along as a dogsbody in an effort to persuade ourselves that the Americans have the money but we have the intelligence.'

'Sounds desperate – and doomed,' said Joan and laughed. Cotton thought both Todd and Katherine looked a little shocked. On other matters Todd was happy to be teased.

'The boys' names are from about Todd's family. Halliday is his mother's maiden name and Foster is . . . who was that again? We did have a go at our surnames but Cotton didn't sound right apparently and Beattie for a boy was considered risky. Emily was lucky and doesn't have to carry all that family responsibility so she just got a girl's name from a suitable list.'

*

On Columbus Day itself, 12 October, Cotton woke early. Standing by the four-poster bed were three children. Emily was holding a glass of milk, Halliday a cookie and Foster a small, bright drawing of indeterminate subject.

'What amazingly pleasant and attentive children! Good morning!'

Cotton sat up.

'That's a very big glass of milk,' he said. 'I may need some help. But you have to promise me something.'

'What?' said Halliday.

'Everybody gets a white moustache.' Cotton felt the biscuit. It was hard. He broke it into pieces on his elbow.

'You've got crumbs on the counterpane,' said Emily.

Cotton held out his hand. 'You snaffle and I'll pick up the crumbs.'

Cotton remembered that exactly a year before, he had been in Madrid on *El Dia de la Raza* – the day of the race or breed – a day when the staff at the British Embassy had been advised to adopt a low profile and to keep well away from the military parade held to celebrate Colombus's discovery. He'd spent the day with Houghton and Marie mostly talking about the Nazi-Spanish-Argentinian connection.

It turned out that the boys were happy with moustaches but Emily favoured lipstick.

'Is there something special you do on Columbus Day?'

'Like what?'

'I don't know. Roll an egg round or do something with three ships.'

'That's Easter and Christmas,' said Emily.

It was agreed there was a parade along Fifth Avenue in New York.

'But that's Italian,' said Halliday.

'Read,' said Foster. 'Read a story?'

Halliday had brought along his book.

So Cotton read from the beginning of *Peter Pan*. He had forgotten how sharp it was, that the age of two was 'the beginning of the end' and that Mrs Darling's broody drawing of cabbages with babies' faces had to compete with Mr Darling's book-keeping, walking rather than taking a bus to work, forsaking coffee at the office.

Cotton knew well enough what was happening. Joan was grilling or more likely smoking Katherine, probably lightly, over breakfast.

'She's a nice girl,' said Joan later. 'She can be a little withdrawn, perhaps, but that's Vassar I guess and all that intelligence.'

'Shhh. She's actually in Intelligence.'

'What? Vassar Hari?' smiled Joan. 'You know, I was going to ask if you were serious about her.'

'I am. She's in analysis though, not the undercover kind of thing.'

'You know what I mean.'

'What can I say? The next idea is I go to her family for Thanksgiving.'

'Really? Well, *hermanito*, I don't think you've done at all badly.'

'There is a problem, actually, *hablando con claridad, un par de problemitas*. '

'Ahhh. Career minded?'

'Career intrigued. Lots of unfamiliar, exciting possibilities. At least I think that's what she thinks.'

'And, quite understandably, you doubt that you can compete with that kind of excitement?'

Cotton laughed. 'I don't know. You could ask her, you know.'

'If you are not careful, I might just do that.'

'Stop. I am not asking you to do that.'

Joan laughed. 'That's either, I suspect, rather considerate or unspeakably caddish. Wait a moment, they don't say cad here. They say rat.'

'I don't think you're reading this quite right. It's not me who is making the decisions here.'

'Dear God, you're not going to turn vulnerable on me, are you?'

He leaned forward as if confiding. 'The truth is . . . I'm not entirely sure what is going on. The signals are . . .'

'Right,' said Joan. 'You *are* looking a bit lost. American girls can sometimes strike Brits as "fresh" . . .'

'Forward?'

'. . . Yes. But they do have other barriers, I assure you.'

'Isn't that my point?'

Joan smiled. Foster was running towards them. 'Are you all right, darling?' she asked and Cotton knew then that Joan would tell Katherine about Emmeline.

Todd was chubby and amiable, with soft eyes. But he was quick and clear. He talked about UNRRA, the United Nations Relief and Rehabilitation Administration, then struggling, 'rather like your Mission', he said, in Washington DC for funds to get refugees through the winter. He had been asked to look over the accounts – 'Appalling. Financial control has barely existed. There is a clever and determined Australian in charge. But getting grain to the Balkans, say, ran up against no desks and fabulous overstaffing, usually with incompetents. Now that the Australian has got in some desks and got rid of a lot of incompetents, he is being attacked for being a foreigner. You know what they are going to do? Call him a Scotsman because the Scots have a reputation for thrift.'

In the afternoon it rained. The rain was heavy enough to make the fall leaves rattle and smack. He held a golfing umbrella over them both as they walked in the garden.

'You must think I am an awful baby,' Katherine said. 'My apartment was burgled and I started shaking.'

'I've done some shaking,' said Cotton.

She nodded. 'Your sister told me about your fiancée. Do you mind?'

'No,' he said. 'I just don't talk about it very much. I feel I am distributing parts of a dead person without permission. At the same time I am giving someone else a burden. Not fair on either. And then a lot of other people have died. And lots have lost someone. I mean you have never said anything.'

'Oh, I've known of people – but nobody I was going to marry.'

'Good point,' he said. He looked round. 'Have you never thought of marrying?'

'My sister calls me that old lady almost on the shelf.'

'When do you get to clamber on to it?'

'When I am twenty-six. That is the cut-off point. After that it is old maid. And I have less than a year to go.'

'Who made this shelf rule exactly?'

She smiled. 'Can I shock you – just a little?'

'Please do.'

'I've always had a taste for . . . well, rather older men. I love Will Clayton, for example. On a more practical level I can have unfortunate taste. The last one was married.'

'A professor?'

She nodded. 'I graduated in '41, did a master's and probably did enough for a doctorate in "will he or won't he get a divorce?". I had bad thoughts for about a year after.'

'How bad?'

'Oh, if the man is this dishonest in his private life what was the master's I did under him worth?'

Cotton smiled. 'All right,' he said.

'You don't disapprove?'

'Why should I?'

'OK,' she said. She nodded. 'How did she die?'

'Bombing raid. November '43. A direct hit.'

She nodded and they walked slowly on.

'Have you been in action?'

'Briefly.'

'And?'

'It is extraordinarily hard to be a participant and a good witness. Action is violent, agitated, a kind of ghastly, forced excitement. And then there's a kind of guilt.'

'At what?'

'Surviving.' Cotton sighed. 'The military love taking group photographs. You probably did the same at university. Look at the photograph again now. Some of the faces are stuck there. It makes you feel not lucky exactly, just more conscious that we were a group of random disposables and how fragile we were.'

'Fragile how?'

'Mostly physically. You remember fingers coming off, that kind of thing. It's the living that look horrified or exhausted or bored.'

'The dead?'

'Vacant, in bits, out of luck.'

She reached up and kissed him briefly. 'Thanks,' she said, 'for sounding honest.'

Later, sitting outside, the children having been given fruit juice and cookies and now running around, Joan turned to Katherine.

'What's it like as a woman in the State Department?' she asked.

'Pretty much like everywhere else. I get to be a mascot, cheerleader, good little girl and debatable.'

'Debatable?'

'Joe in Section E wouldn't kick me out of bed, but Jim in Foreign Aid saw a truly hot stenographer over in the Asian section. I have seen several tactics for survival. You can be one of the boys, you can be little Miss Frigid, in later years the schoolmarmish spinster, you can cry in the rest room or you can imply that you have a powerful protector, preferably a no-brooker.'

Cotton smiled. 'A no-brooker is . . .'

'. . . someone old who gets furious when girls are not treated cleanly and protectively. Generationally, better a grandfather than a father. Father figures can start looking reflective over the cigars and have to clear their throat when they start purring.'

Cotton laughed but noticed his sister did not look comfortable.

'There are drawbacks to the arrangement. If you actually work with that powerful old personage it is easy to become a handmaiden, fetching coffee, listening up appreciatively. And they get a sense of ownership. You can be snapped at, to show you are appreciated. If you don't cry you're OK and some way to being almost a grandson. And of course you are a sensible young woman for listening to them rather than paying attention to the young. You've got the flattery the right way round.'

She smiled. 'I'll stop. I know some things are off-limits and for a woman to talk of misogyny can be taken as vulgar of her.'

Emily ran up to her.

'Are you going to be my aunt?' said Emily.

'Would you like that?'

'Oh yes, I'd like that a lot.'

Katherine nodded. 'I'm considering it,' she said.

'Like Mr Darling?'

Katherine glanced at Cotton. He mouthed, 'From *Peter Pan.*'

'Ah,' she said, 'there are, there are indeed, considerations.'

'Yes,' said Emily. 'Like what?'

'This Peter's feet, for example. Are they webbed? Do you know?'

'No,' said Emily, 'I don't.' She looked at Cotton, a little worried.

Cotton shook his head. 'They're not. There might be a little soap I suppose, but there is no thread and my shadow has never escaped.'

'Well, does he blow bubbles when he sleeps?' Katherine persisted.

This did not go down well. Emily frowned and then shot off.

'When Foster was born,' said Joan, 'she'd watch him ready to pop any bubble that appeared on his lips. It wasn't a frequent occurrence but she is very patient.'

'Where did she get that?'

'No idea. She thought he needed the air.'

Around his shoes Cotton felt some fiddle. Foster was trying to undo his shoelaces.

'Hello there. Of course, you are right. Let's look at my toes.'

He lifted his nephew and they set to removing his shoe and sock.

'Emily! Foot!' Halliday called.

Still sulking, Emily came back.

'Check for webbing,' said Joan.

Emily looked. 'I don't think so,' she said.

'Good,' said Katherine. 'But I'll make a list of potentially horrible habits. You have brothers, don't you?'

Emily nodded.

'But I don't have any . . . horrible things!' said Halliday.

Emily was in love and embraced Katherine again.

22

WHEN HE went to work on Monday 15 October Cotton learned that Hugh Dalton, the British Chancellor of the Exchequer, had sent a cable turning down the American offer over the weekend. Cotton saw the Embassy and Chancery reaction as both gloomy and embarrassed. He heard someone say, 'Communications and distance are always a problem,' but heard no irony in it.

Jim Gowar was still trying to get back to being Jim Gowar. 'Keynes claims that Hugh Dalton was an imperialist but after a drunken undergraduate night with the poet Rupert Brooke, he became a Fabian socialist and has never, ever wavered. Dalton actually included the phrase "sweet breath of justice" in his cable.'

'How are you?' asked Cotton.

Jim Gowar thought. 'Pretty shitty,' he said.

On his desk Cotton had the latest updates from Dr Aforey. 'At last,' he wrote. 'The Pan-African Congress begins today under the banner *Socialism Unites. Imperialism Divides.* It might be possible to say Socialism Unites what Imperialism has divided. I fear that the speeches will be prescriptive but not realistic.'

Cotton doubted that Dr Aforey would ever be happy with his or others' choice of words.

Around lunchtime he called Katherine. She was amused that Brian had 'cut and run'.

'He's gone! Left a note saying I'd left *him* alone.'

'Have you spoken to him?'

'No. Apparently he didn't show up for work today. I tried him at home and he is not there either.'

'Are you all right about being in the apartment by yourself?'

'Of course, I am. Didi's father had words with the police apparently.'

On Wednesday 17 October, Cotton got back to his British efficiency around 6.30 p.m. Around seven he received a telephone call.

'Hello?'

There was no reply.

'Hello?' He waited and then hung up.

About five minutes later the telephone rang again.

'Hello?' he said again, this time a little sharper. There was no reply and he was about to hang up again when Katherine spoke.

'Can I see you?'

'Of course. When?'

'Now?'

'Yes. Are you all right? You sound . . .'

'I'm on the corner with Wisconsin Avenue.'

'Right. I'll be directly down.'

Cotton got his hat and coat and trotted down the stairs. As he came out he saw her Chrysler Royal coming down the street. She pulled up and parked. He walked to the car and got in.

'Hello,' he said. He moved to kiss her. She held up an arm.

'Brian's killed himself,' she said. 'He put a revolver to

243

each temple. His father's pistol on one side and his own on the other.'

'Dear Jesus,' said Cotton.

She took hold of his forearm. 'Will you come with me to the funeral? I want somebody from outside.'

'Of course. I understand.'

For a time that was it. She behaved as if relieved she had asked what she had come to ask. He waited.

'Can we walk?' she asked.

Cotton got out of the Chrysler, walked round to her side and opened the door.

'I don't want to talk about it.'

'All right.' He helped her out and they started walking slowly along the sidewalk.

'He went to see his mother,' she said. 'Asked her for more money. She said no.'

Cotton nodded.

'He . . . told her she was an old bitch, that it was his father's money in any case and . . . then he told her he was a faggot.'

Years before, when Cotton had been about to go back to school in England, his father had seen a British employee outside the bank at home in Mexico City. The atmosphere had been one of sensational discretion round the term 'overdrawn'. In some, almost casual, distant way, Cotton had been waiting for circumstances that matched the extravagant horror his father had put into the word. Through his father's study window he and his sister had heard him say, 'Don't you realize you are putting your entire future in jeopardy? Your prospects will be ruined if you carry on like this. You're overdrawn, man. Overdrawn!'

Beside him his sister had whispered, 'Ooh, this is better than the Day of the Dead!' and raised her arms ghoul-style.

A moment later they had heard the young British banker break down and start snivelling.

'You can start by being a man!' his sister had mouthed.

His father had been not quite as direct. 'I say, come on now. This doesn't help. Stiffen up there. And let's get to the bottom of things.'

Brian had overdrawn.

'How do you know this?'

'His mother talked to mine. I've just translated back, if you know what I mean. I think his mother said effeminate. She didn't understand the passive part and asked my mother about it.'

'What did your mother say?'

'That he had gone crazy and that was why he had killed himself.'

He took her hand. She started but then, after a few steps, even smiled a little.

'You're good at that,' she said. 'Some men have . . . unhelpful hands. You know, no use at all.'

'You knew him for a long time?'

'Oh, we were diaper-little together, you know. There are photographs of us in the same sandpit.' She made a face. 'It's all so stupid.' She stopped walking and squeezed her eyes shut. 'It all looks just so . . . cruel and simple.' She sniffed and started walking again.

'Tell me about him.'

She blinked. She looked unwilling.

'Try.'

She nodded. 'Elderly father. I mean always called the

Admiral. First War. Medals, rank, then wife. Old enough to be sentimental and think of decorative when he saw women. She is physically delicate, if you know what I mean. Never could travel. So very infrequently Brian got the stickler father, but was mumsied to death in the meantime.' She looked up. 'He once told me his mother hated men. They weren't nice, they were gruff and abrupt.' She sighed – it was a sound as if she were about to be sick. 'I don't know when he started drinking, certainly by fifteen. He was drinking before his father died.'

'When was that?'

'Nineteen thirty-five. And then Mummy took on Daddy's role as well. You know? Brian kept flunking . . .'

'What's that?'

'Failing. His grades went way down. So she took advice from high-ranking navy personnel and sent him away to acquire discipline and manly virtues. He was hopeless at math and his father had been a hotshot. They got him into Princeton but then, I don't know, they got him a desk job in the Navy Office where they have a photograph of his father on the wall.'

She stopped. She looked puzzled.

'Sorry,' she said. 'I really can't think of anyone else I could tell this stuff so directly to. Would you know what I meant if I said I felt smothered?'

'Yes.'

She breathed out. 'The worst thing, if I am honest, is that we were not that close any more. He was just there, you know. Sometimes funny, not so often now. And then I think, oh, that was a horrible way to impose your death on other people. Is that mean?'

'No.'

She started weeping. Cotton embraced her, contrived to open his jacket and wrap her up.

'He said she wanted her men ideally emasculated.'

She turned a wet, soft face up to him and kissed. The kiss was warm and, though she pressed, curiously hopeless.

She blinked and swallowed. 'I can get home.'

'Are you sure you can drive?'

'I'll call you,' she said, 'and tell you about the funeral.'

'Yes. You will.'

He kissed her. Her face already felt hotter and drier as if she had a fever. She wanted to get away.

'OK. Thank you.'

He shook his head. 'No need.'

Cotton was still standing in his room with his coat on, when Tibbets walked in. Cotton grunted and took his coat off.

'Your shirt is all wet,' said Tibbets.

'A man called Brian Kirkland committed suicide early this morning.'

'Oh,' said Tibbets. He frowned. 'Shit,' he said. 'I think . . . look, I forgot to tell you. Brian someone . . . or somebody calling himself Brian, telephoned when you were away, wanted to speak to you. Urgently, he said. But I didn't know where you were.' Tibbets cleared his throat. 'How did he do it?'

'Put a revolver to each temple and pulled both triggers.'

Tibbets flinched. 'That really is crossfire. I mean, he could have blown both his hands off. Well, it's difficult to press both triggers at exactly the same time. I'd have thought anyway. I say, a bit . . . gory for everybody else, what? He can't have been right in the head.'

Cotton had seen actors in films slap hysterical women to bring them round, if not to rationality at least to shocked quiet. He thought with Tibbets this would be better in slow motion, possibly with a closed fist. He resisted the impulse. He smiled without smiling.

'Well, you're pretty cool about it,' said Tibbets.

'I've still got two hands,' he said.

'Bit of a sore head, have we?'

'Fuck off, will you? And try knocking next time.'

'Oh well,' said Tibbets. 'If you're going to be like that . . .'

23

ON 18 October the Americans reduced their offer. Instead of $5 billion, they thought $4 billion in all would be enough to see Britain through its difficulties.

'Did you hear that very faint groan from the Embassy?' said Jim Gowar. He called out, 'Reaction from London?'

'Consternation!'

Ayrtoun called Cotton in.

'Morale is going to go. Everyone here is more or less pro-American; in London they are anti-American. Keynes has his drawbacks. He oversold what he could do and has now got bogged down in detail. Do you remember Acton?'

'Discretion?'

'Bear that in mind.' He paused, glanced at his tin of cigarettes but did not touch it. 'I've heard a distressing phrase,' he said. 'Not borrowing from the Yanks is somehow "nobler".

'At the same time as London was wittering on about nobility, Harry Dexter White was chairing a secret US Treasury meeting. It agreed we had exaggerated our balance of payments difficulties and would not need as much as five billion dollars.'

Cotton nodded. 'Right.'

Ayrtoun gave in. He opened his tin of cigarettes and removed a Senior Service. 'One American agency says White has collaborated with the Soviets. Another department allows him to carry on dismantling us. What the fuck do they think they're doing? What is going on?'

'What does Keynes say?'

'He has already asked the Americans whether or not he should just go home. Do you know what Vinson said? "In Kentucky we never ask our guests to leave." Oh, fuck,' said Ayrtoun. He put the cigarette between his lips and lit it. He inhaled, held the smoke in his lungs and breathed out with relief and satisfaction.

'That's better,' he said. 'I take it Keynes has no choice but to press on fighting London and trying to deal with the Americans.'

'He may even be in a bigger hurry now to head off the "nobler" way of life coming from London.'

Ayrtoun drew again on his cigarette. 'What are the chances of the Soviets signing up to Bretton Woods?'

'Nil,' said Cotton.

'Do you think London will come up with an alternative or two?'

'Nothing plausible.'

On 19 October Cotton read that President Isaias Medina had been overthrown in Venezuela in a coup led by army officers.

During the night of 20–21 October, at about 1 a.m., Cotton's telephone rang. It was Mullins.

'Sorry, sir, you're closest and the matter requires urgent attention.' He gave Cotton an address in Prospect Street NW. 'Board of Trade. The police have been called, sir. I'll be along as soon as possible.'

Cotton got himself there at about one twenty-five. The

police car and ambulance outside the house helped pick out the address. He asked the policeman outside the door to call the investigating officer. A bad-tempered captain came downstairs.

'What do you want?'

'I'm from the British Embassy, Captain. My instructions are to provide any assistance possible.'

The captain paused and looked him over.

'Are you a policeman?'

Cotton shook his head. 'Captain, I'm a soldier on clean-up duty. There's another man coming who deals with this kind of thing. I am here to help, not cause problems.'

The captain sighed. 'Yeah. What did this guy think he was doing?'

'You're going to have to tell me.'

The captain jerked his head and they went inside and started climbing the stairs.

'They've given him morphine.'

'Was he shot?' said Cotton.

The captain gave a kind of laugh.

Cotton found a British subject, about forty-five years old, on the floor being tended to by the ambulancemen. Across the room was a very muscular Negro man wearing a blue satin dress. He had stepped out of his red high heels and was showing red-painted toenails. He had taken off his wig. His lips were swollen and smeared with lipstick and blood.

'He's definitely broken his hip,' said one of the ambulancemen. 'We're not sure about the extent of the internal injury.'

'Isn't this what they call the English vice?' said the captain. He pointed at a baseball bat on the floor.

The Negro spoke. 'Wasn't my fault.' That was what Cotton thought he said. 'Customer ask, customer get. I only do what he tell me. He say go, I go. He say go, go — and then he start hollering.'

'Shut your mouth,' said the captain. He turned to Cotton. 'Do you want to press charges?'

Cotton shook his head. 'Truly? I'd really like to kick my own man but I think he is in enough pain as it is.'

The captain nodded. He didn't quite smile. 'He's let you people down, right?'

'Let us down a lot.' Cotton was unsure as to how to play the next part. He wanted no publicity and no record.

'Captain,' said the policeman at the door. 'Another one to see you.'

Cotton was pleased to see Mullins.

'Captain O'Donnell?' said Mullins.

The captain nodded. Mullins handed him a business card and leaned towards Cotton.

'If you'd like to accompany the gentleman to the hospital, sir, I'll attend to matters here.'

'Where's Fielding?'

'On his way.'

'What hospital?'

'We have a medical plan here, sir,' Mullins told him.

The British delegate, shivering but drowsy from the drugs, was put on a stretcher, carried downstairs and put in the ambulance. Cotton stepped in and shook him.

'Who are you?' he groaned.

'We're going to say you slipped,' said Cotton.

'What?'

'On some steps.'

The delegate frowned. 'I'm married.'

'Stone steps.'

The man winced. 'What have I done?'

'Broken your hip, I think. Keep your mouth shut. Is that clear?'

At the hospital the patient was patched up and put into a private room and sedated again. His injuries were listed as 'hernia and broken hip'. The work on him lasted for some time. Cotton slept a little on a bench but by the time everything had been done it was past eight on the Sunday morning.

Cotton went for a cup of coffee and then went directly to the Chancery.

'Rough night?' said Ayrtoun.

'Long.'

'You haven't shaved.'

'How did Mullins get on?'

'Well. I don't ask, of course, but we've had to trade.'

Cotton nodded.

'Do you want to know what?'

Cotton shrugged.

'Information,' said Ayrtoun. 'Poor trade. What I had was juicy. And all to save somebody's arse.'

Cotton doubted that the Board of Trade delegate would be saved.

'Fielding's useless,' remarked Ayrtoun.

'Where is he?' said Cotton.

'I've sent him to keep guard at the hospital.'

Cotton saw Mullins briefly and thanked him.

'No, sir, it was another contact.'

'Who else was there?'

'An FBI agent arrived, sir.'

'What happened to our man's companion?'

253

'I didn't enquire very precisely, sir, but I imagine they'll be hanging on to him.'

Cotton went home. Tibbets was in the bathroom 'having a soak. It's something I like to do on a Sunday,' he called.

'Tell me when you're finished,' said Cotton. He made himself a cup of coffee and read Cissy Patterson's newspaper while he waited. The fall was the loveliest in years. There was a plentiful supply of turkeys for Thanksgiving. In France women had been given the vote for the first time. Cotton decided that, once he had finished in the bathroom, he'd go out and eat brunch.

24

ON MONDAY morning Ayrtoun learned that a journalist from Cissy Patterson's Washington newspaper
was on his way to ask a question about an 'incident involving the police in Prospect Street'.

'Fucking Lord Acton,' he said.

Ayrtoun did not fiddle with his cigarette tin. He opened
it and lit up.

'This is yours,' he said to Cotton. 'Handle it, will you?'

Cotton spoke to Mullins and Mullins used his police
contacts to find out the latest information.

The journalist was short, had wiry hair, needed a shave
and was wearing a blue-and-silver tie. He said his name was
Wolfe, 'of the Hungarian Wolfes'. He was smoking and
rubbing together the thumb and middle finger of his
smoking hand. And he was chewing gum.

'So you've met the man from Protocol,' said Cotton.

The journalist shrugged.

'This could be embarrassing,' said Cotton.

'So?'

Cotton raised his eyes. 'Not to us, man!'

'No? What's your version?'

Cotton shrugged. 'The official police version. What
would yours be?'

'What do they say?'

'I can tell you what they've done. They've arrested a man

who has been charged with aggravated assault while committing a robbery. We understand he has a criminal record.'

The journalist shook his head. 'Not for that.'

'I wouldn't know. I do know he is a Negro.' Cotton allowed a pause. He knew Negroes rarely made it into the press. And a transvestite Negro? 'We are not making a big thing of it because our man is, or was, involved in negotiations with your government. We really don't want to be causing them problems.'

'What was he doing at that time of night?'

Cotton stared at him. 'These men are living in two time zones,' he said. 'They work a minimum of fourteen-hour days. In this case we are talking about a statistician, a man with a slide-rule and bits of paper. He comes from Hemel Hempstead. He has never been to Washington before but he has been put up in a house in Georgetown because we can't afford hotels for all of the delegates. And the poor mutt decided to go for a walk. I did the same when I arrived. I almost got killed.'

The journalist removed the gum from his mouth and wrapped it in the paper he had just taken off the new piece.

'Do you want?'

'No thanks. If you need more . . .'

'. . . I should speak to someone on our side.'

'Exactly.'

The journalist scrunched up his face. 'Where would I go for this?'

Cotton told him 'the name I've been given at the FBI'.

'Shit,' said Wolfe.

'What?'

Wolfe shook his head. He gave Cotton his card. 'Here,' he said.

'Thank you,' said Cotton. 'Why would I need this?'

'This is America. We're optimistic.'

Cotton nodded and smiled.

Brian's funeral was on Monday 22 October at 3 p.m. The hymns were 'Onward Christian Soldiers' and 'The Lord's my Shepherd'. The eulogy was brief and mentioned his father. Brian Kirkland was buried as 'Son of the Admiral. Died at age 25. October 17 1945' in Arlington National Cemetery. The day was dull. Light mist rolled by, sometimes thickening, soon clearing. The grass was damp underfoot. An air of discreet denial prevailed and the mourners behaved with dignity, some of them evidently doing so in contrast to Brian's lack of the stuff. Cotton heard someone say 'Calvin'. Calvin Brandt was a big, beefy naval lieutenant with very regular features but decidedly flat feet. As requested, he accompanied Katherine.

There was a very hushed wake at Brian's mother's residence. Cotton followed Katherine in shaking Mrs Kirkland's hand and received a gracious little nod. There was a moment when he thought she was about to speak but that turned out to be a whisper to someone else that her throat was awfully dry.

As they left the house Katherine passed him a note.

'Do you want me to look at this now?'

She shook her head. 'No, I'll drop you off. You read it then.'

'All right.'

She drove to P Street. 'Call me,' she said.

Cotton went upstairs. He made himself some tea and unfolded the note.

K

I'm so lonely I am frightened of seeing myself in mirrors. I think that was why I was trying to write. But detectives rarely face themselves, do they? They help others or they take it out on them. Then I met a man who told me pulp fiction was nothing like a real, pulped face.

B

Cotton folded Brian's note, put it in his pocket and went directly to Katherine's apartment. He must have been looking very grim.

'I don't want you to be angry with him,' she said.

'I'm not. I'm sorry. When did you get the note?'

'It came by post. A few days ago.'

Cotton winced. 'Are you all right?'

'Yes. I just wanted you to see it.'

'I understand.' He blew out. 'You haven't shown it to anyone else?'

'No. I don't really know what to do with it.'

'Why should you?'

'Yes.'

'Do you feel let down?'

'No,' she said and shook her head.

They sat down and he took her hand.

'Why didn't you tell me about the note sooner?'

'I didn't know what to say.'

'It's not your fault.'

'No.'

'Good. Do you want to stay here?' asked Cotton.

She blinked. 'Do you?'

He smiled. 'Of course, I do.'

'But?'

'No buts.'

She started crying.

'Shh, hey,' he said and put his arms around her.

She cried for some time. She looked exhausted. He carried her through to her bedroom and sat with her until she fell sleep.

Before he left Cotton wrote her a short note:

I liked watching you sleep. Call me.

25

THE NEXT morning, 23 October, Cotton received a letter at P Street from his sister Joan. He thought it would be a reply to his letter thanking her for the weekend in Centre Island and it was. Right at the end of the letter, however, she asked for his help.

I am not sure, you see, that Todd hasn't strayed. Please understand, I don't blame him and I don't have vulgar 'evidence' involving lipstick on collars or anything like that. It's just a sensation that he has drifted away. If I blame anybody, it is probably myself.

He is going to be in DC on the 5–6 November. In the way of things, you'll meet and I don't know quite what I am asking you to do, only that I am asking you for something.

Cotton closed one eye, then two. He wrote back: OK. And dropped his reply into a mailbox on his way to the Chancery.

When he got there Mullins came to see him. 'A word, sir?'

'What is it?'

Mullins unfolded a letter but kept it towards his chest. 'Mr Ayrtoun had Beryl checked out, sir.'

It took Cotton a moment to remember that Beryl was the wife in Crewe. He nodded.

'It appears,' said Mullins, 'that her father could face a charge of black-marketeering, sir.'

Chops under the counter or the black market blackmailed, thought Cotton.

'Mr Ayrtoun told me not to be . . . combative was the word he used. I thought I'd check the letter over with you, sir.'

'Right.'

Cotton looked it over. It was short and suggested that it might be in both Mullins' and Beryl's interests to accept 'the facts as presented' and institute divorce proceedings. There existed a fast-track procedure meant to dissolve unfortunate wartime marriages 'undertaken in desperate times' and while theirs had been pre-war, the breakdown had occurred during 'the dark days of war'. Mullins had good reason to believe that they could make use of this procedure 'in which there are no guilty parties and none is sought' and 'people are able to remake their lives, rather than having them ruined'. He was hopeful for her agreement; the official forms would be sent to her home address and he sincerely wished her the very best in the rest of her life and hoped she would find happiness. He signed himself 'Respectfully yours, Robert Mullins'.

'Yes,' said Cotton. 'The only things I'd take out would be "rather than having them ruined" and "in the rest of your life". Otherwise, it is clear.'

Mullins was pleased and Cotton was impressed by Ayrtoun's reach.

'Thank you very much,' said Mullins.

'When are you due to be demobbed?'

'I don't rightly know, sir.'

'Keep me up to date, though.'

'Yes, sir.'

'One more thing,' said Cotton. He wrote down Katherine's address and gave it to Mullins. 'There was a man called Kirkland living in this building in the apartment above for a few days, let's say October the 10th to the 15th.'

'This is Miss Ward's place.'

'Yes. Mr Kirkland was staying there. He shot himself later in his own apartment. He was buried yesterday.'

'And you would be interested in knowing whether or not he received any visitors while you and Miss Ward were in New York.'

'Can you find out?'

'It might take a day or two. It might even cost you a little.'

'Fair enough.'

Cotton had expected a call from Katherine. At about noon, however, he received a special delivery marked PRIVATE AND CONFIDENTIAL. It was a strengthened brown envelope carrying a red seal. He opened it. It contained an expensive white card.

A room has been booked at the Statler Hotel in your name for tonight. You should not worry at all about the expense. The night will be entirely on me. K
  P.S. Sign in at six, attend to your social round and be there at nine.

At 6 p.m. Cotton went to the Statler. He was welcomed as an old friend and shown to a room one floor above his original accommodation but identical in every respect. He showered, changed, and went to his reception.

He was back at the Statler by eight thirty. At a little after nine there was a knock at the door. He opened it and was handed 'a message for you, sir.'

He opened the envelope. It contained another card with a number and floor on it. 'Top floor,' it said. 'Nine fifteen.'

Cotton went up. Katherine was waiting for him. She was dressed in a towelling robe. She kissed him and shrugged the robe off.

'I was worried,' she said, 'you were thinking I was a tease.'

'No,' said Cotton.

'Not now anyway.'

'No.' Cotton placed his hand on the nape of her neck and kissed her.

'Mm,' she said. 'You know I think we are on the same floor as Lord Keynes.'

'I don't really care about that,' said Cotton. He kissed her again and smiled.

'What is it?'

'You are more than remarkable,' he said.

'Go on.'

He smiled. He wanted to say more, found he couldn't.

'It's all right,' she said. 'We don't have to talk.'

The next morning, when Cotton left his single room at the Statler, he was told the bill had been paid. He picked up a newspaper and took a cab to work. '*1st Negro Player ever to be admitted to organized baseball – Jackie Robinson.*' He put the paper down and closed his eyes. He felt tired but happy, impressed and touched.

At the Chancery, however, Moses had had a letter from Dr Aforey:

I am hearing very bad things of the Pan-African Congress. It has been a procession of Soviet approved texts.

My own suspicion is that this meeting of ambitious men will merely have stoked those personal ambitions. Do you know what thrills them about Soviet Russia? The power Stalin has!

Of course, he regrets, he apologizes that Workers' Rights have been sadly neglected but industrialization has been a complete success. It is a base lie, pure alchemy.

But it does not matter to my Pan-African colleagues because Stalin has achieved and kept power. They like his name, steel. Molotov means hammer, I believe.

My poor colleagues even believe Africa will escape the awkward problem of the stubborn Russian peasantry. Why? Because Africa has no Russian peasants. I am very ashamed of them for this way of thinking, particularly if it is not a pretext.

What worries me now is that this Congress will obtain credence because it was organized and conducted by Negroes, and that other Negroes will defend it simply because of that.

I will stop now and write again when I am less agitated.

The Pan-African Congress had, of course, been observed by the British, names taken, statements recorded. The report writer came close to calling it a non-event of extraordinarily lengthy, utterly tedious speeches. There had been next-to-no press attention. Despite the name, interest had been almost entirely local, 'amongst the Negro populace of

Manchester' (Cotton had not known there was one), some trade unionists and a few fellow travellers. 'Banda, Kenyatta and others have white wives or concubines.' He also added, 'To what extent this Congress will make news in Africa remains a moot point. The expression "blueprint" was heard several times but no plan of any coherence emerged. Instead a number of motions, for example, against Fascism, Racism and Imperialism were carried by the entirety of the delegates to the satisfaction of them all.'

Cotton shrugged. He picked up the telephone and called Katherine at work. They agreed to meet. At the weekend they went away. Cotton was amused that this was more what he thought of as a log cabin. The fall was almost over but there were still a few autumn colours, yellows and reds, mostly on the trees. They did not go out much but lit a fire. She wanted to know about his childhood in Mexico, private education in England, his time at Cambridge, his mother, and in return told him about herself. She was delightfully assured, generous and adventurous. He woke once to find her naked on the verandah.

'I thought you'd like some cold skin,' she said.

They did not talk at all about work.

On 29 October news came through of a bloodless coup in Brazil. After fifteen years, some of it spent pro-Axis, then shifting to the Allies, President Getúlio Vargas was obliged to resign by the military. There was some talk of democratic elections being held.

Coincidentally, the same day, Spruille Braden was confirmed as appointed Assistant Secretary of State for Latin America.

*

Mullins told Cotton that his enquiries about Katherine's apartment had cost $20. He had found out that the police patrol had been told to stay away from 'that part of the street' for four hours on Saturday 13 October.

'Who told them them to stay away?'

Mullins shrugged. 'Only one agency really has that sort of relationship with the police,' he said.

26

NOVEMBER OPENED unpromisingly. The Anglo-American negotiations had degenerated into what the British delegation dramatically termed 'horror'. And Dr Aforey announced that he had dried up or, as he put it, 'I procrastinate, I fear.' He would be stern with himself.

On Monday 5 November the cover of *Time* magazine showed Spruille Braden, the new Assistant Secretary of State for Latin America – 'a bull in the Latin American china shop' said *Time*. It was just one more very clear and public sign that IRIS was moribund and Braden had been brought in, amongst other things, to kill it off. Braden was not lacking in self-confidence. Ridley had a note that Braden had been heard to dismiss IRIS as 'collectivists, do-gooders and what-nots'.

Cotton had arranged to have lunch with his brother-in-law on 6 November. Todd was a little late and while he waited, Cotton glanced at a newspaper. '*House warned of Red Trend in Halls of State. Rep. Shafer (N.Mich.) charged today that the State Department is being "Stalinized" after reviewing recent appointments.*'

Another item said: '*2,533,000 discharged since VE Day.*'

Todd wanted to eat at the Florida Avenue Grill. A white clapboard place, it reminded Cotton of an Essex pub in England he and Jim Gowar had had to run past when training.

'The food is down and dirty,' said Todd, 'but indulge me, it's been years since I ate catfish. And it's November.'

'Catfish are seasonal?' asked Cotton.

'In summer they tend to hunker down in the mud and that gives the flesh . . . well, a murky flavour.'

'And now?'

'Cleaner. Just a white fish. Can have a kind of zing though. Try the short ribs.'

'No. I'll try the catfish.'

'And the hushpuppies?'

Under the taste of the frying Cotton found the flesh of the fish insipid, but without the slip of cod. This was more mushy and there was indeed an undertaste. Cotton inclined more to murky than zing. The hushpuppies, deep-fried balls of cornmeal bread, were heavy and after a while Cotton flagged. His mouth felt dull with grease and he wouldn't have wanted to smell his own breath.

Todd was a neat, quick eater and had tucked himself round the meal within a few minutes. He sat back and lit a cigarette.

'Best tastes are acquired in childhood.'

'This is Southern, isn't it?'

'My mother's family was from the South and she made sure I knew that part of my heritage. Used to send me to an aunt. She had what we children called a fattening farm.' Todd belched and stubbed out his cigarette. 'It's what I do,' he said. 'Eat.'

Cotton smiled. Todd sighed.

'I know about Joan,' he said. 'In a way it is kind of flattering, I suppose.'

'Look . . .'

'It's OK, Peter. But what can I tell you? I'm getting older,

I have the job and I'm grateful for my life, that's all. I mean I was sent to Mexico, met this nice English girl. Joan's strong, you know. And she's . . . respectful. I don't know if you understand that. I never chased skirt, you know. Hey, I'm plump and shy. I'm family. I want to see more of the kids.' Todd blinked. 'Do you want dessert?'

'No.'

'Coffee?'

'Please.'

Todd ordered coffee for Cotton and some cheesecake for himself.

'I worry she's disappointed,' he said. He looked up. 'I'm getting old and I'm tired. I am forty years old, Peter. And that thing about settling down? I mean that's settling down. I'm just not as frequently attentive as I was.'

'It's all right,' said Cotton.

Todd sighed. 'But it looks like I am, well, letting her down by settling down. I don't know. I don't know what I can do about it. I have to show her how much I value her but that the ways have changed. I can't help it.'

They agreed that Todd would buy Joan a present and Cotton would write her a note.

We talked shopping – I gave lame advice. Don't worry. He is devoted to you and the children. But you are, of course, both getting very old. Perhaps you should encourage a sport that gives more exercise than golf or gentle sailing?

On 8 November Cotton saw in the American press: '*British jet plane establishes world air speed of 606 miles an hour.*' A couple of hours later a note arrived on his desk saying the same and that the name Gloster (not Gloucester) was actually correct as the company name and that the aircraft itself was called Meteor (not Meteorite). The 'feat' had taken place 'over Herne Bay' on 7 November. The pilot was Group Captain H. J. (Willy) Wilson.

Cotton spent the weekend with Katherine in her apartment. She quizzed him further on his childhood and on Mexico, asked to make love in Spanish and then in French.

Monday the 12th was Armistice Day and Cotton was sent out in uniform and medals to salute the American war dead on behalf of a stout ally alongside other stout allies, and a large but slightly separate contingent from the Soviets. There was a keen wind – it blew the military music away from them – and being in position long before the dignitaries arrived to lay wreaths made for a cold, stiff wait. Cotton for the Army and two other officers for the Navy and the RAF had been driven there by Mullins, wearing his sergeant's uniform for the first time Cotton had seen.

Cotton looked at the other uniforms there. The British, Canadians, Australians and New Zealanders at least had reasonably comfortable, practical outfits – some of the others looked spectacularly difficult to wear, particularly at the neck.

Then his attention was drawn to a kerfuffle with the Soviets. They weren't happy about something. The Soviets had huge hats, wide shoulders and several had stripes down the side of the trousers and something like riding boots. Cotton saw 'Slonim' there, in his colonel's uniform with enough medal ribbons to form a patchwork block on his chest. He wondered about the medals, if they had been won by the original Colonel and Trapezoid was just borrowing them, or whether they belonged to Trapezoid himself for services to the Soviet government.

The wind had taken on an occasional shrill howl. He relaxed into what he thought of as military patience. Later, various religious personages, their robes billowing and tugging, intoned various prayers into a skittish microphone, and a number of Ambassadors, some dressed in nineteenth-century grandeur, some with the high wing collars of the early part of the century, laid wreaths after Secretary of State Byrnes. The American parade was elsewhere.

Bugles played, Cotton saluted and then waited for the ceremony to break up. The officer from the Navy or 'senior service' took out a cigarette case, offered – Cotton shook his head – and then moved to light up, shoulders hunched, hands cupped.

Cotton strolled towards the wreaths. As he did so he saw Slonim lift a finger and start walking over. When Slonim was near he turned, stood to attention and saluted. Slonim nodded and, without really breaking his stride, saluted back.

'My respects, Colonel,' said Slonim. 'I have come to say goodbye. Now I leave this place.' He switched to Spanish. 'I have other duties.'

'I am sorry to hear it.'

Slonim gave one of his small smiles and chose a cheesy chess simile. 'We are pawns, you and I,' he said. 'But even as pawns we can show respect the one to the other. You have very good woman in Mexico. True operator.'

'Operative,' said Cotton. 'We've adopted the American word, operative.'

Slonim shrugged.

Cotton took off his right glove and offered his hand.

Slonim, Musin, Trapezoid and whatever other names the man had tugged briefly at it.

'Sir!' said Mullins.

Cotton turned. Mullins offered him a cigarette. Cotton shook his head.

'Smoke, comrade?'

Slonim raised his chin.

'To celebrate the peace, comrade,' said Mullins.

Slonim doubted. 'What are they?'

'Capstan Full Strength.'

Cotton held up a hand. 'No, they really are very strong.'

'No,' said Slonim. 'I'll try one.'

He did. His eyes widened and he had to stifle a cough. He nodded.

'I did say,' said Cotton.

Slonim shook his head. 'No,' he said and drew on the cigarette again. He frowned. 'Not . . . sweet,' he said.

'There is no obligation,' said Cotton. 'And this wind is freezing. Farewell, Colonel.'

'Farewell,' said Slonim. But he still had not had enough comradeship. He held up the cigarette and nodded. 'Good,' he said to Mullins.

'What was that about?' said Cotton as they walked away.

'Say Comrade and the Soviets always respond,' said Mullins. 'It's tripe. They still have ranks.'

Cotton grunted. 'Let's get out of here, shall we?'

On 13 November Moses Campbell received a note. In it Dr Aforey said his paper on Pan-Africa had been turned down by all the journals he had approached. 'I do not consider the cowardice to be mine,' he wrote. 'I am left

272

either with approaching those organs that would make use of my paper for their own ends and destroy my reputation, or with retiring the paper from perusal.'

He wrote back (as Moses) and suggested (again) that Dr Aforey consider the press. He also suggested that it was perfectly legitimate to give a brief account of what had happened in Manchester and to contribute some thoughts on other matters to consider in the struggle for freedom, emancipation and economic development.

'I can offer you only short shrift,' wrote Dr Aforey. 'I do not know how much you appreciate the extent to which a kind of code operates in academia. It can degenerate very quickly into sneer and smear, as exalted but closed minds spit odious words (those I will spare you) with the vigour of righteousness. It is not limited to Negroes. Consider the Sovietophiles in Ivy League universities who apparently consider the regime there as merely the New Deal with a gratifying degree of firmness. Those who doubt Stalin, take solace in Trotsky.'

Cotton lost patience. He wrote an article himself.

Recently, in Manchester, England, something remarkable took place. Although not much reported in the press, the fifth Pan-African Congress considered the future of British Colonies in Africa and the West Indies. A delegation of American Negroes, amongst whom was W. E. B. DuBois, also contributed.

It is fair to say that the viewpoint of the many delegates there was Marxist and that the aim of the Congress was to consider the possible forms of political and economic independence that have opened up post-war.

The fact is that the bell has tolled on the British Empire. As yet, it is not possible to say how long the process of dismantling British Imperialism will take. It is possible, however, to consider what will follow.

We talk of freedom but what will follow is a degree of independence. After many years of oppression, it is vital that the difference between freedom and independence is seen.

Freedom entails emancipation but, as our American friends point out, emancipation does not automatically lead to power. To be master of your own fate is as nothing if you are poor.

The Pan-African delegates favoured very heavily the industrialization of Africa.

In my only criticism of the valuable work done in Manchester, I should say that Africa must favour a flexible, self-reliant and modest approach, eschew grand plans but lay strong foundations, while populations are educated to face the uncertain challenges of the future.

Cotton was not sure he had Dr Aforey's tone but sent it to him 'to consider and change as you see fit'.

On 15 November he had dinner with Katherine. She had never made mention of the difficulties for IRIS in the State Department and did not do so now. She was cheerful, relaxed and affectionate. She asked Cotton about his taste in décor and he was stumped.

'I have to admit I have never thought about it.'

She laughed. 'Can·you cook?'

'Not very well.'

'Probably better than me. My mother says if you can read a recipe book you can cook.'

Towards the end of the meal she remembered something.

'Oh,' she said, 'you heard about that man? We met him when we were flying to your sister's. You called him Nemesis, a Soviet Nemesis.'

'Slonim?' said Cotton.

'Yes, that's it. Well, he met his. Poor man died.'

'What? What did he die of?'

'A heart attack, I think. Something like that.'

'When was this?'

'I don't know. A day or so ago? In Mexico City, just after he had arrived. The altitude, I suppose.'

Cotton looked at her. He knew the British claimed to have cried off murder as a weapon in times of peace, but did not know whether all or indeed any of the American agencies had.

'Keynes' plane had to fly low, didn't it, because of the strain on his heart,' she said.

'Yes.'

Cotton was quiet for a moment. While counting possibilities, a real heart attack, the Soviets themselves, various South-American government agencies and the Americans, what struck Cotton was that he had no idea of how much Katherine had known about Slonim.

'What are you thinking about?' she said.

He smiled and lit her cigarette. He suddenly remembered the cigarette Mullins had offered Slonim. Capstan Full Strength.

27

O N SATURDAY 17 November, Cissy Patterson's newspaper led with 'BRITONS CHARGE U.S. OVEREATS WHILE OTHERS STARVE'. The article had been written by the journalist Cotton had seen and whom he thought of as 'of the Hungarian Wolfes'.

He also saw the headline: '*88 Nazi scientists land under heavy guard in New York.*'

On 21 November, in the same paper, he read, '*President Truman's health plan, compulsory health insurance, ran into tremendous opposition in Congress yesterday. Also with other groups, including religious. "Another step into Socialism" says Cardinal.*'

It was no accident that on the third page was an article attacking the British government's policies: '*US to fund English Socialism.*'

Katherine Ward's parents had a 'holiday' house on the Severn River south-east of Washington. Early that same afternoon, she and Cotton drove down in her Chrysler Royal. The house, white, neoclassical colonial, a main block with two lower wings, was not as grand as Todd and Joan's on Long Island but was still of some size and came with more land. But it was, as Katherine said, 'hunkered down' in the landscape, sheltered by a belt of trees and with a pleasant view across the river.

Cotton liked her family. The welcome was not noisy and, within the formality and the circumstances, quite relaxed. Her father, Henry, was small, what Cotton's mother had called 'clean bald', and had kept himself very trim. His clothes were tailored or custom-made and expensive – 'just don't ever call him dapper,' said Katherine. He was wearing a jacket the colour of brown tweed but of a lighter material, and a yellow shirt. He had a moustache no thicker than an army bootlace and cheerfully offered a manicured hand.

Katherine's mother, Eleanor, was rather taller than her husband, looked a little distracted, probably from her habit of wearing her glasses halfway down her nose. She was from Wisconsin and had inherited a fair bit of money. He was a lawyer 'turning back to international trade'. Her younger sister, Barbara, took after her mother, was on a bigger, broader-shouldered scale than Katherine. Cotton also liked her. At dinner, he understood why. They weren't a family that competed amongst themselves for attention. The parents were genuinely interested in what their daughters were doing; the daughters were obviously fond of them.

Henry Ward showed Cotton round the house. He was happy to say he had bought it in 1932 'when cash was king, of course'. It had not before occurred to Cotton that his own father might have done similar. He knew that James Cotton had bought his Peaslake house 'outright' when on leave, but would never have said so.

The Wards' holiday house was traditional but, outside the formal rooms, comfortable. Cotton particularly liked the library. This wasn't all leather bindings that would creak if the books were disturbed. The books here had been read and the shelves were shelves rather than architectural bookcases.

'It's a little worn and torn,' said Henry Ward, exaggerating quite a bit. 'We use it as a family room. When I come here, it's where I like to be. Over there.'

He pointed at an area to one side of the fireplace. It contained a leather armchair, a writing table that swung round on one side and a small table with a reading lamp on the other.

'That's my Voltaire chair,' said Henry Ward. He looked around the room. 'You will take care of her, won't you?'

Cotton nodded. He had, of course, thought of marrying once before. But nobody had ever quite known where Emmeline's father had got to and her mother, who was far too self-involved to care very much, had given her blessing by telephone.

Cotton talked to Katherine later. She looked happy to be there and very happy everything was going smoothly.

'I suspect you are going to be grilled tomorrow.'

'On Thanksgiving Day?'

'They have someone to do that for them,' she mouthed.

'Who?'

'Wallace Chater.'

'All right.' Cotton smiled. Wallace Chater was her 'no-brooker'.

Cotton spent the night in a fairly girlie room in a single four-poster bed curtained with self-spotted white material. He didn't know if that was dimity or not. There were a number of books for a guest to choose from by authors that included Michael Arlen, Pearl Buck, Dorothy Parker and Axel Munthe. In the end he decided not to read, got into bed and thought. After a while he was impressed by how quiet the house was.

There were several guests for Thanksgiving. Wallace Chater came with his daughter, an unmarried lady of about forty called Dorothy, and one of Henry Ward's partners; the Simon in the legal firm of Ward, Simon and Lowell, came with his wife, Rose, fifteen-year-old son Herbert and ten-year-old daughter, Elspeth.

After Thanksgiving dinner, Wallace Chater asked if he could 'borrow this charming young fellow'. He and Cotton went through to the library and Chater sat in the Voltaire chair and asked for a brandy.

Cotton poured him his drink.

'You won't join me?'

'No,' said Cotton. 'I don't drink very much.'

'I approve,' said Wallace Chater. 'That's a good thing in a young man.' He inhaled and supped. He lit a cigar.

'Nothing like a Cuban,' he said. 'This is a Romeo and Juliet. This is what Winston smokes, right? Or maybe that's Montecristo.' He paused and looked directly at Cotton. 'Shall we get to it? You're a man of the world, Colonel, so I am going to speak . . . plainly.'

Cotton nodded. Wallace Chater's hair, not much and entirely white, was centre-parted. He looked puffy and pale and one of his eyes was clouded, while the other, still blue, had one of the smallest pupils he had ever seen. He thought he might get some folksy talk but waited to see how plain he'd be.

'I am pretty sure you'll have seen how much Katherine's

parents take care of their daughters. You yourself have par-taken of their very generous hospitality.'

'Yes, I have.'

Chater was not listening. 'Now I am not saying they are anxious exactly but I think we might use a word like uncertain. Not about you, you understand. They have great faith and trust in Katherine's judgement. But let's say there are circumstances they want to see clarified. I am sure you know what I'm driving at.'

'Yes,' said Cotton. 'Like many others, I am still doing my national service and I have not been released from that. I don't know when that will be and until that time . . .'

'Yes, yes. But what about after your service, Peter? Have you fixed anything up yet?'

'No, sir. I've had a couple of suggestions but I have made no decision on them.'

'I have your word on that? As a gentleman?'

Cotton blinked.

'Come now, Colonel. That girl means a lot to me. That's why I've helped her career along. You just consider how much more she means to her parents.'

'The only doubt I've had, Mr Chater, is whether she'd have me or not. Is that clear enough?'

The old man smiled and blew out smoke. 'As it should be, as it should be. She's no fool.'

'Indeed not.'

The old man nodded. 'Am I right in saying you have a darling sister in the US?'

'Yes, I do. She's married to an American and they have three children.'

'Yes, Todd. I know of Todd. He has been helping out in Washington recently. His dear late father I knew more.

Good banking family. Mm? You studied economics at Oxford, I believe?'

'At Cambridge, yes.'

The old man smiled. 'Let's not beat about the bush, Colonel. You could have prospects in this country. How are you on loyalty to your great nation?'

Cotton contrived a smile. 'I have,' he said, 'discharged my duties loyally during the war and will continue to do so until the day I am decommissioned. But since I have been here my priorities have changed. I've met Katherine and, if she is agreeable, our possible joint future has changed my way of thinking about my own professional future. There has never been any suggestion that she should give up her career and move to Britain. I would never ask her to do that.'

'You'd come here. To New York, say.'

'I've talked a little to Todd. Of course, there are visas and . . .'

Wallace Chater waved his cigar hand at any difficulties. Some ash fell off.

'Colonel, this is a wonderful country. It has untold possibilities. Katherine is a lovely girl and she'd give you good children, I have no doubt.' The old man puffed at his cigar. 'Couple of days ago I sat in on a meeting. Government wants women to go back home, have children, bring them up.' He sighed. 'I get too sentimental, I guess. But I know my old friends would love some grandchildren. Nothing wrong with being a clever mother.'

'My only problem would be my father. He's been at something of a loss since my mother died seven years ago.'

Wallace Chater shook his head. 'Oh, I know how he feels. Lost my own wife, you see. Awful thing, you know.

But you have your sister, don't you? And now the war is over
. . . well, a man who spent his professional life in Mexico
would want to be with his family in his declining years. I'm
only guessing, of course. But I do tend to get sentimental.
Especially after this excellent brandy.'

Cotton got him some more.

'Thank you. You have another problem, though.'

'What's that?'

'Your own country. I'm a patriot, Colonel, and I hate the
notion of turning a man against his own birthright. But we
are a nation of immigrants. Can I speak frankly?'

'Certainly.'

'Your working class are like our Negroes, except they
are in the majority. What just happened? They voted
themselves into socialism.' He shrugged. 'Great Britain is
finished bar a posture or two and a crisp salute. You've
overstepped yourselves. That won't happen here. Why?
Because if you are poor you can make it and people will
always want to emulate you. They won't sneer at you out of
self-pity. They'll want to be like you. And the Negroes have
that open to them. Difficult? You bet. But that's the forge of
strong men who will contribute positively to the nation.
That may take time, of course, but the Negroes have the
chance to earn their place in this country and, if they have
good leaders, they will, they'll do it.'

The old man mused for a while. He was enjoying his
cigar. He smiled.

'Well, I think I have spoken plainly enough,' he said.
'Now, if you'll permit me, I'll be honest.' Cotton had to
wait for an uncomfortable second or two and another puff
of smoke before he learned what Wallace Chater meant by
the word honest. 'The fact is, Katherine thinks she is at a

crossroads.' He waved a hand. 'This job of hers? It's worse than a dead end. She's on the losing side.' He nodded. 'Show her you love her – get her out of it.'

There were games, what Barbara called 'fun stuff', and there was more to eat, Mrs Ward played the piano, very well, and it was late before Cotton and Katherine talked.

'What a darling, absolutely poisonous old man,' he said.

'Oh, you don't know the half of it. Old sweetie had his wife committed. So sad. His daughter is quite cute but definitely nervous about precedent.'

'Why do your parents love him?'

'Daddy's law firm handles some of his affairs.'

'Yes, the practicalities of love.'

She smiled. 'Are you surviving?'

'Of course. And you haven't met my father yet.'

She laughed. 'Is that a problem?'

'He is a little monothematic. On my mother.'

'Right. What did Wallace say? Without the folksy flourishes.'

'Let's see. I should jump nation and get a job in banking. You should lie back and have clever grandchildren, preferably near Park Avenue.'

'That sounds like Wallace. Did you get a threat?'

'Perhaps I missed that. I certainly can't recall one.'

'Then he definitely liked you, enough to think he could do something with you.'

Cotton thought about that. 'I don't think he can quite remember what liking is. In England there is a thing called golden syrup. It comes in a tin. I think he keeps his sentiment in something similar. The tin is quite difficult to get open and the contents are very sticky.'

'My mother says he drops cigar ash everywhere.'

'Yes, he does. Syrup and ash, that's about the combination.'

Whatever Wallace Chater had said, Katherine's parents were delighted. The next morning Katherine's father invited Cotton into the library. Cotton expected a fatherly chat but Henry Ward proved to be timid.

There were magazines on a table. A new *Saturday Evening Post* had a cover called 'Home for Thanksgiving'. It portrayed a dark, rather old trooper, his knees up and his loafer shoes on the higher of two rungs of a rush-seated chair, peeling, without much confidence, what was probably a potato. His greying mother discreetly but proudly considers him. To one side of her on the wide-planked floor is a large, ripe pumpkin and behind them red gingham, cooking utensils, vegetables and fruit.

Henry Ward smiled. 'Do you know Norman Rockwell's work, Peter?'

'No, I don't.'

'Rubicund nostalgia,' he said. He shook his head. 'I shouldn't be unfair. He was a good part of keeping up morale. His *Freedom from Want* in '43 is something of a classic. You know, Mom at the head of a long, happy family table at Thanksgiving, the table just groaning with food.'

Cotton smiled dutifully. Then he realized Henry Ward was in some way apologizing for popular American culture.

28

ON THEIR way back to Washington DC on the Sunday after Thanksgiving she took a detour and stopped at a motel. It was a little after 10 a.m.

'I urgently need some relief,' she said.

'Tawdry, I'm sure, but wonderful,' she opined later. She then got out of bed and walked about naked. 'I need some freedom. And some more when you're ready.'

He laughed.

'Would you really marry me?' she said.

'Haven't I just spent the weekend being examined on that?'

'I meant privately,' she said, 'away from all those people.'

He nodded, knew what she meant by 'privately'. 'Would you marry me?' he asked.

'Yes,' she said. She smiled.

Cotton smiled back. He suddenly felt not so much a pang, more a twinge, but physical and quite painful, on the right side of his head above the eye, and somehow instantly felt that something was wrong, but it was not in him.

But then she said, 'How would you like me?' She was trying awfully hard to be needed. 'Who is it who normally kneels on these occasions?' she asked. 'Let's not be so traditional.'

'You're suggesting we both kneel? OK.'

*

They ate lunch about one and were on the road by two.

'I have a problem,' she said.

'Tell me.'

She smiled. 'It's not that easy.'

'All right. Take your time.'

'I had thought, well, that I had gotten away from teaching and nursing. Do you know what I mean?'

'Traditional areas of concern for well-brought-up young ladies? The Spanish call them the "Marias", the Mary subjects.'

'Yes.'

'And you haven't. Not yet anyway.'

Evidently that surprised her. 'Not yet?'

'No. It's not entirely to do with your being a young female. I was part of the British Economic Warfare Unit. It no longer exists. Worse, I suspect it has disappeared. My old boss is fuming somewhere. And now I get to kick around as a dogsbody.'

'It's not the same.'

They drove on for a while. It was a grey day. The leaves beneath the trees had turned black and clumps of grass had become brown, straw and white-bleached where they had been frostbitten.

'Hoover has Negro blood ,' she said.

'Mm, I've heard something like that,' said Cotton.

'What do you mean?'

'Well, if he does, he isn't going to admit to it or advertise it. Quite sensibly, I'd have thought.'

'But don't you see? He's lying.'

Cotton blinked. 'Come on, that's almost British. "It's not, your Honour, that the defendant has Negro blood, it's because he lied about it".'

'Don't you see what dynamite this is? We can stop him.'

Cotton frowned. He didn't understand. 'By saying he is part Negro? That's the same as calling his male assistant Ma Tolson. These things are said not because they are true but because people resent his power.'

'He abuses it.'

'The point is he has got it.'

'You don't understand how much we have.'

Though Cotton had read the British files on Hoover, he nodded. 'Tell me then.'

'What kind of a man only produces a birth certificate at the age of forty-three in 1938?'

Cotton was beginning to get irritated. 'The kind of man whose much-loved mother had died the year before.'

'I don't follow,' she said flatly.

'He could easily have been protecting his mother's reputation. We know that his father died of what they called melancholia in those days – he'd been institutionalized for years. We know his brothers are at least fifteen years older than he is. What if his adored mother had slipped from the path of abstinence? I even read he could have been adopted.'

'We know that FBI agents visited Mississippi and looked at Hoover family birth records.'

'And what does that tell you?'

'That his family were originally from Pike County.'

Cotton smiled. 'Which is where, exactly?'

'Right at the south of Mississippi bordering on Louisiana.'

'So his family are from the South. My brother-in-law Todd's mother's family was from Georgia. But Hoover was born in Washington DC, wasn't he? Or is that in doubt?'

'No,' she said. She sounded disappointed, low.

287

'There was a nineteenth-century novel called *Lady Audley's Secret*. I read it in the Highlands of Scotland one Sunday because it was raining and there was nothing much else to do. I think Trollope called it the best shocker plot he had ever read but it remains that the Lady in question goes around murdering people because she imagines they are about to find out her secret. Her secret is that her mother was mad, but probably not as mad as she is. You can call that very clunking irony or you can quote Chesterton on Dickens, "the telling is sensational, the secret tame". Tibbets once asked if Hoover was one of the vacuum-cleaner family.'

Katherine didn't say anything.

'It's absurd,' said Cotton. 'You can't suggest Hoover has not married and had children in case they turned out black and revealed the awful secret.'

'You just don't get it, do you?' she said.

'There is one person who can sack Hoover and he can really only sack him for messing up, for failing in his job, not for some bloodline. Yes, I've heard Truman wanted to sack him but, well, he somehow decided against. That's because Truman has his priorities and Hoover has his uses. And Hoover has his own back covered.'

'He didn't cover my back,' she said.

He had never heard that tone from her before. It was flat, almost mild, as if she were saying 'these things happen' but Cotton instantly grasped that he had taken far too long to understand she was angry, then how angry, let-down and betrayed she felt.

'I had my apartment burgled and trashed, men urinated on my clothes, placed a bug behind my bed! A fragile friend ended up shooting himself because maybe he received a little too much pressure, maybe a threat or two of exposure and disgrace. And what for? A warning? As intimidation? Humiliation? To what end? These are *my* people, *my* side and they treat me like the enemy.'

'Look,' said Cotton. 'I agree. I do.'

She glanced at him. The glance contained despair, pride and belief.

'I'm sorry,' he said.

She shook her head. 'It doesn't matter.'

'Oh come on,' he said, 'it obviously does.'

She shook her head again. 'I don't want to talk about it.'

'Listen . . .'

'I mean it.'

She dropped him at P Street.

'Thank you for . . .'

'It's OK,' she said. 'It is. I just need a little time.' She even gave him a little smile.

He went upstairs to his room. It took him a long time to write her a letter.

> My apologies. I made a mess of that. I'll make the excuse that I was thoughtless because I was happy. We'd done Thanksgiving, we'd been talking marriage, I thought we were relaxed and honest, was happy for that because that is what I would like in a life with you in the US. But perhaps we should have tackled the hard things more directly. Of course I will do that and I won't do it with preconceptions or a particular line to push.
>
> Think about it and we'll talk later.

Cotton was not convinced he had the tone right but he wanted to get something to her. He signed the letter and posted it.

Afterwards, he went to his usual restaurant and ate some veal. It tasted a little metallic but he was not sure that was not his mouth rather than the meat and a squeeze of lemon juice.

29

ON MONDAY the 26th he telephoned her. Miss Ward was 'not at her desk'. He left a message and his number. She did not call. In the evening he telephoned her at home. Nobody was in.

By 27 November Cotton was in a mood to notice an article in Cissy Patterson's Washington paper, syndicated from the *Chicago Tribune*.

Smitten Kitten Act Not Good, Girls Warned.

Why, anyone will admit that love is lovely but it happens to nine out of ten girls, and they get over it – so take it easy, sister!

He may be everything you ever imagined in brain and brawn, a Van Johnson, but just be sure he IS for you, before you start telling the other guys and gals all about it.

'Who's Van Johnson?' asked Cotton.
'Actor fellow,' said Jim Gowar. 'Next-door nice, rather wet?'

Cotton called Katherine at work. This time she was 'in a meeting'. That evening, before going out to another reception, he called her at home. This time he got Didi Johnson.

'Hello Didi, I didn't know you were back.'

'Katherine asked me.'

'Right. I'd like to speak to her if I could.'

'Oh Peter, she needs a couple of days I think.'

'I don't really know what is going on.'

'I am not too sure myself. But she is pretty cut up.'

'Tell her I am sorry. I sent her a letter.'

There was a pause. 'I wouldn't know about that. Really.'

'Thanks. How are you and Joe?'

'Well, Joe's Joe, you know.'

'Right. Could you . . .?'

'I will,' said Didi and put down the telephone.

Cotton had no idea what to do. He considered another letter. In the end he sent her some flowers.

The 28th was no better.

On the evening of the 29th somebody knocked on his door in P Street.

'I say, old boy,' said Tibbets. 'I hope you don't mind. But Katherine, Katherine Ward has contacted me.'

'What about?'

'Well, I am not entirely sure,' said Tibbets. 'She sounded quite cheerful. Thought she and I should meet up.'

Cotton paused. Then nodded. 'All right.'

Tibbets squinted at him. ''You don't mind?'

'Do you know what she wants to talk about?'

'No.'

'So how can I mind?'

Tibbets frowned. 'Right,' he said.

Cotton tried to consider. Did this mean she was going to use Tibbets as a go-between? Tibbets, the fine mathematician? Cotton could not understand it. No, he loathed the idea. And if she were trying to make him jealous? Cotton groaned.

'Fuck,' he said.

Cotton had some help getting through the days because he had been dogsbodied into all the frenetic, sometimes farcical activity spilling out from Keynes' negotiations.

The problems were not Anglo-American so much as British: those in Washington exasperated by the government and Treasury in London, those in London indignant and disappointed with the British negotiators in Washington.

On 30 November the Mission rebelled against its revised instructions from London. On 1 December Edward Bridges arrived to take over from Keynes, to find the Mission had not, like the government, lost confidence in Keynes and was refusing to co-operate with the changeover.

On Sunday 2 December Fred Vinson understood what was happening and helped calm the British down. Bridges stepped amiably aside but the Mission was obliged to present the proposal from London.

The Americans brushed the proposal aside as quite unrealistic. London immediately capitulated and went back to the Keynsian deal, $3.75 billion of what was termed 'new money' and $650 billion to settle lend-lease.

On 4 December Cotton was at the Willard Hotel as the delegates waited for a telegram from Prime Minister Attlee. There was very little to do. Cotton read a newspaper report that the entire State Department was to be subject to a probe – it was 'honeycombed with communists'. Cotton was struck by the word 'honeycombed' instead of 'riddled' or even 'infected'. It seemed a very sweet word. In the event Mr Attlee did not send his telegram and many people, including President Truman, were told they could go to bed about 3 a.m.

The Anglo-American agreement was finally signed on 6 December. At the reception in the British Embassy to celebrate the signing Ayrtoun approached Cotton directly.

'Where the fuck is Tibbets?'

'I saw him last two days ago, in the morning. He asked me if I had any tie cleaner.'

Keynes and Lydia called in to take their leave of President Truman on the 7th and took a train to New York. The atmosphere in British Washington went flat.

Ayrtoun called Cotton in.

'What will happen now that we are getting some money?'

'I suppose we'll spend it,' Cotton said. 'It will all be gone within a year, maybe less.'

'And then?'

'More austerity, more rationing,' said Cotton.

'Jesus,' said Ayrtoun. 'Have you seen Tibbets yet?'

Cotton shook his head.

'Tibbets can't do this,' said Ayrtoun. 'He can't go AWOL. Not with what he has seen. Do you understand me?'

'I understand. But I have not seen him or had any communication from him.'

'Shit,' said Ayrtoun. 'I can't let this go. We have to find him. I have to tell the Americans.'

'Right.'

'He wouldn't have gone to the Soviets, would he?'

'I don't think so.'

'Right, I don't think so either. But then what the hell is he doing?'

*

Cotton telephoned Katherine's apartment. There was no answer. He called her at the State Department. There was a clumsy kerfuffle before a click and an enquiry as to who was calling.

Cotton went to see Wallace Chater. He worked out of a small room off a rather grand affair, presumably for receiving important people, more like a drawing room with a desk that was too polished to be much used.

'Peter,' said the old man, 'I'm flattered but I am pretty busy, you know.'

Cotton got directly to the point. 'I don't know where Katherine is.'

'You're the jealous kind,' said Wallace Chater.

'What?' Cotton realized this was some kind of pleasantry. 'No, you misunderstand me. I don't even know who knows where she is.'

Wallace Chater shed his good humour instantly. 'She's in trouble?'

'She very well could be.'

'Wait outside.'

Cotton got up and went into the grand room. He looked out of the window. The Washington light had the look of grey ricepaper. After about ten minutes Walter Chater came out of his room.

'What the hell is going on?'

'That's why I came to you,' said Cotton.

'She hasn't been seen at the State Department for some days. What did she say to you?'

'She told me that Hoover had black blood.'

'What's that got to do with anything real?' Chater stared in disbelief.

'Her apartment was burgled, listening devices had to be removed, Brian Kirkland . . .'

'Yes, I heard about that. Terrible thing.'

'Brian may have been threatened, Mr Chater, by the FBI. In the State Department, well, you know how things have gone.'

'I told you,' said Wallace Chater. 'I told you to get her out of there.'

Cotton didn't bother to reply. 'She couldn't be with her parents?'

'They're travelling.'

'Well?' said Cotton. 'Couldn't she have joined them?'

Wallace Chater thought, then shook his head. 'I spoke to them yesterday. They assumed she was with you.'

'I can't be absolutely sure there is a link but we have someone missing too. A man called Tibbets. He usually works out of Arlington Hall.'

'What are you saying? These two . . .'

'I don't know. I wouldn't call him very strong-minded.'

Wallace Chater stared at him. 'Arlington Hall?'

'Yes.'

Wallace Chater started moving. 'Give me your details,' he said. 'I'll start working my connections and get back to you.'

Cotton wrote down his address and telephone number and his office number. Wallace Chater took the paper they were on.

'I'm disappointed in you,' he said.

Cotton shrugged. 'I didn't help get her a job,' he said and started walking out.

He did not think his last remark had been wise but late in the afternoon he called Wallace Chater's office. Mr

Chater's personal assistant told him that Mr Chater had already left for the weekend. If Wallace Chater had found out what was going on he had not thought it worthwhile to tell Cotton.

Cotton rarely drank but after the usual tedious reception in an embassy he bought some whisky in a packet store.

30

I N T H E late afternoon of Sunday 9 December snow began
to fall. Washington wind joined in. The stuff came as
flurries, hit the window with a mix of stick and click.
Cotton watched a snowflake become a crystal, all sym-
metry within irregularity. The thing was fuzzy with cling.
Behind the rapid flicker, in the street below, the fallen snow
had begun to mount up but the wind was pushing through
it, diminishing the flakes into specks and whittling uneven
paths of its own. Cotton put a fingertip against the glass.
The pane felt cold, then warm, and a flake melted and slid
about an inch before turning to ice. Cotton drew the
shades.

At eight he received a telephone call from Ayrtoun.

'Is Tibbets there yet?'

Cotton already knew he wasn't, but walked through the
bathroom and looked in. Back on the telephone again, he
said, 'No.'

'Have him call me when he gets in. It doesn't matter what
the time is.'

'Right.'

Cotton made himself some supper. He cut up a tomato,
ground some black pepper on to it and laid it inside an
omelette. He had a cup of coffee and washed up his supper
things.

At nine he caught the news on the radio. It was mostly

about the storm that had hit the East Coast. All airfields were shut down. In another item it was reported that General Patton had been gravely injured in an automobile accident near Mannheim in Germany. He was paralysed from the neck down. Cotton knew little of Patton, had only the British impression of someone strong-willed and loud-mouthed and the soldier's suspicion of squabbling, self-publicizing generals on both sides. He noted however that Patton was not the lead item. He doubted that any weather would have taken precedence over Montgomery in Britain.

Cotton turned off the radio and started reading Dr Aforey's notes, pencil-written in the margins of a book he had sent him. He had written some remarks on witchcraft as a 'closed system of beliefs', something that both explained and contained cause and effect. He had placed a large asterisk by a demure, almost diffident, allusion to mankind's craving for stability and explanation – that could be witnessed in societies far away from the Azande people of North-East Congo and South-West Sudan.

Cotton dozed off. He could see a man standing on one leg in a shallow river being joined by a stork. The stork flew in and imitated the man. That woke him. Surely it was the other way round? It is difficult for a man to stand motionless on one leg. The man held a spear and a net, the stork had a beak and soft under-neck, like a pre-digestive hammock. Cotton blinked and groaned. He realized he had translated a film seen at school on a tribe in the Amazon, to a never-seen Africa.

He felt stiff. He had been sweating. Cotton got up and felt the heating pipes. They were very hot. He drank some water. He parted the drapes and looked out. The snow was not so much falling as rushing by the window. The window rattled sometimes but the snow was muffling the sound of the wind.

Around ten thirty he undressed, brushed his teeth and hair and got into bed. He was, in a dull way, surprised that he should feel so tired but almost immediately fell asleep.

He was woken by someone banging on the door. At first he was so fuddled he looked at the window, as if the storm might have got worse; he did not know where the noise was coming from. He reached for the light switch by the bed. Whoever it was thumped on the door again.

'Yes!' said Cotton. He rubbed at his eyes. He got out of bed and went to the door. 'Who the hell is it?'

'Mullins, sir.'

Cotton blinked. 'Right,' he said, and opened the door. 'What is it?' Something occurred to him. 'Your baby?'

'No, sir,' said Mullins. 'Mr Ayrtoun requests that you dress and come with me, sir. It's very urgent.'

Mullins was dressed in an overcoat and had taken off his hat. Cotton breathed in the chill from him. He shivered. He shook his head to get rid of the sleep.

'Do you know what this is about?'

Mullins shook his head.

'Right,' he said. 'Come in.'

'No, sir. I'll only wet the floor.'

The snow on Mullins' boots was almost melted.

Cotton turned and started getting dressed.

'How cold is it out there?'

'Well, sir, it has stopped snowing for the moment.'

Cotton felt foolish. Of course it was cold out there. He pulled on thick socks, heavy trousers, his boots, put on a pullover over his shirt and a jacket over that, then a scarf and an overcoat. He jammed on a hat and started putting on his gloves.

'All right.'

He and Mullins went down the stairs and outside. The street was deserted, the snow unmarked except for Mullins' steps coming in. When they walked it made a soft stuttering sound as the flakes compacted under their weight. The snow came up to their shins. Mullins had driven there in the Humber Super Snipe they had used to rescue Mrs Ayrtoun from the Flying Boat. He had left the engine running. They got in and shut the doors. Mullins shifted gear and pressed gently down on the accelerator. There was a little wheelspin and then the car began trundling forward at no more than four or five miles an hour. Instinctively, Cotton looked over at Mullins.

'It's urgent, sir.'

Cotton nodded.

At the first junction Mullins turned down into Wisconsin Avenue. The Humber was large and heavy. The noise of the snow changed from a soft, crumpling sound to something more like a groan but once he had managed the turn, Mullins shifted gear and they were soon up to twenty-five miles an hour.

'Candy, sir?' asked Mullins. 'Butterscotch. In the glove box, sir. Not for me.'

Cotton unwrapped the sweet and put it in his mouth. He felt he was in a travelling waiting room. A very chilly one.

'I may have to ask you to rub the windscreen, sir,' said Mullins.

'Just say when.'

Cotton looked out ahead, but kept an eye on the

misting-up of the windscreen. Mullins turned again when they came to M Street. He changed down with at least a couple of hundred yards to go, then again till they were creeping along. A streetlamp by the corner was buzzing and flickering. Cotton used his sleeve to rub at the windscreen.

'Thank you, sir. Anything?'

Cotton looked out on his side. There was no other traffic.

'No.'

Mullins turned towards the Potomac River. This was not what Cotton recognized as any route to the Embassy. Mullins picked up speed again and then they went through the same routines again as they turned north again to get on to Canal Road.

The longer the drive lasted, the more difficult it became for Cotton to remain calm. Was he like his father? Anxious for things to be settled? He knew he was getting nervous when it occurred to him that the drive might concern him or his behaviour. But what was he? Some kind of Slonim, living in a world of ghoulish banishments and secret police?

'Wipe, sir?'

'Sorry.' He leaned forward and rubbed again. As he did so he became aware that their surroundings were no longer lit or urban. There were bare trees to one side. The headlights picked out a black locust tree that had fallen against a sycamore. He then saw that the road ahead was not unmarked snow. There were a number of tyre tracks. And almost immediately afterwards, he picked up that on the other side of the wall ahead of them to their left was another sort of white below them, slightly greyer. It was ice on the C & O Canal.

Mullins changed down.

'It's icing up under the snow,' he said. 'And the ridges are. . .'

Mullins had to work more now. He kept in second. A wheel would hit a patch of ice and he'd have to adjust. The Humber, a stately vehicle designed for officialdom and senior managers, wobbled and started to slide. Mullins worked the clutch and steered with the skid to avoid locking up. Despite the cold, Cotton found he was sweating into his scarf.

'Eyes peeled, sir.'

'What am I looking for?'

'Don't rightly know, sir.'

Cotton peered ahead. Then faintly, about two hundred yards ahead, he could make out a cluster of low-level lights. Almost immediately someone with a torch stepped out into the road and flashed a torch at them. A policeman in a cape approached.

'Gentlemen, you should turn back.'

Mullins showed him his identity.

'You'll have to walk, gentlemen. We have to keep the road clear.'

Mullins followed the policeman's parking instructions and they got out.

The air was extraordinarily cold. It was very dark. The policeman's torch lit up the snow on the ground and on the trees as he swung round towards them.

'Have you light, gentlemen?'

'No,' said Mullins.

'Then just aim for the glow ahead.'

Cotton and Mullins began crunching their way forward. Mullins began breathing quite heavily quite soon.

'Is this Gina's due date?' asked Cotton.

'Imprecise, sir. Sorry I didn't bring a light.'

Cotton shook his head. He was not accustomed to apprehension. It was his habit to wait. But here he was frightened of his own stupidity. Ignorance is one thing, a failure to see something worse. But the cold overtook his sense of apprehension. And the snow was beginning to fall again.

The road dipped a little, not much but enough, he thought, to have caused the Humber problems in this weather if it had come as far. Ahead of them, four or five vehicles had their headlights on and he could see blurred shapes moving around. In the headlights were sections of exhaust rising against the falling snow. And then, like a silhouette, like those charts for identifying enemy aircraft in outline, he was presented with a puzzle. It took him five steps to pick out a tow truck with a crane attached. Hooked to it, front wheels raised, was a black Chrysler Royal with the front screen punched out.

'Where's the fucking ambulance?' someone said.

Cotton looked around.

'Yeah,' someone was saying. 'The back just went. They just slid backwards into the canal.'

'What did they die of?'

'How would I know?'

'You mean they drowned?'

'You can't survive that kind of cold. You go into shock pretty damned quick. You've got ten feet of water there.'

Cotton felt a heavy thump on his back. He turned. Ayrtoun, wearing some sort of deerstalker hat with the ear flaps down, was squinting and grimacing at him. He was carrying a torch.

'Come with me.'

Cotton followed him behind a Chevrolet. On ground-sheets were two vaguely human shapes covered by blankets that were already gathering snow. Ayrtoun beckoned Cotton and lifted back one of the blankets.

Tibbets had his mouth open. Whether it was the light from the torch or not, his skin had a pale grey-blue colour.

Cotton nodded. Ayrtoun indicated he lift the other blanket himself. Cotton did. Her hair was flat and wet. Her head was to one side. Cotton saw that the snow falling on her face did not melt at once. He brushed it off gently and covered her again.

'Hey! That's the ambulance!' someone shouted. Cotton turned. He thought he was about to go into shock and start trembling uncontrollably. He took a deep breath and then held it. Without siren but with red light flashing, the ambulance was creeping closer.

Ayrtoun gripped his arm.

'They were pulled out dead. You see me later this morning. Mullins will bring you. If you need him he'll stay with you until then.'

Cotton nodded. He did not want more instructions and began walking away back the way he had come.

There were practicalities. It took Mullins an age to turn the Humber round, so long the ambulance had already crept past on its return journey. The snow was getting far worse, was being blown in almost horizontal gusts from the Potomac.

When they finally got going, Mullins asked for a butterscotch. Cotton gave him the sweet without comment. He had to rub the face of his watch to see what time it was. It was just after 4.30 a.m. He wondered where the time had gone but didn't really care.

They took an hour to get back to the bunkhouse on P Street. Mullins came upstairs with him.

'Do you mind if I make a call, sir?'

'Of course not. Coffee?'

'Sir.'

Cotton made coffee while Mullins telephoned Gina.

'She's uncomfortable,' he said.

'Labour?'

'I don't know, sir.'

'Go.'

'I've been told to stay, sir.'

'It's that – or I can go with you. Or,' he added, 'we can be sensible. I can stay – and you can go. I don't think you need me now and I have enough to think about until I see Mr Ayrtoun.'

'Are you sure?'

'Yes, I am. Thanks. Go on. Good luck.'

Mullins paused, then shot off.

Cotton closed the door after him and went to the bathroom. The door through to Tibbets' room had been locked. He went out again and tried the corridor door to Tibbets' room. That too was already locked.

He went back to the bathroom and started running the bath. He undressed and got into the warm water. He soaked until he could feel his toes again, put his head under the water, then got out, dried off, combed his hair and shaved in a mirror that kept misting over.

Cotton then dressed as for the office and made himself some fresh coffee. After a while he thought he should eat something. He was at the very beginnings of alarming himself that he was not reacting. He did not think he was in shock. He was not trembling. He was not nauseous. His throat felt dry, though, and his chest was a little tight. And he realized he did not want to sit down.

He squeezed the bridge of his nose and shut his eyes. He tried to imagine her Chrysler Royal skidding in the way he had heard, slipping backwards into the canal. He did think the skid could not have been that slow or they might have been able to get out. He wasn't sure if what the Americans called the trunk and the British the boot could have provided some moments of buoyancy. Perhaps it had luggage in it – or water had poured in very quickly.

He started walking up and down. He was aware that he wasn't imagining the deaths, wasn't wondering at the shock, panic and struggle as they fought to get out of a vehicle sinking into ice-topped water.

Cotton had read somewhere – Robert Louis Stevenson? – the description of a young man being 'parsimonious of pain'. He even smiled slightly. He did not think that was the case. What he couldn't do was grasp what had happened. He could not get purchase on it. He was sliding off it.

Behind this, he had to be aware this was a version of self-protection. He was also, even more faintly, aware of a highly chilled version of anger, but he wasn't even sure that it was his own anger. He shook his head, breathed in and made himself sit down.

At this stage he was looking not for answers: a good question would have done. What were they doing in the car together? Where had they come from? Where were they going?

The questions came and went because they were not right. He tried again. Tibbets had worked out of Arlington mostly. Katherine had worked for IRIS in the State Department, beside the White House. The weekend had just ended. They might have been away together. He considered this. He checked himself for jealousy.

She might have moved on from him to Tibbets. He didn't quite believe it and distrusted himself. But was he allowing his judgement of Tibbets to brush it off?

31

A T EIGHT o'clock Cotton was in the Chancery. He went directly to Ayrtoun's office.

'No self-importance, no self-pity,' snapped Ayrtoun. 'Clear?'

Cotton nodded.

'There'll be a single, not a joint, statement.' said Ayrtoun. 'From the Americans, of course. It has been approved by her family's representative.'

'Wallace Chater?'

Ayrtoun ignored the name. 'It will suggest that Miss Ward was kind enough to offer a lift to an allied worker, Tibbets, from Arlington Hall. Because of the appalling weather, you see. He thought it only fitting to provide company and possible assistance to a lone female in such adverse climatic conditions. Unfortunately, etc.'

Cotton raised his eyebrows.

'She gets distinguished family and dazzling future cut off, he gets the boffin treatment.'

'What?'

'The mathematical wizard stuff. Halfway to other-worldly harmonies even in this life.'

Cotton breathed in. 'What were they doing?'

'That's not your concern.'

Cotton shut his eyes. Spanish has the expression *vergüenza ajena*, shame or embarrassment for someone else because they are behaving badly or stupidly. The degree of sympathy varies. Cotton heard his own lips come apart with a popping sound. He did not know if he was thinking of Katherine or Ayrtoun or even himself.

They can't, he thought, really have been doing ground research on J. Edgar Hoover's bloodline. Can they? Ayrtoun was playing the blunt, buffeting part. Cotton had little idea of what he himself was doing.

'What else was in the car?' he asked.

'Apart from their bags? I have absolutely no idea.'

'Do you think they found anything?'

Ayrtoun gave Cotton to understand, a kind of groan but only in the face, that he was being indulged. 'It's of no importance if they did,' he said.

'Nobody is going to investigate?'

'Don't embarrass yourself,' said Ayrtoun. 'I didn't say that. I said *you* weren't going to investigate.'

Cotton nodded. 'Who is?'

Ayrtoun cleared his throat. 'You have three choices,' he said.

Cotton frowned. 'Like the three-card trick? Find the lady?'

'It's as you wish,' said Ayrtoun. 'One – it was an accident. Two – it wasn't. Third, it was a suicide pact.'

'Suicide?' said Cotton.

'It's a possibility. I didn't say it was probable. If it was an accident, you get to be very sorry. If it wasn't, you can't do anything about it.'

Cotton looked up.

'There are all kinds of humiliations when you lack power. You just have to accept them – chew your heart in your own time.'

Cotton said nothing. From somewhere he remembered Blinker Hall from the First World War, removing a heart and handing it back when he had chewed on it. Ayrtoun insisted. 'You have no means of redress. To be clear. Try anything and I will have you stopped. To help you . . . well, I imagine you want to get away home for Christmas.'

Cotton could not have spoken even if he had wanted to. The grip in his chest had become so strong that he could barely breathe. He got some air down his nose.

'We've got you on a flight later this week. Friday. From New York.'

Cotton realized he was shaking. Ayrtoun tapped on his cigarette tin to get his attention.

'If I were you, I'd accept accident. Accidents happen, particularly to the overwrought and the preoccupied. I don't know if she let her patriotism get the better of her; I do know she is dead and that there are more important matters. Now I am going to tell you things you shouldn't really know. With me?'

Cotton did not think he was but nodded.

'We need an American partner. I've chosen the FBI. *I* have. We are not excluding the other agencies by any means but the FBI is the nearest the Yanks have to a civil service. It's unelected, conservative and consistent. We know who and what we're dealing with. In addition we are closely involved with them on . . . large Soviet business. I can't tell you about it but I can tell you we can provide something they need. It's not a formal alliance but it is as good as we'll get.'

'Is the Soviet business what Tibbets was working on?'

Ayrtoun chose his words. 'Let's say he was privy to privileged information that made his going missing a matter of considerable concern,' he said. 'Did he say anything to you?'

'No. Tibbets never spoke to me of his work or even of what he planned to do this last weekend. I do know that Katherine resented Hoover's tactics. That's all.'

'All right. But let me make this clear. Hoover is too important for us to doubt that it was an accident.'

'Have the FBI asked for our co-operation?'

Ayrtoun shook his head. 'No,' he said firmly. 'They are wholly confident it was an accident.'

Cotton rubbed his eyes, briefly left his hands over them, then took them away.

'All right?' said Ayrtoun.

'I don't know,' Cotton said.

Ayrtoun sighed and moved on. 'Your Dr Aforey has written a letter. Says you're just what the colonies need,' he said.

'It was my cover.'

'Quite,' said Ayrtoun. He sat back and closed one eye. 'You're not really on for the Soviet thing, are you?'

Cotton shook his head.

'Then you'll be playing in the second eleven, you know.'

'Possibly,' said Cotton. He looked up. 'Did we find out what happened to the real Slonim?' he asked.

'The tank commander. We think the real Colonel Slonim may have been killed at Kursk.'

Cotton nodded. 'I'll say goodbye to Mullins.'

'Ah, that might be difficult. I think what's-her-name — Gina? — I think she's in labour. In any case he's a free man now. His demob came through.'

'Really?' said Cotton. 'I didn't know. When was that?'

'Dated the 1st November, I think.' Ayrtoun paused. 'But

you know how these things are – there's always some delay.'

Cotton nodded. 'And trade-offs.'

'Well, we are not entirely hapless, you know,' said Ayrtoun. 'You'll be back in the Statler. Your stuff will be delivered. You'll attend to your social duties?'

Cotton stared at him. He remembered he should say goodbye to Jim Gowar. 'Absolutely,' he said.

Cotton went back to the Intelligence Room. He found Jim Gowar wasn't really up for much and that their goodbye was shuffling, awkward and nearly silent.

He then sent a telegram to his sister Joan.

```
KATHERINE DEAD IN CAR ACCIDENT DURING STORM
STOP RETURNING TO UK ON FRIDAY BY AEROPLANE
FROM NEW YORK STOP CAN I SEE YOU BEFORE OFF
LOVE PETER
```

On his desk there was a note from the P & Q, listing his engagements. The P & Q had clipped on his personal business card. On the back he had written – 'My Condolences.'

There was also a note for him from Mrs Duquesne. 'Do come and see me. Any time. Evelyn.'

And another from Dr Aforey. 'I am most sorry to hear of your imminent departure. I hope you will permit me to say farewell.'

He decided to deal with them both as soon as possible, largely because he could not think of anything else to do.

He took a cab to Dupont Circle and Mrs Duquesne's mansion.

'Oh darling,' she said, 'they've taken the bloom off you.'

Cotton nodded. 'Not much sleep,' he said.

'It's utterly tragic.' Mrs Duquesne put her hand on his forearm and dropped her voice. 'Some are saying she strayed. I do hope she strayed with you.'

Cotton looked at her. He thought his face probably twitched. He did not want to have his emotions prodded – rather more than not wanting to hurt a rich old lady. He lowered his lids and cut her off. 'Thank you.'

'Oh darling,' she said. Her lips quivered. She turned her head away.

Dr Aforey he saw in a mixed-race cafeteria on Georgia Avenue called Martha's. He was already there eating a large piece of pecan pie when Cotton arrived.

'My friend,' said Dr Aforey, 'I understand your mission is completed and you will now go on to pastures new. I am very sorry to hear this thing. I regret in particular that I am only an academic sort of man and, as such, too prone to fastidiousness and timidity.' Dr Aforey shook his head. 'I lack the sweet touch that our Lord brought to the world. It is a sin, I think, but also a damning parable on my own insufficiencies.'

'You have your students,' said Cotton.

Dr Aforey winced. 'Oh, I feel I am but a dull and digressive teacher, Mr Cotton. Research is my forte.' He blinked. 'But despite the rationalists, the brain is not the soul. Mr Cotton?'

'Yes?'

'May I offer you my friendship and active correspondence?'

Cotton nodded.

'I should say that I have taken the liberty of writing to your Foreign Office, praising you but censoring myself.'

'I hope we meet again, Dr Aforey,' said Cotton.

'Oh, sir. You are too kind.'

Dr Aforey took out his wallet and removed a small newspaper clipping. He handed it to Cotton with a certain ruefulness.

Sir, the Fifth Pan-African Congress was held recently in the undoubtedly great city of Manchester. While the organizers are to be sincerely congratulated, would it not have been in all cases better and more in the majority interest of citizens of the British colonies if those in favour of plural democracy — the recently elected Labour government of Great Britain, for example — had taken a greater interest in such a seminal event?

'Is this the *Manchester Guardian*?' asked Cotton.

'The *Manchester Evening News*,' said Dr Aforey. 'I regret it is not a bigger contribution.'

Cotton handed the clipping back and shook hands,

'Farewell, Doctor.'

'And to you, my good friend.'

Cotton did not manage to see Mullins until 13 December. He had recently returned from the maternity hospital.

'A girl,' he said. 'We are calling her Lucia, Lucia Mullins.'

'Congratulations!' said Cotton. 'I'm delighted for you. How is Gina?'

'Tired,' said Mullins. 'It was a long labour.'

'But is she well?'

'Yes.'

'What are you going to do?' asked Cotton.

'Make my life here,' said Mullins. 'We're hoping to get married soon. Maybe move to Chevy Chase.'

'Good. More congratulations. I should have brought a cigar.'

'I don't really smoke, sir,' said Mullins. He paused. 'I did smoke on Armistice Day though.'

Cotton nodded. 'Capstan Full Strength?'

'Yes, sir.'

'Thanks.'

Mullins shook his head. 'I can't help on this, sir. I was put to finding Mr Tibbets when he had disappeared. The last sighting was on Wednesday evening, December the 5th.'

'Five days?'

'More or less.'

'Do you know where they went?'

'My sources say the Shenandoah Valley. In Virginia.'

'FBI sources?'

'Sir. It was out of my hands then.'

'Yes, I understand that. Do you know what they planned?'

'Not really, no. I guess that Miss Ward thought Mr Tibbets had information that could help her. And she was preparing something.'

Cotton shook his head. 'Do you think she really believed she could bring Hoover down? Believed that?'

'Perhaps she wanted to believe it, sir. That was a lot of pressure she had to take. And not only her. That friend of hers who took his own life, for instance. She could have felt responsible.'

Cotton nodded. He realized he was looking for answers he was never going to get.

Mullins looked apologetic. 'Sensitive security matters, well they really do cause very strong reactions.'

'Did they kill them?'

'I'm afraid there will always be a doubt.'

To his own surprise Cotton laughed.

'Or they could have assisted the accident,' said Mullins. 'Following someone from very close can make them nervous. The weather was terrible. They couldn't see ahead very well. And just a nudge can cause . . . well . . .'

'It's all right,' said Cotton. He groaned, Of course it wasn't all right. He swallowed. He held out his hand to Mullins.

'Thank you for all you've done. May I wish you and your family the very best?'

On Friday the 14th Cotton took an early train to New York. He was travelling much lighter than when he had arrived. His uniforms and the rest were being shipped.

At Penn Station he was met by Todd and Joan and driven to the airport.

'We haven't told the children yet,' said Joan.

'It's all right. You decide.'

Todd was worried about the flight.

'Look at the wings,' said Todd. 'If there is ice on the wings, don't get aboard. Call it off. I mean that. That's for Newfoundland too.'

As he flew north, Cotton looked out. He was impressed by how bleak the landscape became. After Newfoundland, he wrapped himself in a blanket and, even though there was a strong tailwind, slept. He was woken by the smell of kedgeree and coffee. At Shannon he stretched his legs and breathed in salty air.

London was grey, damp and sooty. All passengers were made to queue and were closely quizzed at Customs.

'Come from Newfoundland, sir?'

'No, the US.'

'Anything to declare, sir?'

The customs officer showed him an extensive list of forbidden items. A few minutes later, the presents given him by Joan and family had been unwrapped and most judged illegal. These included chocolates and some very hard-to-get, even in the US, leather gloves for his father, certain foodstuffs and tanned goods being on the customs officer's list. 'Do you know how the skin was cured, sir? We have to be careful, sir.' He was back in Britain.

He retained a painted plaster ashtray from Halliday, a drawing of a horse or possibly a dog from Foster and a pressed flower from Emily. These were only of 'sentimental value'. He baulked at them confiscating the scarf for his father.

'He's old and feels the cold badly.'

'Oh, there are a lot of people like that in Britain, sir.'

But the customs man nodded, chalked his bags and left him to repack.

Cotton took a cab to Waterloo, a train to Dorking and had to wait an hour for another cab to take him to Peaslake. The weather was misting up, the dew beginning to freeze. His father heard the cab draw up and came out to see who it was. The porch light had gone. There was a scratch of matches.

'Who is that?'

'I'm back from the US,' said Cotton.

There was a pause.

'Have you brought your coupons?'

His father was lonely and not pretending. The house was old cold.

'I'll light some fires,' said Cotton.

'You don't seem to appreciate something,' said his father.

'What's that?'

'I haven't got the fuel.'

Cotton touched his father's elbow. His father looked at him.

'I am perfectly happy,' said Cotton, 'to go scouring for firewood tomorrow. I'll even cut down some of your trees. But I am – and I will clean out the grates – going to get the place warm for once.'

His father blinked. 'I'll see what food I've got.'

Cotton began lighting fires. The drawing room was icy. He set fire to the kindling and old pages from newspapers. His father had bundled them far too tight. The kindling flared, the newspaper smoked and then the coal began to crackle. More smoke than hot flames.

He stepped back and replaced the fireguard. Cotton's nose was dripping. He saw there were two letters on the mantel-piece addressed to Lieutenant Colonel P. J. B. Cotton.

Cotton considered, then opened the first envelope between teeth and gloves. It was the offer of a job after he was demobbed. It would involve 'strategic security' within the British Commonwealth with 'close attention to the economic implications for His Majesty's Government.' The salary offered was £650 per annum pre-war scale, though this would be coming under review i.d.c. – in due course.

He remembered something Tibbets had said: 'I'm beginning to think peace is rather a let-down.'

And he remembered Katherine turning, pleased, beginning to smile, about to say something. He shuddered.

The other letter told him his wartime service was over. From 1 January 1946, he would be a civilian again.

'I can do you two rashers of bacon, some toast and some stewed apples,' called his father.

'Have you any whisky?'

There was a dull clinking sound.

'Actually, I've got a bottle of Châteauneuf-du-Pape I've been keeping. Would you be on for that? Oh, and there is a bottle of Beaune. From the year your mother died.'

Cotton nodded. 'Beaune,' he called. 'Let's get a room up to temperature and put the wine in it.'

Afterword

A number of names mentioned in the story may now strike readers as odd or even incorrect. For example, Ashanti is now usually Asante. Annamese is now usually Vietnamese. These were, however, the versions used in late 1945 and I have kept them, rather than use possibly helpful anachronisms, as part of the atmosphere of that time.

Similarly, David Eisenhower was not born until 1948, his grandfather not elected until 1952, so that what is now Camp David was still called Shangri-la, the name F. D. Roosevelt had given it.

Some names of real people have been used. John Maynard Keynes is the subject of a biography by Robert Skidelsky. Keynes died in April 1946 and the British finally paid off the loan he negotiated in 2006. Given inflation and the low rate of interest, the deal turned out to be a very good one for the UK.

The twice-mentioned MacLean is indeed Donald MacLean, with Burgess and Philby rather more famous now as a spy who defected to the Soviets in 1951 than as First Secretary to the Embassy when Cotton is there. His code name was 'Homer'. Philby's code name was the Livingstonesque 'Stanley'.

A little more difficult to pick up is that the 'pillow-diddling' attaché was Roald Dahl whose exploits are recounted in a recent book, *The Irregulars* by Jennet Conant.

The woman Ayrtoun mentions as having named Harry Dexter White as a Soviet agent to the FBI was Elizabeth Bentley. She did so again in front of the House Committee on Un-American Activities in July 1948. Two weeks later, in August, White appeared before HUAC and denied the charge. After testifying, he suffered a heart attack. He died on 16 August 1948.

On organizations, the American OSS really was broken up in September–October 1945 and, after a period of infighting and reorganization, the CIA was formed in 1947.

A great deal has been written (and surmised) about what became known as the Venona Project – the extraordinarily painstaking work of cryptologists in deciphering Soviet coded messages. Although Tibbets does not say so, he is involved in one part of this project. In 1949, American codebreakers identified 'Homer' as being one of three or four people in the British Embassy in 1944. MacLean was only able to escape because Philby was then in Washington DC and privy to the discoveries as they appeared. It is fairly certain the FBI did not inform the CIA of the full extent of the Venona Project until as late as 1952.

Rumours about J. Edgar Hoover were rife in 1945 and continued until his death. Possibly homosexual, possibly a cross-dresser, possibly of some black descent, possibly compromised by organized crime, his tactics, some illegal, and his willingness to spy on and harass all kinds of people in his fight against 'subversion', finally meant that, on his death, FBI directors were limited, less by principle than by time, to ten-year terms.

Hoover served from 1935 until 1972, as a Spanish friend points out, almost the same length of time as Franco ruled Spain, 1939 to 1975, both men sharing an extraordinarily stubborn desire to die in office.

Acknowledgements

Many thanks again to my editor Kate Parkin for all her time, patience, hard work – and hard questioning – and to all the team at John Murray.

Thanks too to my family – and especially to my husband who has been endlessly calm and encouraging.